SCOT MIST

SCOT MIST

Catriona McPherson

SEVERN
HOUSE

First world edition published in Great Britain in 2021 and the USA in 2022
by Severn House, an imprint of Canongate Books Ltd,
14 High Street, Edinburgh EH1 1TE.

Trade paperback edition first published in Great Britain and the USA in 2022
by Severn House, an imprint of Canongate Books Ltd.

severnhouse.com

British Library Cataloguing-in-Publication Data
A CIP catalogue record for this title is available from the British Library.

ISBN-13: 978-0-7278-9033-7 (cased)
ISBN-13: 978-1-4483-0735-7 (trade paper)
ISBN-13: 978-1-4483-0734-0 (e-book)

All Severn House titles are printed on acid-free paper.

Typeset by Palimpsest Book Production Ltd.,
Falkirk, Stirlingshire, Scotland.
Printed and bound in Great Britain by
TJ Books, Padstow, Cornwall.

This is for all the essential workers,
with deepest admiration and endless gratitude

scotch mist: **1.** (lit.) a barely detectable fog; **2.** (fig.) an unconfirmed belief, a rumour; **3.** (inevit.) an alcoholic beverage

ONE

Friday 13 March 2020
Cuento, CA

There were only three of us at the summit meeting in the Skweeky-Kleen Laundromat attached to the Last Ditch Motel. Kathi stood behind her folding table, in her SK polo shirt, both fists clenched on the shining melamine top. Her wife Noleen was over by the door, standing four-square like a club bouncer and wearing one of her most uncompromising slogan sweatshirts. The front read NOPE and the back read STILL NOPE. I knew she meant it.

I was standing halfway between them, backed right up against the rank of dryers.

'I'm closing the motel and the Skweek,' Kathi said. 'There's nothing to discuss.'

The other five permanent motel residents waiting downstairs in the car park would beg to differ. Todd *had* begged, *and* differed, while I'd had him on speakerphone, until Kathi made me hang up.

'But would you hear me ou—?' I tried to say.

Kathi jabbed a finger at Noleen's sweatshirt before she spoke. 'Disneyland is closed. The federal government has offered a tax-filing extension. A. Tax. Filing. Extension. Lexy, they've admitted that the only sure thing is death.'

'I don't know what the Brit equivalent would be,' Noleen chipped in.

'Me neither,' I said. 'Taking down the *Bake Off* tent?'

'I swear to God if you crack one single joke,' said Kathi. Her jaw was clenched so tight she sounded like Sean Connery. Doing a surprisingly good American accent.

'I'm not joking!' I said. 'We haven't got a Disneyland to close.'

'Look,' Kathi said. 'I don't know how many people are sick.'

I did and, going by the way she shifted her feet, I think Noleen did too. 'But they didn't all catch it in Wuhan and they're not all on that floating petri dish down in the docks. Some of them are in the city and some of them must be leaving the city and this is a motel ninety minutes from the city and so it closes today.'

'Kath—'

'So help me, Betty White, if you tell me not to worry and it's not so bad and it's going to be fine I will never speak to you again. *And* I'll ask the City to tow your boat.'

Now, the permit process to moor a houseboat on the slough that gave the Last Ditch Motel its branding disaster of a name made Brexit look like a PTA meeting in Pleasantville. So, on hearing that, I was sorely tempted to nod, smile, bow – she was holding a pretty handy-looking steam iron now – and back away. But I loved Kathi and I understood better than almost anyone what this moment felt like to a serious, clinical, lifelong germaphobe.

'I'm trying to help yo—' I said next, because I might be a counsellor trained in family, relationship, and personal therapy, but I'm also a moron.

'I don't want to "grow",' Kathi said. 'This isn't an "opportunity". I am not interested in being "brav—"'

I changed tack. 'It's going to be bad. It might be very bad. It might be so bad we look back on very bad with nostalgia. Do you know what else Gav the Gov did yesterday, besides the tax and Disney stuff? No? The executive order about grabbing property? No? Well, listen to me now because if this motel is empty when it gets really bad – if it gets really bad – then it might be turned into an overflow hospital.' Kathi's mouth dropped open. 'Or emergency accommodation for street people.' Her face started to drain from her usual sallow to a kind of putty colour. 'Or shelter for first responders on the front line.' She put the iron down and spread her hands flat on the folding table, as if for balance. 'So my advice, as your friend, is stuff growth and courage. Fill the motel as quick as you can with people you trust, then circle the wagons and let's get through this together.'

'And close the Skweek,' Kathi said.

'No,' I said. 'Todd can run the Skweek. Della can run the motel. I'll help her. You two can take care of each other. And—'

'And Roger goes to work every day in a goddam hospital ward in goddam Sacramento and comes back here every night in his goddam scrubs and kills us all?' This was Noleen. Kathi didn't have enough bite left in her.

'No,' I said again. 'This is what I've been trying to tell you. Roger goes to work and stays there. Well, stays with another doctor up there. And that doctor's wife is one of the people who comes here and stays with us. Barb wants to come too.'

'Todd's mom, Barb?' said Kathi, like she knew several.

'Todd's mom, Barb,' I agreed, because I supposed she might. Like me and Morags. 'We can fill this place, Kathi,' I went on. 'But we need to get going.'

'But if Todd runs the laundromat,' Kathi said, 'that means people in and out all day long.'

'No. No, it doesn't,' I told her. 'It means people drop off binbags of washing at the fence. Todd sprays them with Lysol, picks them up with tongs, empties them into the machines and then drives the clean washing to people's houses and dumps it out at the kerb.'

Kathi looked around as I spoke. She loved the Skweeky-Kleen. The name was her life's philosophy and it described the place to a T. Every surface sparkled, gleamed, glittered or glowed, depending on whether it was glass, steel, tiles or wood. The fluff catchers were forensically free of fluff and the soap dispensers were forensically free of soap. If there was ever a new religion as nuts about fabric-softener residue as old religions are about other stuff, their strictest adherents could eat their soup with the Skweeky-Kleen fabric-softener drawers in place of spoons. Kathi, and this should seal it, polished the coins before she stacked them in the coin machine.

But if there's one person who could be trusted with the spankingly antiseptic pride and joy of a severe germaphobe, it's surely the cleptoparasitosis-ridden, out-of-work anaesthetist who lives in her motel because she gets insecticide from her cousin in Costa Rica that kills not only ants, beetles, mozzies, wasps, and the imaginary bugs that ruin cleptoparasitatory lives,

but could take out a raccoon if you made it up double-strength.
In other words: Todd Kroger.

Devin, the college kid who'd moved into Room 101 after he
was driven out of his dorm by bullies, always said there was
no point knowing an anaesthetist on long-term sick leave. But
that's college kids for you.

'You thought of all that?' Kathi was saying when I started
paying attention again. 'Filling up with safe people before we're
filled up with bio-bombs? And no-contact laundry drop?'

'Wait till you hear what we've got in mind for food shopping,' I said. 'You're going to be fine. Really.'

'But what I mean is,' Kathi said, 'you thought of all that
for *me*?'

I hesitated.

'What? What? What?' she squawked. 'What aren't you telling
me? What's the catch?'

'I knew it!' said Noleen. 'And after all we've done for your
bony ass!'

'Wait a minute,' I said. 'Why would it matter whether we're
doing it all "for you" as long as we're doing it? Why would
that make a difference?'

'So why not just *do* it for me?' Say what you like about
blind terror; it doesn't half make people straightforward.

'Because it makes no odds to you why it happens,' I said.
'It's still safety, sanctuary and succour, no matter what.' She
was frowning. 'Suck-hour, not suck-er. But it's going to make
a big difference to the rest of the town and the county and
the country, afterwards, whether you were "pulling up the draw-
bridge" or "protecting vulnerable strangers". One is heroic and
the other is . . . less heroic. Think of the press. Think of your
business.'

'How does Barb moving in make us heroes?' Kathi said.

I nodded, acknowledging the point. Barb Truman lived in a
palatial McMansion up in the tree streets, the fanciest of
Cuento's neighbourhoods, complete with looping roads, lack
of pavements and the kind of personal space that only a lot of
money can buy you in California. (That always puzzled me.
It's huge! Why are the houses packed in so close together?
After two years, I still didn't know.)

'She's giving away her house for someone else to stay in,' I said.

'Who?' said Kathi.

'Immuno-compromised parents of an ER security guard.'

'That's nice of her.'

'Well, they're her gardener and housekeeper so it's either that or she cracks out the Dyson herself, and you know Barb.'

All three of us nodded. Barb hadn't been rich for long – that's another story – but hoo boy had she ever caught on quick.

Kathi thought a moment and then said, 'Who else do you think might come?' She was crumbling. 'How would we vet them? How could we control them? How can we be sure they won't sneak off at night to . . .'

'Lick a bus stop?' I said. Because there's a limit to the amount of pussy-footing around I can do, outside a therapeutic setting. 'They won't. They'll be too grateful.'

'But who are they?' Kathi said.

'Well, Della and Devin have got three different pals lined up who need to get out of troublesome home situations.'

'Troublesome how? Would they bring the trouble here?'

'OK, one's not trouble. It's just . . . what do you call it when a family's happy and normal, not frozen and weird?'

'Huh,' said Noleen. 'No judgement. Do you mean a multi-generational household?'

'That's the one. Elderly grandparents need to leave a flat where the young adults are teamsters.' I didn't actually know what teamsters were, so this sentence was a risk. And I do get heartily sick of being laughed at. But right now neither Kathi nor Noleen were giving me the kind of look they dish out when I talk about schoolkids buying new rubbers for the start of term, so I guessed I was good. 'And then there's this one woman who's been planning to leave her pig of a husband and thinks she better get out now in case there's a real crackdown and it "isn't to his liking", if you catch my drift. Plus – get this – an IT guy from UCC who needs to leave behind his sow of a wife for much the same reason. Talk about a meet-cute!'

'I make that five,' said Kathi. 'Add the regulars – us, Todd, the 3Ds – and it makes eight. This motel has twelve rooms.'

'It's more than eight,' I said, because Kathi had a room she

used so she could keep the owner's apartment clean, and Todd
had a spare room in case of night spiders. I reminded her of
that. 'And Devin wants to keep his own room from before the
wedding – just for working in, same as usual. Plus the doctor's
wife is a dancer and wants a room to practise in.'

'She can't have one,' said Kathi. 'The secret police won't
swallow that when they come round.'

'So we'll call it a crèche,' I said.

'A what?'

'A nursery. Her kids are tiny and the domestic-abuse-survivor
wife has got twins. Not sure about the IT guy. But that's five
kids already including Diego.'

'Still leaves us one body short,' said Kathi. 'What's the point
of any of this if the deep state can sequester our leftover room
and billet plague victims in it. Oh, you think they won't shred
the constitution?' she said, clocking the look I couldn't help
giving her. 'They've closed *Disneyland*.'

'Honey,' said Noleen, who'd been astonishingly quiet, for
her. 'You sound a bit . . . What's the word I'm after, Lex?'

'Barking mad,' I said. 'We can keep one room free for if
someone needs it, Kathi. No one's going to billet anyone in a
single room in a motel full of kids and old people, and that's
not what "sequestering" is anyway. I think you mean "comman-
deer". And the deep state isn't a real thing. Is it?'

Noleen shook her head, but Kathi looked at me as if I'd
questioned the existence of narwhals. Just for instance. Totally
random example. From months ago. And anyway, I'm not a
zoologist, so leave me alone. 'Of course the deep state is a real
thing!' she said. 'You call them the civil service because that's
how you roll, Your Royal Majesty on a big red bus, but there
are thousands of them with a reach around the globe.'

'I know you're under a lot of stress, Kathi,' I said, 'and I
love you dearly. You are one of my best friends now and your
friendship shows me that I never really knew what friends were
until I moved here and met you. So I'm going to cut you a lot
of slack for the duration of this difficult time. But . . .' I held
up a finger, 'those red double-decker buses are English.'

Kathi has a range of derisive snorts she could take on the
road. She learned the core snort from Noleen who uses it daily,

but she added a panoply of specialized snorts with a breadth and specificity that continue to amaze me. The snort she delivered now was made up of genuine remorse, performative weariness and a wide stripe of heartfelt contempt. God, I loved her.

'Right,' she said. 'I know. You're "Scottish". Not "English". Totally "different thing". Jeez.'

'Fine,' I said. 'Come the Fourth of July we'll all stand up and sing, "Oh, Canada".'

'"We all" meaning Todd and Roger and us and you and the Ds, right?' Noleen said. 'Not the wives and the old folks and the IT guy and Barb. Right? I mean, this is going to be over long before then, isn't it Lexy?'

'Of course,' I said. 'A month tops. We won't even have to teach anyone how to use the AC. By the time it's too warm for Californians, everyone'll be back home.'

Yeah, we really did say that. We believed it too. How were we to know how long we'd all be banged up together in the Last Ditch like some sitcom slash commune slash cult? And how could we have guessed that one of us wouldn't make it out alive? As if 2020 wasn't already a latrine pit of a year plus a warm bin-juice chaser, without adding murder.

TWO

I let myself out of the Skweek, on to the walkway that made the Last Ditch such an enduring thrill. Seriously. I come from Dundee, a city that doesn't have motels, or outdoor swimming pools, or drive-through stuff, or burrito wagons. A city that has only two vowels. So there are some bits of iconic America that never fail to tickle me. Waiting at the barrier while a goods train goes through town makes everyone else in Cuento spit tacks, but makes me feel like I'm in a Tom Waits song. Getting so much ice in your Coke at the pictures that you can give yourself goosebumps in August? Chilly heaven. Parking your arse as soon as you get into a pub and having a waitress bring the beer right to you? It's maybe not sensible and if it ever took off in Scotland, with our booze habit, people would be leaving in body bags at closing time. But I can't deny that it's lovely. Until you stand up to leave and can't feel your legs. But even then . . . Uber!

And the best thing of all, the thing that makes my life indistinguishable from a Hitchcock movie shot in an Edward Hopper painting, is the top-tier walkway that runs round the horseshoe of rooms that make up the Last Ditch Motel. It's disappointing that the car park's full of SUVs and hybrids instead of tail-fin Cadillacs but maybe that would be too much of a good thing.

Anyway, as I let myself out, leaving Kathi to celebrate her last afternoon at work by polishing the insides of the washing machines, I leaned on the railing as if I was standing in the world's highest pulpit and addressed the crowd below. Todd was there, bristling with diamonds like he always is whenever he's stressed. Well, on any given day he wears stud earrings as big as mistletoe berries and his eternity-style wedding ring, but today he had added the cross I once thought was cubic-Z from the size of the stones, two tennis bracelets, and – I saw when he stretched his arms above his head and his work-out sweats rode up – a belly-button ring with a diamond solitaire the size of a grape. I shuddered. Belly jewels always looked a bit like pustules to me.

The 3Ds were there too – Devin and Della and wee Diego. Della was in the neat tunic she wore to her job as a spa receptionist and Devin was in the collection of surferesque rags he wore to his job as a slacker hacker who'd downloaded his coursework already and wouldn't need to go back to campus till graduation day. They'd been married a month and were very much still in the honeymoon phase, always gazing, often touching. Diego was deep in a honeymoon phase of his own. He'd got a stepdad who made his mum too happy to nag, and played Fortnite and skated. What six-year-old could ask for more?

'Wait, why's Diego here?' I said. 'Oh God, estás enfermo, cariño?'

'He's perrrrfectly healthy,' said Della, rolling her R in an abysmal *Star Trek*-style attempt at a Scottish accent to pay me back for speaking Spanish near her. 'They've closed the schools.'

'In Cuento?' I squeaked. If there was a flare-up right here and Kathi found out about it she would need tranquillizers. In fact, it might be an idea to set her up with a little something anyway.

'State-wide,' said Devin, which was simultaneously better and so much worse.

'No school! No school!' Diego chanted, with a little burst of that floss dance that looks cute when you're six but should be banned on your seventh birthday.

'Lexy,' said Todd. 'Not to be forward or anything, and do let me know if something's come up that's preventing you, but when you get the chance, would you mind letting us know what happened in there?'

He didn't use my accent but he was definitely trying to make some point or other about British speech. Probably that we were a bunch of wittering turnips who'd have to butch up to play table-top croquet. That was his usual take on things.

'Sorry,' I said. 'Yes, of course. Um, basically,' I paused. This was a moment of some import. Usually I just bumble along, doing no active harm and remembering to sort my recycling, so it wasn't every day I was in charge of announcing an actual plan to bring about a public health initiative. 'Operation Shuffle is go. Meet me onboard in five minutes. Bring snacks.'

'Snacks! Snacks! Oo-ah! Oo-ah!' chanted Diego. I reckoned his teacher might have handed out some blue lollipops before she sent her class away. He was as high as a phone mast.

'Da fuq's Operation Shuffle?' said Devin.

'This is,' I said. 'We're moving Roger out, Mrs Doctor in, a wife in, a husband out, granny and grandad in, housekeeper and gardener in, Barb out. Kathi out. You in. Noleen out, Della and me in. Operation what better name than Shuffle?'

'Operation Nelson,' said Todd. 'In honour of Willie.'

'Willie Nelson! Oo-ah! Oo-ah!' said Diego, still flossing as vigorously as dental hygienists are always telling us to.

'Why?' I said. 'I don't get it. And I won't wear a bandana.'

'Duh,' said Todd. 'Cos we're gonna get by with a little help from our friends!'

'That was Joe Cocker,' I said. 'And we are *not* calling it . . .'

'No,' said Della. 'We're not.'

'Oreos!' sang Todd, arriving onboard my houseboat ten minutes later and letting a torrent of packaging tumble out of his arms on to the coffee table. 'Pringles. Onion dip. Guac. Parm chips.'

'What the hell?' I said. I'd seen Todd excise the central rib from a kale leaf because it was too much starch at the end of the day. 'Did you have all this in store somewhere?'

'Hey,' he said. 'If I'm not gonna see ma honey for a coupla weeks except on a video call where I can apply filters, I'm gonna make the most of it. One week of chips and dips, then back to normal for him coming home.'

'But we're not starting right now, are we?' I said. 'I know I had to push it to get Kathi signed up but I thought it was still hypothetical. Kind of just in case?'

'Of?'

'A black-out or a shut-down or whatever we're going to call it. Beteo County isn't closed. And Gav the Gov hasn't said anything about closing it.'

'Lexy,' said Todd. 'Gav the Gov is going to shut the whole state. I'm surprised he hasn't done it already. And we need to be ahead of the curve. So tonight Roger comes home to pack and tomorrow . . .'

'Right,' I said. 'OK. Tomorrow we kick off Operation Coc— Damn you to hell and back in a woolly thong, Todd! I'm never going to be able to call it anything else now, am I? But, even so, if Roger's coming home tonight, what's with the Oreos?'

'It'll all be in my gut till after he's gone tomorrow,' Todd said. 'It won't hit my butt till Tuesday.'

'And you'll have time to work it off before he's home again?'

'Just,' said Todd. 'If I give myself a week to binge and a week to cleanse, I'll be back to my normal perfection to welcome him home.'

It would sound like bragging if anyone else said it, but Todd was one of the most beautiful people ever born. He had glossy black waves that tumbled over his smooth forehead unless he slicked them back. In which case just a single gleaming strand fell over one eye. I mean, Todd pushed it but it still fell. His skin was the colour of an almond shell, but without the pock-marks – the man had no pores. His eyes were the colour of the skin on a discarded bowl of guacamole – not quite brown but not quite green – and his teeth were miracles. Not even those diamond studs could outshine them. Of course, he was in perfect physical shape. Course he was. Muscles as subtle as they were stupendous; muscles that looked as if he'd got them hewing logs to build a cabin, instead of pumping weights while he gazed at himself in a mirror, but beautiful manicured hands that had clearly never hewn so much as a disposable toothpick. If he wasn't my first, dearest, and would be outright best if it wasn't for Kathi, friend in America, I'd hate him. Because when I saw pictures of myself alone, I looked normal. But when I stood next to Todd, I looked like Baby Groot. Or Baby Yoda. Perhaps Baby Shrek. Definitely someone short, beige and lumpy.

Della arrived as I was opening wine. Della, who was so beautiful she made me not care about Todd: black hair like a skein of silk that sat in a bell shape against her back. Complexion like the peeled almond inside the shell, lips so red she only ever put Vaseline on them even for the grandest occasion, and a body I couldn't believe had produced a child. Her breasts were like little buns just under her chin and the rest of her front was as flat as an ironing board. Her legs were two-thirds the length of my entire body. I knew this for a fact, because once I'd borrowed her yoga pants and I had to roll up so much at the bottom I looked like I was wearing ankle weights. She did have ugly hands. There was that. But they were those strong ugly hands, like an artist or a chiropractor, that made ordinary women's hands look kind of pathetic.

Right now one of them was holding her phone as she spoke into it in such rapid Spanish that I only caught one word in ten. That word was 'Cocker'. 'Sí, sí,' she said. 'The Beatles song.' Then she hung up. 'Do we need Devin?' she asked us. 'I left them playing.' I wondered if she realized how it sounded when she spoke of her husband and son in the same breath that way. 'My good friend Meera is very happy to come but it's got to be early tomorrow. Her husband is doing a night shift and she needs to be out before he comes home again.'

'In case he's been exposed?' I said. It still didn't feel real. It was a few hundred cases, a handful of tragic deaths, but in a state this size I couldn't bring myself to worry that a random little town like Cuento in a random little county like Beteo was in any real peril. 'What does he do?'

'No, in case he stops her,' Della said. 'He's a cop.'

'Jeez,' I said. 'Wow. Really? And yet she's scared of him?'

Todd and Della shared that look; the one that says 'Whitey gonna white' and I nodded and held a hand up to acknowledge it.

'If she gets away, he'll probably accept she's gone,' Della said. 'He'll be glad the kids won't talk over the game any more. But if he had to watch her pack and then see her literally pick up her keys and walk out the door, he might have a "bad reaction to the beer", you know.'

'He sounds quite the catch,' I said.

'Enh,' said Della. 'He's just one of those guys. He loved her tiny waist and her shiny hair. Then she had the twins. Her waist was gone and her hair was full of spit-up. He's still sulking.'

'Do you think she'll go home again once this is all over?' I said.

Della shrugged. 'He has a big paycheque and great health

insurance,' she said, sounding sadder than I'd often heard her. 'She's a beauty therapist with twins. Life is real.'

'Would she be willing to do some sessions with me while she's here?' I said. 'Free of charge.'

'If you're a hammer,' said Todd, 'everything looks like a nail.'

'I hate that expression,' I said. 'It sounds filthy. Oh!'

'Oh, what?' Todd had just loaded more onion dip than seemed physically possible on to a Pringle and barely managed to get it to his mouth.

'Those things are a miracle of food technology,' I said. 'What tensile strength.'

'Oh, what?' Todd said again, through a mouthful, which was gross beyond measure.

I really didn't want to tell him that talk of hammers and nails had reminded me that if we were going into whatever we were going to call it – purdah, quarantine, isolation – tomorrow morning, then tonight was my last chance for a week or so to hang out with Taylor.

'Phone him,' said Todd. He's very annoying.

I *would* phone, though. We'd met just after Valentine's Day, and we'd been taking it so cautiously it was more like bomb disposal than dating. My excuse was that I was a marriage-and-family therapist and had seen too much too many times to go tra-la-la-ing into a new relationship like I was taking a basket of snacks through the dark woods to my grandmamma. I don't know what Taylor's problem was. He was forty-four, single-never-married, a career ornithologist at the local wetlands reserve, with a night job in a phone shop to make ends meet, who could usually total thirteen separate pockets on any given day: six in his combat trousers (which went down to two if he unzipped the legs and they turned into cargo shorts, but it was only March); six in his sleeveless khaki jacket, the thing he called a fishing vest; and the most important pocket of all, on the breast of his short-sleeved shirt, lined with a protector and home to five pens, one of his three penknives and a whistle he used to make duck calls.

In other words, he was perfect. So far outside the meat market of mainstream dating that I felt like an anthropologist when we went out for our first burger. It had been a hard evening to dress for. I'd plumped for a boatneck linen shift with a high split up the back and he'd told me I had lovely clavicles, then told me why geese fly in a vee and swifts fly in an oval, explaining it so clearly and – get this – so *quickly* that I asked three follow-up questions to keep him talking. That had never happened before in the history of men talking about their passions. Ever. Even the Emperor Hadrian, out on a first date, would spread a napkin and draw a sketch of his wall.

From that night on, I really liked Taylor. He was honest and funny and, if he had an ego at all, he was keeping it in some fourteenth pocket he'd forgotten about. Also – this might be work, where I mostly hear about problems – he was just so *normal*.

Normal, that is, except for the go-slow, which is why I welcomed the prospect of a sequestering or whatever we were going to call it: I could invite Taylor round tonight and proceed full-steam ahead in a way I'd never dare to if we were going to have to see each other again, all freaked-out and regretful, in another day or two. This way we could spend the circuit breaker weeks recovering.

Sometimes, when I meet people for the first time and they hear that I'm a therapist, they try to ask me a question they can never quite frame. It would boil down to 'Are you all sorted out then?' if anyone ever actually boiled it. And there's the answer: no. I'm as weird and hung up and stupid as everyone else. Just not at work.

When I stopped thinking about Taylor and started listening to Della again, she'd moved on to the IT guy.

'His wife's . . .' she was saying. 'I don't know how much I can say.'

'Unfaithful? Addicted? Abusive?' said Todd.

'She punched him when he caught her making out in a taxi with her coke dealer,' said Della. 'So, I think, all three. Only, he's very religious so it was taking a lot of work to get him ready to leave. But they have a tiny apartment – one room with a bed in the wall – and he knows he needs to get out before the music stops.'

Todd and I had exchanged a look. I said it. 'Very religious?

How is he with "the gays"? Not that we all have to hang out or anything, but if he's going to be a pest . . .'

'Oh, he's good,' said Della. 'I mean, I think. I think he would be good.'

'Why?' said Todd. 'Why so breezy, Della? I've never met a man religious enough to make divorce a problem who was "good" with any other kind of fornication. Which is totally what he'd call my long happy marriage where no one makes out in taxis with coke dealers.' Todd was speaking quite fast and shovelling onion-dip-loaded Pringles into his face *very* fast, as if he thought he could plug up with carbs and stop himself from scolding his friend. He was failing.

'I don't want to gossip about him when he's not here,' Della said. 'But believe me, he'll be OK.'

'Oh really?' said Todd. He'd washed down the Pringles with a huge slug of wine and was now wrestling open the Oreos. He dipped one in his glass and ate it whole. I was beginning to think he could definitely be fatter by the time Roger got off his shift and drove home. 'Have you ever actually broached the subject? Has it come up? Why would a hardcore Catholic macho man who's too embarrassed to admit his wife hits him be such a willing volunteer for the rainbow coalition?'

'He's Muslim,' Della said. 'And trans.'

Todd, dipping another Oreo, let it go. We all watched it sink to the bottom of his glass of Zin.

'That could be delicious,' I said, nodding at the dissolving biscuit. 'We could call it a . . . dirty . . .'

Before I could think up the end of the sentence, the door opened. It was Roger, home from the children's ward of the hospital in Sacramento where he made babies better, made straight men consider turning, made women rail at the gods, and made Powerpuff Girl scrubs look sexy. Truly, like me standing next to Todd and turning into drain hair, when Todd stood next to Roger he turned into a daytime-cable, mall-opening kind of gorgeous celebrity, whereas Roger was the billboard in Times Square, movie-greenlighting kind. He looked as if he'd sold his soul to some Silicon Valley demon and been given the world's first real-life filtering app. Details? Well, he had skin the colour of good Georgian mahogany and he wore his hair shaved off so his head looked like a sculpture. His cheekbones and jawbones and the bow of his top lip bounced light around like a disco ball and his eyes shone like eighty-five per cent cocoa solids liquid chocolate, the minute you lift the piece of fruit out of the fountain, before it cools and loses its shine. And did I say he saved babies' lives?

As I looked around my three friends, I wondered what the balance of outlandish gorgeousness would be when the new arrivals turned up. Kathi and Noleen were average on a good day, Devin was basic, Diego didn't count because all kids are officially beautiful . . . and why was this bothering me tonight when it had never bothered me before? Could it be that I didn't believe Taylor's light was really as far under the bushel as all that? That if I scared him away with declarations of . . . marked partiality . . . maybe some other woman who didn't look like Groot, Shrek, or Yoda would scoop him up before I was on the street again?

'You know something?' I said. 'You are three of the prettiest people I've ever seen in the same place.'

'Don't worry,' said Todd. 'He's not going anywhere.'

God, he really was infuriating. I quirked a look as if to pretend I had no idea what he was on about.

'Taylor?' said Roger. 'He's totally into you. Why would you question it?'

'Not everything is looks,' said Della. 'My first husband was a handsome man, like a god, but I never had a happy day with him. Devin looks like when *Star Wars* has a scene in a bar, and I wouldn't change him.'

'Thanks,' I said, because saying 'Piss off out of my boat with your scumbag honesty and I hope you all get boils' might come off a bit brusque. Then my phone rumbled in my back pocket and I took it out. A text from Taylor. 'Hey, beautiful!' it said.

Which should have helped, if I thought he meant it, but all I concluded was that he too was going to go deep for a while till we could see what was what and this was his 'nothing-to-lose' final gambit for the first stage of courtship, ending tonight.

THREE

'Tonight' ran over. Taylor left me early next morning after what I can only call a magnificent send-off and headed north to his mother's house. He didn't usually live with his mother. He had taken great pains to assure me of that the first time I'd met him. Which was obviously a clue that he liked me already, right? Or why would he have cared what I thought?

'It's because she's blind,' he had reminded me, during a refreshment break the night before.

'As a hawk,' I pointed out. She *was* visually impaired, true, and frail with it, but she still made her own bed when she got up in the morning, spurning fitted sheets in favour of hospital corners you could cut yourself on, and she still gardened her quarter-acre of roses and velvet lawn.

'But she doesn't drive,' Taylor pointed out. 'Obviously. And I don't want her gadding about in Ubers if it gets bad.' Gadding? Was he mocking me? None of my friends ever mocked me with anything I'd actually say – like *ned, pluchs*, or *swadger* – but they got a lot of mileage out of things like *serviette* and *lady's maid*. Scotland was England to them, and England was fifty per cent *Downton Abbey*.

'Wouldn't it be safer for you to drop off your mum's shopping on the porch but stay at home . . . or wherever . . . than if you come and go from work to her house every day?' I said, when he got back to my bedroom after his shower in the morning.

'I don't think I'll be in the store much longer,' he said. 'If Beteo goes full-on bunker I don't see phone stores being classed as essential.'

Just as well he wasn't hoping to rise through the ranks and get a manager's name badge and his own pen anytime soon.

He was one of the few Californians who'd genuinely think tagging goose legs was more life-or-death than upgrading an iPhone.

By the time he'd left and I'd peeled myself off my mattress, showered the goofy grin off my face and the film of sweat off the rest of me, and tottered round to the car park to see what the day had in store, Operation . . . I bet Willie Nelson had the song in his set list at some point, so where would the harm be? . . . was up and running.

At least, there was an elderly couple with a lot of luggage waiting serenely on the pool loungers, and the chain-link gate on runners was closed and padlocked over the Last Ditch driveway. Noleen was cable-tying a notice to the inside, facing out to the road.

'What does it say?' I asked her, hoping she had channelled her business course rather than her wardrobe when she composed it.

'Please call Reception at this number to be admitted.'

'Clear and concise,' I said. 'But why are you going to admit people?'

'Oh, I'm not,' said Noleen. 'I'll tell them to fuck off over the phone. Only, I thought the City might kick up if I wrote it right on the sign.'

'Huh,' I said, and went to greet the couple by the pool. These must be the parents of the . . . I really had no idea what team-sters were. They were tiny and ancient and, apart from their little arms and legs, almost completely spherical. The man wore long silky shorts and had pulled his white socks up so far there was only a rim of knee showing. The woman had on – I'm not kidding – a muumuu, but she'd bought it exactly the right length and width, so she looked like a paper lantern. I wanted to hug both of them, or maybe take them to the boat and sit one on either end of the mantelpiece like those bloody elves. Except cute.

I got a hold of myself. It must be a total gutter to start being found adorable when you hit eighty. 'Hi,' I said. 'Are you Della's friends? I'm Lexy. Welcome to the Last Ditch. Can I help you with your stuff? Do you know what room you're in?'

'Hello,' said the wife. She had such apple cheeks that when

she smiled her eyes turned into little glinting crescents, like a vintage Santa. Her husband might have had a smile to match but his moustache was the size of a well-fed housecat and pretty much covered that bit of his face.

'Hello,' he said. He pointed a finger at himself and said 'José.' He pointed at his wife. 'Y Maria.'

No way, I thought. Then I took a punt, more for my own entertainment than because I really believed it. 'And you're Jesús's parents, right? Della knows your son?'

'Sí,' said Maria. 'Della knows our son.' God, how I loved this country. 'But his name is Mateo.' Oh well.

The rest of the morning was a bit of a blur; thank God I've stopped seeing clients on a Saturday. I used to but they cancelled all the time. That wasn't really such a surprise because anyone can feel depressed or anxious when work was looming then suddenly find themselves OK when nothing was being asked except to stroll through a farmers' market and start drinking at lunchtime.

So today I was free to assign rooms, lug bags, explain temperamental shower heads and assure an anxious parent that the pool fence was as sturdy as a fence can be – i.e. sturdy enough to be called a beautiful wall – and her babies were in no danger.

This was not the wife of the doctor letting Roger live at his place while we were all under house arrest, or whatever we were going to call it. *She* was quite another story. Her name was Blaine and so was her face: Botoxed despite being thirty, with those blocky eyebrows and that thick pale lipstick that always makes me think of long-distance swimmers covered in goose fat. She had a figure like Jessica Rabbit, if a mutant bee had just stung her buttocks, and almost as many diamonds as Todd. He took to her like a duck to gravel, smiling with his lips closed and asking her to be sure and let Noleen in the office (subtext: not him) know if she needed anything.

That was a first. Todd was the nosiest person I'd ever met, and the bossiest too. He hated to let a guest stay at the Ditch for even a single night without getting in on the act one way or another: adding pillows and arranging them; suggesting attractions and downloading a ticket app; stripping off someone's perfectly fine outfit and making her wear what he decreed would suit her.

Me? I liked Blaine at first. She was so catastrophically hopeless with her kids that you'd have to be a rock not to feel some sympathy. One was two-ish, as far as I could tell and I'm no expert. He specialized in lying screaming on the ground, writhing and pounding his heels, bellowing for his mum and then squealing like a greased balloon if she asked him what he wanted. When she picked him up, he started in on a round of full-body bucking, hitting her in the chin with his head and in the thighs with his feet. I'd have been tempted to drop-kick him, but Blaine clung on.

The other kid was another age I couldn't name: she could support her head but she wasn't mobile yet. She just clutched things and yearned for movement, desperately trying to coordinate her legs and feet to start advancing, but in fact just kicking and grabbing and going round in a circle like a break-dancer.

'Do you want a cookie?' Blaine asked her, ducking out of the way of her brother's next knock-out blow. 'Do you want to watch *SpongeBob*?' The big kid stopped bucking. 'I'll find an episode,' said Blaine, putting him down and taking out her phone. Before she had navigated to the site, he had started writhing on the ground again. Even I knew you didn't mention *SpongeBob* until the opening credits were rolling, and I know nothing.

'Do you want me to take the baby?' I said. She was grey with dust all down the side she was spinning on and I was sure she had gum in her hair.

'Would you?' said Blaine, turning a dazzling smile on me. 'I'll lug this little angel if you carry Navy.'

'Navy?' I said. Then I took a step back as Blaine's eyes flashed with a shot of pure murderous hatred.

'Yes,' she said in a cloyingly sweet voice. 'Navy is my daughter and Salem is my son.' I liked her even more then. She had given both her kids Paltrow-level daft names when she was off her head on the good drugs and now she was mortified. Who wouldn't be?

She headed for the stairs with Salem – Salem! *Salem!* – under one arm and was halfway up them when I called to her.

'Wouldn't you rather have something on the ground level?'
I said. 'For safety?'

'No,' she said. 'It's safer up here. People break in all the
time to first-floor rooms.'

'I meant for the kids,' I said. 'Hurling themselves over the
railings.'

'Ohhhh!' she said and stopped dead. Then she nodded. 'Good
call.'

'I'll ask Noleen to reassign you before anyone else gets
here, will I?' I said. 'José and Maria might not be up to the
stairs, and someone with twins is on her way, but the other
guy should be fine.'

'More people are coming?' said Blaine, stopping dead on
her way down again. 'I didn't know that. Are they all from the
hospital? Phil's co-workers?'

Poor Salem was still pogoing away, banging his head into
her stomach and his legs into the small of her back, since he
was now tucked under one arm like a yoga mat. The baby was
wriggling quite hard in my arms too and, every time she moved,
a noxious stink puffed out of her nappy waistband It was an
impressive guff for such a tiny, sweet angel of a creature to
have produced, I must say; the sort of smell that's shown in
cartoons as thick wavy lines, or yellow clouds. All round, it
seemed weird that Blaine wanted to chat about who else was
moving into the Last Ditch.

'I don't think so,' I told her. 'Sorry. It would have been nice
for you to have friends close, eh?'

'Pfft. Shehh. Right,' she said. 'It would have been juuuust
dreamy to be banged up with a buncha doctors' wives telling
me what to feed the maggots and when and why.'

I couldn't help but nod.

'I call them the carrot Nazis,' she went on. 'Sworn to fight
M&M's wherever M&M's are eaten.' I laughed. 'These chicks
have some serious paper and all the time in the world but you
wanna see them.' She didn't have much room to talk, mind
you: although her look was obviously high maintenance, it
wasn't all that attractive when you got close. The crazy make-up
was bad enough against the Kardashians' raven tresses, but
Blaine's hair was a walnut-brown colour that clashed epically.

Or, I didn't understand style these days. That was another option.

'Phil rides my ass about networking,' she was saying now. 'Like it matters to his patients whether his wife is bored to death in a parenting group or having her own kind of fun.' Then she narrowed her eyes at me. 'You married?'

'Nope,' I said. 'Sounds like he needs to back off and let you live *your* life instead of *his* job.'

I blame first ladies. That great dollop of the 1950s at the tippy-top of American society is the only thing that really does trickle down. I've lost count of the number of clients who complain that they need to cater brunches and cocktails, even full-blown dinners with fish courses, for their husbands' colleagues. And these are not ambassadors or CEOs of just-about-to-float companies. These are ordinary blokes. The sort of men who, if they were Scottish, would go to the pub or have a kick-about.

'Exactly,' said Blaine. 'Why does a doctor need Donna Reed in his kitchen?'

'Exactly,' I said too. I had no idea who Donna Reed was. 'So this is free,' I went on, opening up Room 102, a choice made to keep night-time crying away from my friends. Devin only used 101 for work these days and he always wore noise-cancelling earphones. Todd's mum could go in 103. Barb was as deaf as a post in her left ear, owing to all the Van Halen concerts in her youth and the Slipknot concerts in her fairly unbuttoned late middle-age.

Blaine stepped inside and dumped Salem down in the middle of one of the queen-sized beds. 'Bounce,' she told him. Salem didn't need to be told twice. He staggered to his feet and started making the most of his mum being the only mum in the history of mums who took that view of bed-bouncing.

I handed Navy over and backed away.

'Phee-ewf!' Blaine said. 'What a stink. No more kimchi for you, young lady.'

I didn't know if she was serious and I didn't care. If she was kidding, I liked her. If she had really given her daughter pickled cabbage then no wonder the other doctors' wives disapproved. And I liked her.

'I'll trundle your stuff in if you dink your car open,' I offered.

'No, you're good,' Blaine said, giving me a hard stare as if I was overstepping. 'You should go see what *she* needs.' She was pointing out of her open door towards a woman in a very shiny stretch mini-dress and teetering heels who had just stepped down from an SUV even bigger than Blaine's and was standing leaning against the closed driver-side door with the heels of her hands in her eye sockets. Noleen, hauling shut the chain-link gate to lock us all in again, caught my eye and jerked her head telling me to take care of it, whatever it was. My friends are really bad at remembering that I'm not on call 24/7. Although, to be fair, they don't try.

'Hi,' I said, strolling over. 'I'm Lexy. Welcome to the . . . motel.' She was weeping quite hard and shaking a bit too and I reckoned the name of the place wasn't the way to go right now. 'Can I help you?'

She took her hands away from her face and sniffed up a hard cry's worth of snot. 'Mirabelle Flynn,' she said. 'Meera. Hi. I'm cool. I'm good. I'm just tired and scared and so grateful and worried and kinda exhausted, you know.'

'I couldn't have put it better myself,' I said. 'Did Della tell you that I'm a therapist and we've got a doctor living here too. We can talk to you about all your worries. Over a glass of wine, maybe?'

Meera had been re-gathering her hair into its high ponytail and she gave me a brave smile as she snapped the scrunchie over it again. 'I'm not scared about the virus,' she said. 'I'm just a little freaked out that I've really left. I've left! I've left him! I should be sorry. I should at least be sorry about the bug, right? But I'm out! I've left him! I've done it. I've never been so happy in my entire life since I had the babies. But this time no drugs and I still feel like I could fly.'

'Ah,' I said. 'Well OK then. Talk about a silver lining.'

Meera gave me a beaming smile out of her haggard face. When her mouth couldn't grin any wider, her lips started to wobble and two more tears rolled down her cheeks. 'What have I done?' she whispered.

I stepped forward and hugged her. 'Taken the first step,' I said. 'I'm so sorry you had to, but what a great thing to have done for yourself and your children.'

She gave a big hiccupping sob and wiped her face on my shoulder. I hoped it was just tears she was leaving. 'Speaking of children,' she said and, extricating herself from my arms, she opened the middle door of the car.

'Oh they're so cute!' I said. They were a pair of little redheads with spatters of freckles across their noses, both dressed in train-driver costumes, cotton caps and all. And they were fast asleep, buckled tight into booster seats round their middles, heads, arms and legs lolling in total relaxation. 'And so chilled.'

Meera gave a small sob. 'I slipped them a little something,' she said. 'Medically approved. Our doctor prescribed it for a long flight back to see my mom in Philly at Christmas.'

'Uhhh-huh,' I said. Many things about American life continue to surprise me, but for sure the three-step response to unruly kids is one of them: 'sedation, Ritalin, military school' doesn't really have an equivalent where I come from. 'So can I carry one into your room for you?'

'Please,' she said. 'You take Joan and I'll take Bob. Thank you.'

Bob, I thought. Joan. Salem. Navy. There surely had to be a middle way. Meera sprung the nearest kid from the booster, leaving me to go round to the other side and grapple with the buckle, trying to spring the other one. It's a mum thing, I think, making a booster-seat belt buckle fly apart at a single touch. I was like a teenage boy faced with his first bra catch in the dark. But I made it, only half-waking up the kid as I snapped straps and randomly hit various knobbly bits. She yawned and held up her arms to be lifted. By a complete stranger. These were either some well-adjusted little railway engineers or that 'medically approved' sedative could bear a closer look from the FDA.

'So how did they get to be such train fans so young?' I said, as I met Meera at the boot of the car.

'We spend a lot of time in the museum,' said Meera. 'When it's too hot outside and it's Daddy's day off so we can't stay home.'

'It sounds like it's been pretty bad.' I had turned round and was bumming open the door of Room 104.

'He's a good father. He's never laid a finger on either of

them. He never would. He's going to be heartbroken when he gets home and finds them gone.' She had stopped in the doorway but not to look around at the fittings. I don't think she was seeing what lay in front of her eyes. She was far away inside her own head, imagining a scene that made fresh tears come. She shifted the little boy on to one shoulder and took her phone out of her sweatshirt pouch pocket.

'Don't call him!' I said. I probably wouldn't have, if I'd been at work. At work, if a woman who'd finally left her horror of a husband told me she was going back after less than an hour, I'd be professionally bound to say it was her decision and I would support her in whatever she felt she had to do. But, like I said, I wasn't at work.

'Of course not!' she said. 'I'm just checking the time. If I go now I could get home before him. And I could leave the car full until he's asleep and have everything unpacked before he wakes up and he'd never know.'

'Because if he found out . . .?' I said.

'He loves his kids,' Meera said. 'If he knew I'd taken them and then brought them back . . .'

'He'd be sorry he made you feel like you had to, and he'd ask what he could change?' I said.

Meera said nothing. She cupped the little boy's head in her hand and laid him down gently on the bed. So I cupped the little girl's head and laid her down too. I was a bit less successful, and I had to untangle her chubby legs from underneath her bottom. Then we both stood and looked at them. They looked nothing at all like her. I pieced together a picture of Wonderdad from their strawberry hair and freckled white skin. Irish ancestry, I thought. Then I hoped that wasn't lazy stereotyping because I knew he was a policeman.

'How old are they?' I asked.

'Four.'

'Can I ask you a question? You said he'd never do anything to hurt them, right?' She nodded. 'Has he ever hurt you when they were around to see it?' She didn't really nod. She did like half a nod, just lowering her chin and leaving it down there. 'So the only reason he hasn't done anything to hurt *them* is a bit of a technicality,' I said. 'When they're five, or six, and they know enough to understand what they're looking at, it's going to hurt them plenty to see him hurting you.'

'Yeah but he'll—' said Meera, then bit her lip.

'He'll stop hurting you in front of them when they're big enough to understand?' I asked. 'Or when they're big enough to tell people?' Meera hitched her skirt up so she could bend, sat down on the edge of the other bed, and put the heels of her hands back in her eye sockets. 'I know you know this,' I said. 'So don't hate me for saying it. But good fathers don't hurt their kids' mums.'

'He has such a stressful job,' she said. 'He sees terrible things. And people can be so suspicious of the police. So rude and mean.'

'Good,' I said. 'Glad to hear it. Sounds like it couldn't happen to a nicer guy.'

She laughed. 'Fair point,' she said. 'I hang out with mostly cop wives when I'm not at work.'

'Yeah?' I said. 'I can't wait to introduce you to Blaine two doors down then. She's married to a doctor but she's seen right through *their* wives.' Meera laughed again. I sat down beside her. 'This is going to be perfect,' I said. 'You won't be lonely with all of us around and he can't get to you. Because of Noleen who let you in.'

'With the sweatshirt?' Meera said. I laughed now. I hadn't noticed but I could remember my own early days of knowing Nolly.

'And there are three more kids,' I said. 'And another spouse, more or less in your situation. I don't know if Della told you?' She shook her head. 'And,' I said, 'Noleen and Kathi are nuts on supplies. They've got enough toilet paper and coffee to see us all good till Doomsday.'

'*Toilet* paper?' said Meera.

'You've had a lot on your mind,' I guessed aloud. 'Not been watching the news?'

But I didn't take the time to explain to her because I could see that the big gates were open again and Noleen was waving in a two-fer.

One of them was Barb Truman, now backing her Toyota Tacoma up to the bottom of the stairs, very gently, but not gently enough to stop the chinking of many, many, wine bottles in the truck bed.

'I'm all set!' she called to me. 'Party at my place!'

'I thought you'd gone dry?' I said, going over. There had to be twenty cases of wine, twelve bottles in each. Where was her actual luggage?

'Dry?' she said. 'No way. Topical oestrogen, baby.'

'God almighty, Barb,' I said. 'I meant I thought you'd stopped *drinking.*'

'I have!' she said. She opened her arms wide and blinked her innocence. 'I haven't touched a drop of Scotch or vodka in months. I'm strictly a beer and wine girl now.'

'Right,' I said. Then Todd leaned over the railing from the walkway above. 'Mom!' he said. 'Welcome! Can I help you . . .?' His voice died in this throat as he spotted what was in Barb's truck bed. 'I thought you were dry?'

I left. Partly because I didn't want to hear Todd's comeback to the oestrogen line and partly because the other new arrival was looking a bit lost. He had parked his Saturn in the check-in bay outside Reception but hadn't got further than opening the driver's door and putting his feet out on the tarmac. I walked over. I was beginning to feel like a cruise director. I should have a clipboard and a memorized calendar of activities.

'Hi,' I said. 'Are you Della's friend? Moving in today?'

'Yes,' he said standing and putting out a hand to shake, then quickly changing it to an elbow bump. 'Arif Jafari.' He had an Oakland As T-shirt on and a pair of denim cut-offs with thick socks and Timberland boots. His legs were skinny and obviously cold because hair was standing out on the goosepimples, making a fuzzy nimbus.

'Lexy Campbell,' I said. 'Do you know what room you're in? I think it'll be upstairs but I'm not sure which.'

'I asked for a quiet one,' he said. He glanced over my shoulder towards where Barb and Todd were beginning to unload the wine. One of Blaine's kids was screaming its head off inside Room 102. But it wasn't transient worry about parties and babies disturbing him that had put the deep line between his eyes and those settled grooves at either side of his mouth. They hinted at a more long-term sadness.

'I'm not a complainer,' he said, jumping to the wrong conclusion about why I had said nothing. 'It's my job: tech support. We're working at home now and we have an office soundtrack to play but it won't fly if there's a background of children and . . .'

'Van Halen,' I said. I decided not to mention Slipknot. 'I see what you mean. Well, your best bet's going to be up there beside the laundromat, probably. You don't mind the smell of detergent, do you?'

He smiled and the lines round his mouth turned into dimples, although the line between his eyes didn't go away. 'I love it,' he said. 'My mom worked in a hotel laundry when I was a kid. Back home in Iran. I spent my childhood napping in hampers.'

'Sounds lovely,' I said. 'So how long have you been here? I only arrived about a year ago. I came to get married.'

'Me too,' he said. His face had fallen again. 'And look how that's going.'

'I'm divorced,' I said. 'Judge to judge in six months flat.'

'But you didn't move out of your house because you were scared to be in isolation with your spouse, did you?' he said.

'No,' I agreed. 'I moved out because I came home and found my husband porking his ex-wife.' Then I froze. Della had said he was religious! And I'd just said something really rude! And *pork*! When the haze of mortification cleared, though, I could see that he was laughing.

'You win,' he said.

'*And* I'm a marriage therapist,' I added. That little titbit is terrible PR but it's great for cheering people up.

Right enough, he laughed again. 'You definitely win. You should put it on your website.'

'Yeah right,' I said. 'Fail at marriage the Lexy Campbell way.'

'No seriously,' he said. 'It would bring people in. Much less intimidating. I might have spoken to a therapist before it had gotten this bad, if they weren't all so perfect and together.'

'Not an issue with me, Arif. Collapsed marriage, terrible relationship with my mum and dad. British teeth.' I grinned to prove it.

'Oh yes!' he said. 'That's tough too. Perfect Americans looking down on the rest of us.'

He was being kind because he was extremely easy on the eye and his teeth were gorgeous, but still I reckoned I could get used to having an ally around here for a week or two.

FOUR

'So . . . how far down the Kool-Aid Highway are we taking this thing?' said Noleen. She and I, Todd and Kathi, Della and Devin were gathered, as we so often gathered, in the back office behind Reception, arranged around the collection of armchairs too knackered to go in the renting rooms any more, along with the office chair Nolly had wheeled through from her desk in front, plus a yoga ball some guest had left behind – and think what a relief *that* must have been, when they realized at the Oregon border or the start of the San Fernando Valley that they were shot of it. Diego was nowhere to be seen. He'd met Salem, Bob and Joan by now and was lording it over them, showing off the motel like the king of the hill.

'He's with Meera, right?' I said to Della. 'With the twins? Not Blaine, with the babies? Because she's a total bubblehead, no offence.'

'The doctor's wife?' said Todd. 'Really?'

'I know people married to doctors who're morons,' said Kathi, making me cheer inside. If she was snarking she was OK.

'How'd you mean "Kool-Aid"?' I asked Noleen. She started to answer but Todd broke in.

'Kathi,' he said. 'And this goes for you two too.' He nodded to Della and Devin, 'Operation Cocker is going to be hard on those of us who're parted from our loved ones, like Lexy and me. Some generosity from your place of privilege would be welcome.'

Noleen drew a huge breath then pursed her lips and ripped a cracker of a raspberry until her lungs were empty again.

'What loved ones?' I said. 'Taylor? He's a liked one. I'm separated from my month-old liked one. Don't pin this on me. So. What Kool-Aid?'

'I mean are we going to cook up big communal meals and have singalongs?' Kathi said. 'Or is everyone on their own? Like regular guests.'

'Are you charging them?' said Devin. 'If you're charging the going rate, I guess they can do what they want. If not . . . I dunno.'

'Where would we be without hot takes like that?' Todd said. '*Are* you charging them though? Because maybe I can pay for Blaine? Since Roger's living in her house. I'll pay for Blaine.'

'I'll kick in for Arif if he's having trouble,' I said. 'I'd like to help him.'

'I want to help Meera,' said Della. 'I want her to have no reason to go back to that man. I know what I said before, but I didn't know how bad it was until she opened up today.'

'And we've already settled José and Maria's billing tariff to mutual satisfaction,' said Noleen.

It wasn't like her to speak so stiffly. I narrowed my eyes at her. 'You're not charging them a cent, are you?'

'I'm a businesswoman!' said Noleen. 'Of course I'm charging them. I mean . . . have you seen them? They look like a coupla little bunny rabbits in bad clothes. So they're paying by cleaning their own room and making their own coffee in the morning. Unless I get their coffee and clean their room.'

'Charge my mom hard cash,' Todd said. 'She can afford it.'

'You could ask Meera and Arif and the bunnies to cook,' I said. 'In lieu of rent. Maria looks like a woman who knows her way around a pot of stew. I'd definitely sing songs round a campfire to get a taste of it.'

'Or we just wing it,' Devin said. 'How many nights are we talking about? If they even shut Beteo County, how long are they going to shut it for? Really?'

'A week?' I said. 'Two?' I was thinking one night of Maria's chili, one night of some Iranian speciality, Todd's world-famous black'n'cracked seafood one night (would Arif eat seafood, if he was religious?). I'd knock up a big batch of mince and tatties unless someone stopped me, and with the taco night, pizza night and breakfast-for-dinner night that were mandated in the city by-laws we were there.

'Hm,' Todd said. 'Well, that's not what I'm hearing now. Roger thinks it could take over a month statewide.'

'A month?' All of us were in the chorus, although Devin was

a bit late because he was swallowing a mouthful of Coke, but he caught up: '—onth?'

'China is building hospitals,' Todd said. 'A month is tight.'

'*We're* not going to be building hospitals,' said Kathi. 'Are we?'

Todd said nothing. Didn't need to.

'It's so hard to believe it's real,' Della said.

'Because you can't see it?' Kathi asked. 'That doesn't make it unreal. That just makes it small.'

'There are scientists all over the world looking at it on slides right this minute,' Devin said.

'I think,' I said, 'speaking professionally, which I know I don't often do and so I hope you'll forgive me' – the truth was that I needed a bit of thinking time to dream up what to say. But saying *something* was an emergency – 'yes, I think the more camaraderie and community we can offer here at the Last Ditch, the less the impact on everyone's mental health.'

'Speak for yourself,' said Noleen. 'Hell is other people.'

'OK, well the less likely it is that any of the guests'll go stir-crazy and sneak off home for some company. That do you? So I'm for the cook-outs. I'll make—'

'God no! Not mince!' said Todd. 'How can your national dish be ground beef and mashed potato? Some of you must have had teeth sometime in history.'

'Our national dish is haggis,' I said, with dignity.

'Which is ground organs *dreaming* of being beef,' Todd said.

'And served with rutabaga!' said Noleen.

'Not just rutabaga,' I snapped back. 'Also . . . mashed potato. Shut up.'

But I'd convinced them about the communal dinners because, if we were eating together, then people wouldn't be sloping off to the supermarket for their own ingredients ten times a day.

'What about entertainment?' said Della. 'If we're not going to the movies – will the movies close, Todd? – or the parks – they can't close parks, can they, Todd? – then we have to make sure no one gets bored.'

'I'm not playing charades,' said Noleen. 'Or karaoke or Scrabble, or Clue, or Monopoly. Or doing puzzles or yoga.'

'Poker?' said Della.

'Poker I can live with,' Noleen said.

'I don't know how to play poker,' I said.

'That,' said Noleen, 'is not a problem.' She smiled wolfishly. 'I can teach you.'

'You know what we really need,' Todd said. I glanced around to check if anyone else knew what he was talking about, but all I saw were blank looks. 'A case! I'd kick over the Scrabble board if we had a case to solve.'

'It wouldn't help Meera and Arif and Blaine,' I said. 'Or José and Maria Cottontail.'

'Those two can sit in the sun and reflect on a life well-lived,' Todd said. 'But the rest of them could help detect if we had something to detect, couldn't they?'

'What about Barb?' I said, going for deadpan.

Todd shuddered. 'What could she detect? Light beer in the keg? Lo-Alco wine in the punchbowl. Did you see what she moved in earlier? She's left all my baby pictures behind.'

'Todd,' I reminded him, 'it's not a wildfire evacuation.'

'Oh yeah,' he said, rubbing his nose. 'Duh.' Life in Northern California does that to you.

'I think you should go with poker,' Della said, 'and not hope for a case. If everyone's home and no one's out getting up to mischief, it seems like the mayhem ratio would tank.'

'Tell that to Arif and Meera,' Kathi said.

'Have you never read Agatha Christie, Della?' said Todd. 'Seventeen strangers thrown together in a remote country house over a snowy winter weekend? Or, you know, the equivalent.'

'A locked room mystery!' said Noleen. 'Who needs poker?'

'A common mistake,' said Devin. 'You don't mean "locked room". You mean "closed circle". That's what we are: a closed circle of seventeen strangers trapped together behind a chain-link fence, refugees from a hostile world outside the gate, with tensions running high and old scores to settle.'

'What old scores?' I said. 'The only old scores are between Barb and Todd.'

'And I would never kill my mom,' Todd said, 'because jail cells have cockroaches.'

He meant it too.

'But that's an essential element,' said Devin. 'The strangers aren't *actually* strangers. They're long-lost siblings and regimental comrades left for dead on a battlefield. Or bigamous spouses.'

'Better not be,' Della said.

'Or just plain old sworn enemies. It doesn't matter. It's the being holed up together with no escape that's key.'

I hoped someone else was going to laugh, because my throat had dried out and I wasn't sure I could manage it. I was still waiting when a knock came at the office door.

'I hope that's not the inspector,' Noleen said, going to open it, 'because he's turned over a few pages at once if it is. We haven't even found the old man with the paper knife in his neck yet.'

It wasn't the inspector. It was Blaine. 'Uh, hi,' she said. '*This* is cosy.'

I cringed. I've never been one of the cool kids before. Even now, Noleen and Kathi weren't cool. Todd was cool on the surface but *such* a dork underneath. Della and Devin were sort of cool, I suppose. Roger was Captain Cool of the Coolship Coolterprise. But he wasn't here. Anyway, before now I had only ever been the one knocking on the door and finding out there was a party and I wasn't invited. So, above my pay-grade as the decision might be, and although Blaine was the least needy of the new arrivals, I piped up.

'We're plotting how to get you all to join our merry band!'

'Not a real band,' Devin said, waving around at the rest of us. 'Because can you imagine?'

Blaine had put on even more make-up since earlier and had surely had her hair in hot rollers to make those blowsy curls. As she smirked at Devin, Della didn't put a proprietorial hand on his arm or anything so crass. She didn't frown and she didn't pout. On the other hand she didn't blink.

'We were thinking we could all eat together,' I went on. 'Take turns cooking and eat family-style?'

'Oh well, I don't eat much,' Blaine said. She spread her hands over her hips as she spoke, smoothing down her figure-hugging trousers. 'But if you want to feed the kids I'd be happy to drop them off. What time?'

'But you have to eat something,' Noleen said. 'And I bet you have a speciality you could whip up for the rest of us one night too?'

'I cancelled my meal-kit delivery service,' said Blaine. 'Otherwise, I'd love to.'

'But won't Phil need the ingredients?' said Todd. 'For him and Roger?'

Blaine frowned at him, then cocked her finger and clicked her tongue. 'Are you the hunk's husband? We've never met but I ran into your gorgeous chunka chocolate candy at a 5K Turkey Trot last Thanksgiving. Hoooo-eee.'

'Ch-chocolate?' said Todd. Fair play to him for being able to speak at all. I was still at the stage of wondering whether to lift my jaw off the floor with both hands or leave it in case I needed it down there again when she spoke the next time.

'Aw, don't be a stiff,' said Blaine. 'Anyway, Phil said there was a dance studio that I could use while I'm here?'

'There's a room you can use to dance in,' Kathi said. 'If you push the furniture back.'

'Perfecto!' said Blaine. 'And who'll take the kids while I'm busy?'

'I'm happy to,' I said, even as the others rounded on me. I had changed my mind about this bint and I reckoned whenever those poor babies got to spend time away from her it was going to boost their future happiness and chances of survival. I wouldn't put it past her to hit one of them in their pillowy little tummies with a flying foot or leave them alone in the other room so she could get her practice done in peace. I decided not to ask where they were right now.

'She's awful!' Kathi whispered, as Noleen dragged Blaine back out to the front office to set her up with a key. 'Todd, you never said she was an asshole.'

'How was I supposed to . . . oh!' Todd slapped himself on the backside. When he took his hand away again he had his phone in it. 'Kick that door shut, Della, would you?' he said, before answering. Then went on, 'Hey, babe, you're on speaker, so don't salivate out loud for my hot little bod, huh?'

'For fuck sake,' said Roger. 'I'm in the break room at work.'

'Ohhhhh!' I said. 'Very informative! So when you're *not* in the break room . . .'

'And I don't do phone sex no matter where I am,' Roger added hurriedly.

'No of course not except yeah you do and now we know it,' I said. 'Ha ha ha ha ha ha.'

Once or twice, over the years, new clients have asked me if I'm really a therapist. I have no idea what they're driving at.

'I'm glad you called,' said Todd, as Noleen sidled back in. 'Is she gone? Good, she's gone. Roger, why didn't you tell us Phil's wife is a grade-A nightmare?'

'I've never met her,' came Roger's voice down the phone. 'Is she refusing to follow your safety protocols? Kick her out and she can come back here then. This was to protect her from us, not us from her.'

'Please don't say that,' Todd said. 'No, it's not virus stuff. And anyway, she reckons she met you at a Turkey Trot.'

'OK,' said Roger. I could never work out if he was 500 per cent gay or 500 per cent married or both, but I believed that he had no memory of meeting a glamorous woman decked out in Lycra and sweaty from running.

'Is Phil an asshole too?' Devin chipped in.

'Wait, who all's there?' said Roger.

'Everyone,' Della told him. I got an attack of the fuzzies, like I always did whenever one of them – all married now, all coupled up, no need to add danglers – said 'Us' or 'We' or 'Everyone' and meant me too.

'Phil's a regular guy,' said Roger. 'I'm not sure they have the happiest marriage in the world but he, you know . . . loves his kids, shares his chips.'

'DON'T SHARE CHIPS!' said Todd, Kathi and me all together, making quite a racket.

'It's an expression,' Roger said. 'Guys, I gotta go. Todd, take me off speaker, huh?'

'Ooooo-ooooo,' said Della and Noleen and me all together, in a chorus, followed up with kissy noises.

'That is *not* an expression,' Kathi said.

'Nope,' I said. 'Cash in your chips. Had your chips. Piss on your chips.'

'Why are all your sayings so disgusting?' she asked me.

'What do you mean?' I demanded.

'So many old proverbs about shit. Your embroidered pillow stores must be something else.'

'What are you . . .?'

'I love you so much . . .' Kathi said. She had a point. The end of that was: I could use your shite for toothpaste.

'And I hope your next . . .'

Shite's a hedgehog, I filled in silently. 'But hope in one hand, shit in the other, is Yiddish,' I pointed out. 'So it's not just us.'

'Anyway,' said Noleen, 'stop wasting my time when I can't get to the sweatshirt printers. We're supposed to be bitching up *other* people.'

'Oh yeah,' said Della. 'We were at: so what if Phil loves his kids. Who doesn't?'

'Blaine?' I said. 'Or at least she doesn't fuss over them.'

'That's more like it!' said Noleen. 'Tell me more.'

'It wasn't sweet nothings,' Todd said, putting his phone back in his pocket after hanging up. 'It was news. One of the hospital board is the wife of a . . . fill in some steps . . . of an aide to the former governor. And she reckons it'll definitely go statewide any day.'

'Right,' said Noleen. 'That settles it. I'm going to the wholesaler's. Who's going to Costco?'

'Not Kathi,' said Della and Devin and me.

'Lexy can go,' Noleen said. 'But hurry back. We need you at dinner. You've met them all and you can introduce them without . . . you know.'

'What?' said Todd. 'Was that directed at me? Without *what*?'

I didn't listen to the answer. The thought was striking me that maybe I wasn't a dangler after all. Maybe I was the lynchpin of the group. The hub, the hinge, the crux. Or did I mean 'crucible'? Maybe I meant 'fulcrum'. Whatever the word, maybe I was all that and a bag of chips. Another fine expression, and totally shite-free.

I'm not a Costco chick at heart. OK, I'm not a chick at heart, but I'm trying to assimilate. See, my kitchen and shower room are tiny, and the rest of the boat isn't choked up with cupboard space either, so unless I want to use kitchen-roll multi-packs as side-tables, or hang bags of tortilla chips on the wall and say they're art, I can't really do stadium groceries. It's not snobbishness, because I *love* IKEA. A three-pack of crap Tupperware with a meatball chaser? I am in. But Costco even on a good day would tax me.

Costco on that Saturday in March 2020, after Gav the Gov said old people needed to stay at home and old people who lived in old people's homes could only be visited if they were . . . well, you remember. There was a crackle in the air as our brainstems told us to hide nuts and pick off impala (not sure what species this is; go with me), while our cerebra said maybe we could share it all and make sure no one went short. And I was shopping for seventeen. It is impossible to shop for seventeen, for ten days, more if we stretched it, and not look like a hoarder.

I stuffed my trolley with the breakfast choices of everyone from José – Bran Buds – to Navy – expensive mush with a name in such a heartfelt font I couldn't decipher it. I bought lamb for our Iranian night (Arif had packed his spices from home for exactly this eventuality, and he talked me through how to choose garlic like an old French man training a truffle dog); I bought beef for our Mexican night ('Fat fat fat!' Maria had said, taking my face in her hands and shaking my head to make sure it went in. 'Grasa! Grasa! Grasa!' I got it. She had probably been fighting a losing battle with the Queens of Lean for all her years here north of the border). I bought chicken for taco night, for the eventual carb crash that Todd was still denying would happen, and for the clean eating requirements Blaine suddenly professed, despite what she'd said about carrots and fascism. I bought bacon for breakfast-for-dinner night, and fish fingers for the under tens, of which there were suddenly five! And bread and jam and peanut butter and crisps and dips and Oreos and beans and pasta and popping corn and a big paper sack of flour because everyone else was buying it and by now I was my lizard brain's bitch. I was practically grunting and dragging my knuckles as I hauled it all out to Todd's Jeep.

'That's disgusting,' said a woman just stepping out of the car next to mine. 'Hoarding should be illegal.'

'I'm catering for a scratch camp of at-risk dependents of first responders,' I told her. Which was practically true.

'Bullshit,' she said. 'But I'm going to use that line if anyone bugs *me*. So thank you.'

'You're not welcome,' I said. 'We're going to have to be better than this.'

But she was gone, leaving me with nothing but two over-the-shoulder middle fingers to remember her by.

'Well,' I said to myself, 'we're going to have to be better than *that*.'

Noleen went a bit *Tenko* with the shopping when I got it home. She marked things off on a sheet attached to a clipboard and double-locked the back office where the crisps were. But then she kept doling out tubs of ice cream as long as anyone asked for one, once the pizza was down to the crusts.

'I can't believe you didn't buy any dipping sauce for our pizza crusts,' Devin said. 'Are we supposed to just eat, like, the crusts?'

Della said something softly to José and Maria and they all nodded and stared at Devin. I had heard Della's 'pot of rice and happy for it' speech a couple of times and I assumed Devin had heard it more than that.

'Jeez!' he said, picking up his crust and starting to chew. 'I'm eating! Watch me eat!'

I thought again that we were going to have to try a bit harder to be extra-kind while this all worked through or we'd end up shredding each other. Somewhat surprising, I reckoned, because there *was* a common enemy, which usually helps, but it was invisible, like Della had said, and maybe invisible enemies don't count.

There was Blaine, of course, since her 'chocolate candy' comment, and what with her steely determination never to cook. But it was hard to bond over loathing her when she was sitting right there. Which she was, despite all the talk of practically being breatharian.

I shouldn't have worried. Our true common enemy was on its way. In the end, Blaine didn't get a look-in.

FIVE

I slept badly.

And waking didn't help much.

As I emerged from dreams, through denial, all the way to the reality of my bladder, I realized the birdsong I'd been hearing wasn't birdsong at all but human voices raised in alarm, and quite nearby too. I scrambled out of bed, threw on a dressing gown and a pair of clogs – Diego's kittens were still making good use of the slough bank whenever they could – and set off round to the forecourt to see what was up.

I'm not great first thing before my coffee but even I couldn't miss it: over the chain-link fence currently keeping the world out of the Last Ditch, someone had tied a couple of bedsheets to make a banner. And on that banner in foot-high red letters was daubed:

COME HOME, BITCH.

Meera in a chiffon and marabou wrap, with matching stiletto slides, stood pale and shaking in the doorway of her room, with Della and Devin both holding her and trying to soothe her. Diego was doing his best too: 'That,' he said, 'is a bad word. Real bad. Not nice. Only bad people say it. That person wrote that bad word is a bad, bad person.'

Meera tried a watery smile. Meanwhile Noleen advanced on the fence and started ripping the sheets free and folding them up into a bundle. Kathi was outside their room, hugging herself and grimacing.

Blaine had appeared in her doorway in a pair of sushi pyjamas. Her hair was tousled but still perfect and her face was invisible inside some kind of poultice.

'Are you OK?' I said.

'Uhh, you tell me,' Blaine muttered. She couldn't really move her lips but she pointed at the sheets to help get her point across. For some reason, Noleen was working left to right, so the BITCH was still plainly visible. 'I thought this place would be dull but safe. What's with the drama?'

'No,' I said. 'I mean, what's wrong with your face?'

'Overnight silicon lift mask,' she said. Behind her, one of the babies started to cry and she raised her eyes to heaven, or as far as she could with a plastic exoskeleton plastered over herself from chin to hairline, and went back inside her room. The screaming rose in pitch towards true terror and another voice joined in. I surmised that Blaine usually took the mask off before she greeted her kids in the morning.

'OK,' I said, going over to Meera. 'We can deal with this really easily. We get a restraining order.'

'He's a cop,' Della reminded me.

'So he should know better,' I said, before Diego cut me off with another dose of six-year-old wisdom.

'Don't go back,' he said. 'Don't go home to a bad man who called you a bad name. That's bad.'

'The kid might need a thesaurus,' I said, 'but you can't fault his reasoning.'

Meera was frowning and seemed puzzled. 'Are there security cams?' she said. 'He's usually so careful not to do anything that would make him look bad.'

'He *is* bad,' said Diego.

'We have a camera pointed at the office doorway,' Noleen said, as she passed en route to the dumpsters, holding the bundle clear of her onesie. 'But not on the fence. If he drove past the police station, though, he'll be on their cams.'

'He's a cop,' said Della again. Then, at a sound from upstairs, we all looked up.

Todd, in a gel eye-mask and a chinstrap, looking almost as freaky as Blaine, had cleared his throat in a communicative way and was now urgently beckoning. 'Can I have some help up here?'

Kathi and I trotted off to the stairway and took them two at a time. 'What is it?' I said, advancing along the walkway. Then I saw Arif standing frozen and waxy – much the same as Meera downstairs – hanging on to the railing. Tears were pouring down his face.

'What's up?' I said.

'Don't throw them in the garbage,' Arif said. 'Keep them. Prints. Evidence. In case.'

'Good point,' I said, and shouted as much down to Noleen.

'You can fish 'em out again then,' she shouted back.

'Ew,' said Kathi, shrinking back as if I was already sprayed with filth.

'Happy to!' I shouted down to Noleen. 'There's no danger,' I said to Kathi. 'I'll wear gloves and shower afterwards.'

'Take a break!' Todd said. 'Arif, did Lexy happen to mention that she's a therapist? Of course she did, she could give lessons to vegans.' Arif almost smiled. 'But did she tell you that she's on a campaign to make Kathi lick a toilet and me eat an ant farm?'

'What?' said Arif. Who could blame him?

'Don't worry,' I said. 'About the sign. Meera's going to get a restraining order. I'll go to the cops once I'm dressed and put it in motion.'

'Meera is?' said Arif. 'Wait, does she think that was meant for *her*?'

'Well, yeah,' said Kathi. 'Because of the B-word.'

'My wife . . .' said Arif, but his voice cracked before he could say more.

'Hang on,' said Todd. 'You think your *wife* would call you *that*?'

'Why would today be different from any other day?' said Arif softly.

I leaned over the railing. 'Diego?' I called. 'If a lady wrote that word on that sheet, what would you think of that?'

'She's a bad lady,' Diego shouted up.

'Out of the mouths of babes and children,' I said. 'Arif, can I hug you?'

He nodded and I wrapped my arms around him, gutted to feel how cold he was, shivery and thin, as if he might snap. Todd wrapped his arms round him from the other side and Kathi tried to get hers round all of us. We rocked and patted a while until Kathi said:

'We might have to can hugging if this virus gets really bad.'

'And we have to stop this hug right now,' said Todd, 'because someone hasn't flossed. Arif, everything you ever heard about Brits is true.'

'Oh sod off,' I told him, mostly because he was right. I only ever floss after barbecue.

I had to talk my way past the chain-link to get to the police station. 'Kathi, Kathi, listen to me,' I said. 'There are sixty million people in California and there are five hundred cases.'

'Five hundred!'

'Oh God give me strength! When the county or the state says we need to do whatever we're going to call what we might need to do, I will do it. But today, I'm going to get a restraining order on Arif's wife and Meera's husband. Or try anyway. Look at it this way: if I succeed then they'll stay away. Which is safer. For everyone.'

She thought it over long and hard and then nodded.

'Thank you,' I said. 'And thank you for hugging Arif earlier. That was kind and brave. Can I say that?'

'I'd rather you didn't,' Kathi said. 'It's like you're always grading me.'

Which sounded really horrible so I slunk off to the cop shop, my tail between my legs and my head hanging.

It's a short walk from the Last Ditch to Cuento PD HQ. Just past the self-storage facility and through the tunnel under the railway tracks, and if I'm making it sound insalubrious, all I can say is I'm not mentioning the dust blowing into town off the acres of tomato fields, or the skunky stink of the bins at the back of the Swiss Sisters drive-thru coffee shack. It's my hometown now and I try not to be too honest about it when I don't have to.

I let myself in and felt a burst of cheer. Either the turnover in receptionist/dispatchers at Cuento PD is indicative of a toxic workplace, or the city's avoiding having to pay benefits by employing a ton of part-timers for a few hours a week each, but I had never seen the same person twice, any of the regrettably many times I had found myself appealing for help at this particular Plexiglas window. In other words, this one was a fresh start.

'Hi,' I said, with a big smile.

'You're that shrink on the boat, ain't ya?' said the total stranger.

'Lexy Campbell,' I said. 'Pleased to meet you. Say, I wonder if you can help. I'd like to start the process of applying for restraining orders.'

'Zzz?' she said. 'Like plural? You need more'n one restraining order, the problem might be you.'

I laughed. 'Not me. They're on behalf of two recently separated spouses both being harassed – well, one is and we don't know which – by their domestic partners.'

'Sound like your marriage counselling is super-crappy.'

'They're not clients,' I said. 'They're neighbours.'

'Huh,' she said. 'OK.' Then she bent her head and carried on reading her magazine.

'So . . . can you help me?'

'Uh . . . nope.'

'Why not?'

'Because this is a police department,' she said, without looking up. 'The neighbours need to go to the court up in Madding. File their forms with the judge and wait for the court to decide, then serve the papers to the parties and turn up on the date to hear the ruling.'

'Oh, is that all?' I said.

'No. They also need to pay the fee.'

'Of course they do!' I said. 'What's the fee?'

'Five hundred and ninety-five dollars,' she said. She looked up this time. She didn't want to miss that little bomb landing.

'Wow,' I said. 'Each, right? Of course right. OK then. Well, in case they can't afford that, I'd like to report a crime. To be going on with.'

'OK.' She turned a page of her magazine and pretended to be engrossed by the small print of the prescription drug advert that had been on the previous page.

'So could I speak to a police officer?' I said. Even as I spoke, I heard the door behind me open and the squeak thump squeak thump of a sizable polis advancing in crêpe-soled shoes. I didn't even have to turn. I'd know that gait anywhere.

'Ms Campbell!'

I turned anyway.

'Detective Rankinson!'

'Sergeant,' she said.

'Oh! Hey! Congratulations.' I was genuinely chuffed. It didn't matter that Molly Rankinson couldn't stand me and I kind of hated her right back. Any time a sister gets a foot on the ladder I'm happy.

'Less surprise would be nice,' she said.

'That wasn't surprise,' I said. 'It was joy.'

'Joy?' said Molly. 'That seems normal.' Sarcasm was her factory setting. If we didn't hate each other so much we could have been good friends.

'So anyway, I'm here to report a crime as I was just telling your magazine reader there,' I said. 'Sorry. Uncalled for.'

'What is it this time?' said Molly. Which was *totally* uncalled for, because it wasn't as if I did it a lot and the three times I had, I was right.

'Not sure what to call it,' I said, only now realizing that I might have worked this out on Google before I set off. 'It's not exactly vandalism, or trespass, and not exactly threatening behaviour or an announced intent to commit a crime. It's . . .'

'Why don't you tell me what happened,' Molly said, 'and leave the category to me?'

She ushered me through the divide from Reception to the guts of the precinct, away from shiny tiles and potted plants and on to scuffed linoleum and hands-down the worst multi-drink vending machine that ever spat powder into cups and added lukewarm water with scum on top. Even now, at the start of the day, when it hadn't been used for hours, it seethed with the stench of tomato soup, cocoa, coffee and worst of all 'tea' spreading a miasma throughout the back corridors that must make the cops yearn for a drunk to come in and puke on the floor, freshen things up for them.

Both of us were holding our breath when Molly opened the door of an interview room and ushered me in.

'Shoot,' she said.

'Someone came to the Last Ditch in the night and wrote COME HOME BITCH in red paint in letters a foot high.'

'I thought you said it wasn't vandalism,' said Molly. 'That's criminal damage. I'll send a car down.'

'Ah well no,' I said. 'It was written on bedsheets that someone hung up.'

'But that's still criminal trespass with specific intent.'

'Well no again,' I said. 'They were hung on the fence. From the other side. Like, tied on at the top and then let fall? You know what I mean?'

'And it said, COME HOME, BITCH?'

'Exactly!' I spread my hands to share with her the horribleness and undeniability of how illegal that must be.

'Pity,' said Molly. 'That's an invitation. Not a threat. Nothing we can do.'

'Aw, come on!'

'I'm not saying it's irresistible,' she told me. 'Only that if it had been "come home or else" or "come home if you know what's good for you", we'd be off to the mall. But as it is, I can't help you.' She waited a beat. 'So, you gonna go?'

'Me?' I said. 'It's not for *me*. That ship has sailed, hit an iceberg, sunk and inspired a long boring movie. The message was for someone else.'

'So what are you doing here?'

'I volunteered to come and tell you. Thing is, we've turned the Last Ditch into a sort of safe haven for various people in case the governor issues a Don't Budge order or whatever we're going to call it. Vulnerable seniors, dependents of first responders, people in danger of domestic abuse. We're calling it Operation . . . we haven't settled on a name yet, but that's what we're doing.'

'Very commendable.'

'And Barb Truman.'

'Does the *Voyager* know?' Molly said. 'They're looking for feel-good angles.'

'Uh no,' I said. 'And it's not going to. Because one of the spouses of the DV victims has found out where they are and came last night to leave a sign that's a clear threat to their partner – whatever you might say – and the last thing we need is the other one reading the paper and finding out where to come to do even worse.'

'I don't say "whatever". You described intimidation. It's not a threat unless there's an actual threat. And intimidation isn't a crime. Sorry, but there's nothing I can do.'

'Until it's too late, right?' I said. 'Yeah, I've heard that.'

'I could move in,' she said.

I rewarded her with a bit of a laugh for her sarcasm. 'Right.'

'I'm not kidding,' she said. 'I might be on desk duty soon, working from home. And home's not great. You got any last rooms going on the good ship *Quarantine*?'

'Wait, you were serious?' I said. Then, 'Why are you on desk duty?'

'I'm not,' said Molly.

'Because I thought cops had to be in tip-top health.'

'I am,' she said.

'And why can't you just go home?'

'I can,' she said.

'Glad we cleared that up then,' I said. 'And thanks for the lesson on the difference between threat and intimidation. I appreciate it.' I put my hand on the door but something made me turn back. She had an unfathomable look on her face.

'I only have one kidney because of a transplant,' said Molly. 'And my girlfriend's a nurse in the ICU at Sutter.'

I reeled out of the interview room. I don't think I even managed to say goodbye. After two years of tight-lipped stick-up-the-arse jobs-worthery and nit-picking, the world's most reserved and repressed woman – including Plymouth Brethren and tax auditors – had just told me in the space of one sentence that she *was* gay, like we knew she was and like she always pretended we didn't, that she was in a relationship, that she was a transplant survivor, and that she was as scared of this virus as the rest of us. Wow.

As to her suggestion? What would the gang think of a cop coming to stay? Kathi's mafia in-laws were long gone, and Roger had had his old tattoos covered in plain black now because he'd got sick of wearing stretchy bandages at work. Della was a legal resident since she'd married Devin. Maybe I could float the idea and not have the rest of them put my head down a toilet and flush repeatedly.

Or maybe I should check with Meera, Arif and the bunnies. If I could work out how to ask sweet little old people in their eighties if they had papers, and how to ask a trans Muslim which identity made him antsier around law enforcement, if either did, and how to broach the notion of another cop rocking up, with a woman whose cop husband had left her in the state Meera was in.

Maybe I should just let it slide and assume Molly would find a place to stay if it turned out that she needed one.

On the other hand, if she moved in, that *was* the last room filled and Kathi could breathe out and stop worrying about the government billeting strangers on us.

In the end I did nothing, because when I got back to the boat, my landline answering service was lit up like a Vegas Christmas tree with clients needing emergency appointments in case Gav the Gov brought the hammer down before their scheduled sessions in the working week.

And I was just as happy to see them today as to try and find out whether all the insurers would cough up for Skype if I had to close my office. (I had heard once that Escher tried to render Covered California as a woodcut but gave up sobbing.)

On the only break I could carve out of the tidal wave of consternation sweeping my client list, I went to find Kathi to see how she was bearing up. Still in the Skweek, which was good; perhaps my short lesson in statistics had gone deep. And not only was she stuffing clothes into washers and smoothing out dry ones on her folding table, she was babysitting too. Diego, Salem, Bob and Joan were busy building a racetrack out of wooden blocks all around the legs of the table and Navy was on top of it, drowsing in her bouncy chair with a Groucho Marx dummy lying slackly in her half-open mouth. As I closed the door, she roused enough to give it a bit of a suck, making the cigar waggle and making me laugh for quite a long time. It was very realistic, and if there's anything funnier than a baby with a cigar then YouTube has missed it so far.

'How come you drew the short straw?' I said.

'Meera's making gumbo,' said Kathi, 'Blaine's practising her dancing, Todd and Della are hatching some plot or another, top secret, Devin's working and Noleen's terrible with kids. They make her swear.'

'She alw—'

'Even more,' Kathi said. She stopped the precision-folding of a T-shirt into a six-inch-square, razor-edged tile and gazed at Navy. The baby had fallen back into a deep sleep and the cigar dummy was balanced on her bottom lip again. 'I never had Blaine down as a pacifier mom,' she said. 'What with the clean eating.'

'That's only for her,' I said. 'She's all about M&M's for the kids.'

'Bain,' said Salem from under the table. 'Mama? Nabby?' His voice went high on the last word, as if he had only that moment wondered where his sister had got to. He clambered out and Kathi hoisted him on to one hip.

'There she is,' she said. 'Sleepy baby.'

'No!' said Salem, pointing at Navy's mouth.

'Irony doesn't develop till age three,' I said. 'It's OK, honey, it's only pretend.'

'No!' Salem said again. He was starting to buck like he'd been bucking yesterday. Since Navy looked sound asleep, I reached over and took the dummy out. She closed her lips with a smack. Salem sighed and settled in Kathi's arms.

'Oh,' Kathi said. 'I might know what the problem is. This bouncy chair belongs to the motel. Someone left it behind. When I found the pacifier in there with the baby, I just assumed it was hers. But if Salem has never seen it before, I better ask Blaine, huh?'

'I'll ask her,' I said. 'I'll be more . . .' normal about the non-existent danger of germs from a baby putting some other kid's dummy in her mouth is what I couldn't work out how to say '. . . measured about the risk of germs, no offence, Kathi eh?'

'Germs?' said Kathi. 'I dipped it in bleachy water and rinsed it at 60. It had been in her crotch right beside her diaper.'

'I'll ask anyway,' I said. Because whenever I can protect Kathi from public gaze I like to. Also, I wanted to see if Blaine had wiped off her palette knife make-up for dancing or if she was just letting it melt and run down her neck.

She was light on her feet, I thought as I approached Room 202, which had been designated as the dance studio. If I'd been prancing around in there, the walkway would have been shuddering. Or maybe she was tied in a knot on her mat or bent like a snapped lily stem at whatever she'd managed to rig up as a barre.

None of the above. I knocked on the door, tried the handle and, when it opened, stuck my head in and said, 'Quick question, Darcy Bussell.'

But Blaine wasn't dancing. She was stretched out on the couch under the window, with a PayDay bar in one hand and her phone in the other. She stared back at me, frozen mid-munch.

'Uhhhhh,' I said. 'So why couldn't you eat pizza last night?'

'Uhhhhh,' she said. 'I can eat anything if I'm alone. I just can't eat much in front of people.'

Which was far more core dancer behaviour than jumping about to music, if my past experience and reading was anything to go by.

'You gonna bust me?' she said. 'Is there anything I can do to stop you?' She held out her half-eaten PayDay bar, as if to offer me a bite.

'As it happens,' I said. 'You could brush off Navy getting a sook on someone else's dummy that was knocking round the Skweek. Kathi washed it.'

Blaine stared and then blinked. 'OK, I have no idea what you just said there, but it's a deal.'

SIX

I wonder what they called it before *Groundhog Day*. I rolled over in bed, heard birds singing, yawned, opened my eyes, then opened my *ears* and realized that in fact the birdsong was a chorus of human voices raised in alarm. I rolled out of bed, shrugged on my dressing gown and clogs and went off to see what had gone wrong *now* before the sun had barely cleared the horizon.

Blaine was in her doorway in the exoskeleton slash face mask and sushi-print pyjamas, Meera in her marabou wrap stood pale and shaking with Della and Kathi comforting her, Arif gripped the railing on the walkway above with Todd comforting *him*, and Noleen was untying the bedsheet from the front fence. Bedsheet singular, not bedsheets plural, making today nothing like yesterday really.

Also the message written in foot-high red letters on this morning's solitary item of household linen was:

OR ELSE.

Needless to say, Molly didn't believe me. I went back to the cop shop as soon as I was dressed and caffeinated, armed with the name and address of Meera's scumbag husband and Arif's scumbag wife, and asked the dispatcher – different chick, same magazine – if I could speak to Sergeant Rankinson about an ongoing case she and I had discussed previously.

'Another sign on bedsheets on the fence at the Last Ditch,' I told Molly when she had shut the door on the smell of the vending machine and we had both breathed out. 'And – Ha-ha! – I bet you can't guess what it says.'

'Probably not word for word,' said Molly. 'But would I be able to place it in a category?'

'Um,' I said.

'Such as "threat",' she offered.

'It says OR ELSE.'

'Of course it does.'

'Yeah, but I swear I absolutely swear that I didn't tell anyone at the motel you'd said that all about intimidation and threat yesterday. Not a soul. I swear on . . . I'll swear on anyone's life you ask me to swear on. I'll swear on David Attenborough. I'll swear on Judi Dench.'

'Oh I believe you,' Molly said.

'Huh,' I said, sitting back. 'Well, good then.'

'And have you kept the evidence?'

'Absolutely,' I said. 'Noleen bundled it up with the paint on the inside and put it in a locked cupboard along with yesterday's.'

'Great,' said Molly. 'So we can get prints off both and compare the paint and find out what was used on the first – let's call it the "real" sign – and what was used on the second – or we could call it the "fake" sign. And we could go around the suppliers and ask them to describe the face and voice of the woman who bought a bucket of red paint yesterday.'

'Woman?' I said. 'So . . . you think it was definitely Arif's wife? Not Meera's husband? But why would you call the second one a fake? And why does her voice matter?'

'Not voice so much as accent,' said Molly.

'Wha—? Wai-wai-wai-wai-wait a minute!' I said. 'You mean *me*?'

'Can you think of another way I could tell you the note needed to say "or else" and hey presto the next day it does, and you swear on Richard Attenborough you didn't tell anyone?'

'David,' I said. 'And I swear I didn't paint the sign either. Who else can I swear on that would convince you? Have you got a polygraph?'

'Oh sure,' said Molly. 'The city gave the PD a polygraph right after they upgraded the coffee machine. Get outta here!'

'So you're not going to arrest me?' I said.

'For wasting police time?' said Molly. 'Nah. I never understood that. Some loser wastes my time and then I waste even more of it on paperwork? Not for me.'

'I meant for leaving a threatening sign,' I said.

'Not if you're not leaving it for a spouse you've been abusing,' said Molly. 'Not today.'

'I'm not going to get into trouble because the addressee of the sign is not my spouse,' I said, nodding. 'That's helpful. Thank you.'

I'm not sure if she knew she'd given me an idea and didn't care, or if she didn't even care enough to work out that she'd given me an idea. It didn't matter. I tucked it away for future reference anyway.

'And how are you getting on with your temporary move?' I said. 'I haven't had a chance to ask the others what they think about you moving into the Ditch.'

'Oh no?' Was it my imagination or did she look disappointed?

'Like I said,' I explained, except it's not really an explanation if you're lying, I suppose, 'I didn't speak to anyone last night. Remember? How I didn't tell anyone about what sign would count as threatening?'

'I do remember you saying that,' said Molly. 'Only, when I drove past you were sitting outside at picnic tables in the parking lot with a chiminea going and you sure looked like you were talking plenty.'

'But you've just told me you don't think lying to the police is really that big a deal,' I said.

'Not quite how I remember it,' said Molly. 'Have a nice day, Ms Campbell. You take care now, won't you?'

'I will,' I said. 'And I'll ask them tonight,' I added. Pretty magnanimously in my opinion, because there was nothing about the prospect of enduring conversations like this one at home every evening that was tempting me. 'I'll get back to you tomorrow,' I finished. 'Since that's starting to be our thing.'

'Whatever,' said Molly.

I stood, curtseyed a bit – not exactly deliberately, but I never know what to do when I'm around people with guns; it's not something I was brought up to negotiate. I've saluted once or twice in my flusterment and that didn't go down well either.

'Six Bay Area counties are sheltering in place,' Kathi called. 'Shelter in place! Like it's an active shooter.' She had come out on to the walkway to hail me. She must have been watching for me coming back.

'I know, honey,' I said. 'I'm sorry. I know. But it's still five hundred and odd cases in a state of sixty million. It's not time to panic yet.'

'You'll be shouting case numbers into the hinge of my coffin at the viewing,' Kathi said.

'Well, I can offer you a distraction today,' I tried next. 'That's something, isn't it?' She made the winding hand signal to tell me to keep talking. 'You, me and Todd on an adventure? One where you don't need to leave the Jeep?' More winding. 'Can't shout it out in the open, though. It's on the side of right but it might not be one hundred per cent strictly legal.'

'I'm in,' Kathi said. 'Do I need to close the laundromat?'

'Best under cover of darkness,' I said.

'Oh boy,' said Kathi. 'Am I ever in!'

I had a full day of clients but just enough time before the first one to swing round by Todd and get him on board too. Arif was there and I recognized the look on his face as soon as I spotted it.

'Oh God,' I said. 'Arif, I should have warned you. Todd has no boundaries. None. But if you say no calmly and firmly he sometimes gets the message. Failing that, you can hit him on the nose with a rolled-up newspaper.'

'What are you talking about?' said Todd. 'I was just showing Arif some photographs of when I had a beard and suggesting—'

'Exactly.'

'But I think he's right,' Arif said. He was sitting at Todd's vanity table, considering his face in the wrap-around mirrors.

'What's he telling you to do?'

'Nothing!' Todd said. 'Just raise the lower level of the beard up the neck a little and shape it into a bandana point instead of a pastor band, and then drop the top beard line to accentuate his cheekbones and clip his moustache. Just a little. You should never have a moustache bushier than your eyebrows. It's a golden rule.'

'It's a golden pile,' I said. 'You made that up this morning. What about Tom Selleck?'

'Well, exactly,' said Todd. Arif nodded along sagely. 'And

fill in his monobrow until it grows back naturally.' Arif stopped nodding. 'Trust me,' said Todd. 'Monobrows are back.'

'Arif,' I said, 'he won't stop at the neck so you need to shut it down now. I'm assuming you're perfectly happy with your clothes?'

'I'm in IT,' said Arif. Todd pressed his hands over his heart, sensing that he was just about to be given his favourite gift: carte blanche.

'Well, on your head be it,' I said. 'But don't say I didn't warn you and don't let him throw anything in the dumpster. In case you change your mind.'

Arif gave me the sunniest smile I had seen on his face since he stepped out of his car on Saturday. Maybe this was exactly what he needed. Maybe I had finally found what Todd was perfect for.

'Get that in case it's the *Voyager*,' Todd said, nodding at his phone, which was charging on his bedside table and had just started vibrating.

'Why would it be the *Voyager*?' I asked him.

'I pitched a listicle about mental preparation for an enforced retreat,' he said. 'Five hundred words for Friday? You don't mind, do you?'

I did mind, and was all set to let the *Voyager* down with a thump. But it was Roger. 'He's . . .' I began, then ran out of steam, because *currently lathering the rather gorgeous and newly single guy who just moved into the room next door* isn't what a banished spouse needs to hear.

'It's you I called to speak to, Lexy,' said Roger. 'But your phone's off.'

'Oh!' I said. 'Yeah, there was a sign in the . . .' I began, then I ran out of steam again, because *police station where I've been every morning since you left your loved one alone here* isn't that great either. 'It's Roger for me,' I said to Todd, and then went out on to the walkway and shut the door before he could argue. His hands were covered in shaving soap and the Last Ditch door handles are tricky.

'What's up?' I said. Down in the car park, Noleen had marshalled all the kids like a little troop of Munchkins and was walking back and forth in front of them, drill-sergeant-style, addressing them very firmly. Diego, Salem, Joan and Bob stood to attention, watching her as she passed but otherwise quite still. Navy, in a pouch on Noleen's chest, was gazing up at her too.

'Ahhhhhhh, just wondering how it's going,' Roger said. 'Operation Cocker.' Either he was lying down or he was gravel-voiced with exhaustion. Maybe both.

'Well, Noleen's holding some kind of youth rally out front, for some reason,' I said.

Noleen, who had ears like a bat, shouted up at me, 'Safety briefing before I let them swim,' without breaking stride.

'Kathi is still working,' I went on, into the phone, 'although she's watching the case count. Todd's found a project.' Roger laughed. 'Della's friend is slowly starting to unfurl. I think this is going to be great for her. She cooked last night and the compliments boosted her a bit. What else? I think we'll have to keep José and Maria when this is over because I don't want to go back to an abuelo-less existence. And Blaine . . .'

'Yeah,' said Roger. 'That's why I called. Blaine. How's that going? Is *she* a keeper?'

'Why?' I said. 'Does Whatsisname want her back?'

'I don't think so. He does want some FaceTime with his kids, which she's not making any effort to make sure he gets. No idea why.'

'She's an enigma, right enough,' I said. 'I think she's maybe just taking a break. Eating PayDays and filling the kids with M&M's and doesn't want to get a hard time about it from the healthcare professional.'

'Oh God!' said Roger. 'We're not talking about Blaine any more, are we? Todd's hit the Cheez-Its.'

'I couldn't possibly comment.'

'And so I'm going to get a three a.m. call when the first zit pops up and I'll have to talk him down from self-loathing and back to celery.'

'Surely not now,' I said. 'Not when you're . . . How is it up there?'

'We're re-tooling,' Roger said. 'Cancelling electives and so on. It's OK. Just no one has bandwidth to worry about home and family.'

'Tell you what,' I said. 'I'll film the wee ones right now on Todd's phone. Noleen's teaching them to swim on the tarmac. It's quite funny. Then I'll send it to you and you give it to Whatsisname.'

'Phil,' said Roger.

'Give me five minutes.' I killed the call and hit the camera. 'Salem!' I said. 'Wave to Daddy! Noleen, hold the baby up so I can get her face. Say "Hi, Daddy!"'

Underneath me, a couple of doors opened. Meera came out from under the overhang and stood with her hands on her hips, looking up at me while I tried not to focus the camera right into the valley between her hiked-up boobs. Today's dress was even more low cut than the first one. 'Are you filming my kids?' she said.

'Oh,' I said. 'Yeah, but only because I'm filming Blaine's kids.'

Meera looked along towards Blaine's door. 'She's filming our kids!'

'Only to send a film to Phil!' I told her.

'Who the hell's Phil?' said Meera. 'What's wrong with you?'

'Phil's their dad,' Blaine said, coming out where I could see her, and standing with her back to me, watching the children. 'My husband. Knock yourself out, Lexy.' She waved her hand over her shoulder. 'Keep him from bugging me to set up a videocall.'

'And don't forget to kick your legs,' Noleen added. She had ploughed on with her tarmac swimming lesson all through the argy-bargy. 'Now who wants to jump in the water?'

'Me!'

'Me!'

'Me me me me me me!'

'Diego?' said Noleen.

'Sure, why not,' Diego said, trying for cool and landing on the cutest thing ever. 'You can use my floaties for the beginners, Abuelita.' He was showing off in so many different ways: he owned water wings, he didn't need them, he was intimately connected to Noleen, whom he'd never called Granny before in his miniature puff. 'Nemo and Dory, SpongeBob or regular,' he said. 'Take your pick.'

I had quite forgotten how comprehensively Della used to encase him in inflatables to put him in the pool when he was tiny.

'Hey, remember when Diego had so many rings and wings and stuff on him we could use him to play water polo?' I said later, as Todd, Kathi and I set off in Todd's Jeep on what Kathi was calling Operation Same Back With Knobs On. In all innocence, I'm sure, since the word didn't have that meaning in America. I was trying not to let on, in case she stopped, same as I did when Todd suggested that, à la Brangelina, Bennifer and Bey-Z, he and his beloved could be called . . . wait for it . . . Todger. I'll never know how I managed to keep a straight face and I prayed he'd never Google British words for male anatomy or hear it on *QI*.

'Happy days,' Todd said, with a sigh. 'You don't know what you've got till it's gone.'

'Is someone casting a production of *Steel Magnolias*?' said Kathi. 'Is this your audition piece?'

'So,' I said, trying to refocus them on the job at hand. 'It's Scumboy first and then Scumgirl? Todd, do you need directions?'

'I was born in this town, Lexy,' Todd said. 'Would you need directions from the pawnshop to the jellied-eel stand in Dundee?' All of the Last Ditch had been gorging on *Masterpiece Theatre* every Sunday night since before I'd arrived, and the mix of midwives and butlers had left them with an interesting take on life in the old world.

'Sorry,' I said. 'And when we get there, you keep the engine running, Kathi's on look-out and I'll jump out and do the deed.'

'Roger that,' said Kathi. Another phrase I sometimes had trouble with if I was feeling lively. Right now my nerves were beginning to thrum. Despite what Molly had said, and despite the fact that I was almost sure she meant to send me a message by saying it, I was still about to do something that felt illegal.

'Here we are,' Todd said, pulling over to the kerb outside a trim little ranch-style house with urns of agaves on the gravel garden and a huge 'blue line' flag in a holder attached to the porch. I hopped out and opened the back door. We had practised

and our bedsheet game was far superior to the makeshift effort
that had been tied to the motel fence the last two nights. This
one was tacked to bamboo canes top and bottom, so I could
unroll it neatly and lay it on the drive for Meera's husband to
read when he came home.

OR ELSE WHAT, LOSER?

is what we had decided on after much discussion. If it was him,
then the message was clear; if not, then it was obscure enough
to be unsettling. Perfect either way.

Except for one small thing: Meera's husband wasn't at work.
He was at home and he opened the front door just as I was
weighting the sheet down at its corners with some of the big
decorative rocks dotted about the gravel.

'Freeze!' he said.

And I might have, except he had what we at the Ditch call
the 'walking truck payment look' off to a T – buzz cut, goatee,
ridiculous belt, silly shoes, terrible jeans, and biceps that owed
everything to gym membership and protein powder. Plus he had
added that thing they call a command presence – mostly clenched
fists, clenched jaw, and clenched attitude – and finished it off
with a stare that screams of practice in the bathroom mirror.

'Oh calm down, Fanny,' I found myself saying. 'I'm just
delivering a message from your poor wife.'

'You are trespassing!' he thundered. He might have had
elocution lessons to lower his register. Something about his
voice was wildly bogus anyway.

'There there,' I said. 'Not to worry. Try to cope.' By which
time I was back in the Jeep and Todd was pulling away.

'Toodles!' he trilled out of the driver's side window, blowing
a kiss.

Scumboy was photographing or maybe filming the back of
the Jeep, which might have been worrisome except that he was
standing with his feet a yard apart and holding his phone in
both hands with his arms straight out in front, as if he was
facing down perps with a loaded handgun.

'What a twat,' Kathi said. 'Seriously, what a total pillock.'

'I'm so glad we stopped the swear jar for limey slang,' Todd said. 'Sometimes nothing else will do. Like now. What a bell-end.'

It wasn't far to Arif's house, just across the freeway on the overpass and round one of Cuento's many parks, into a neighbourhood I didn't know very well but, with enough American life under my belt now, could place: the streets were straight but the trees were large and half the little craftsmans underneath had been flattened and rebuilt twice the size with cathedral windows. The other half had been left standing and added to at the back, so they looked as if they were wearing bustles. Arif's home-sour-home was on a corner plot with raised veg beds in the front garden, lots of little beans and lettuces poking neatly through the rich dark earth. I wondered who was the gardener, thinking I could get Arif a couple of grow-bags and some tomato seedlings to put on the walkway in case he was missing his hobby.

When Todd parked, I hopped down again, took the second sign from the back of the Jeep and unfurled it on the drive, facing the street so she could read it as she arrived home at the end of the day. She was the manager of a mall security operation up in Madding, Arif had told us. Sounded like a wannabe cop, if anyone was asking me. More of the same, with heels on.

And more of the same it turned out to be. I had just weighted the fourth corner of the sign, with a brick wiggled out from one of the raised-bed walls, when the front door opened.

'What are you doing?' She was a tall, high-breasted woman; Amazonian wouldn't have been exaggerating.

'I'm delivering a message,' I said.

She squinted at the upside-down writing. 'What does that mean?'

Todd, hanging out of the window again, said, 'Yes, we'd love to stay and chat but you seem awful so we're gonna bounce. Later!'

I climbed back in. 'Have a shite day now!' I sang out. And Kathi added a raspberry and two flipped birds.

'Well, maybe it's better we ran into them,' said Todd. 'Let them see we're not scared, even if they've managed to flatten their spouses.'

'Do you think it'll work?' I said.

'You know what?' said Kathi. 'I really think it will. I don't think we'll be having any more trouble now.'

A prediction that was right up there with 'this might take as long as a month' and 'he's a bit of an arse but he'll rise to the office, won't he?' when we look back at it now.

SEVEN

I get that cops react like rockets to shouts of 'officer down'. It's only natural that the death of someone you count as a brother is going to cut deep. But 'officer pissed off' shouldn't merit special attention. So it was dispiriting to see, when we rolled back into the Last Ditch car park ten minutes later, that Scumboy had already gone crying to his mates and one of them had run Todd's plates and Molly had leapt into action and beaten us back here.

'Aw man,' said Todd. 'I promised Roger I wouldn't get into any trouble while he was away and a visit from Molly R was mentioned specifically.'

'Leave it to me,' I said, jumping out before the Jeep had even stopped and strolling over to where she was waiting, leaning against her car. I could see Noleen hovering just inside the office, watching.

'How did you get in?' I said.

'Master key,' said Molly. 'This is a Calfire clear-route.'

'A what?'

'The fire department have a key to the gate in case they need water from out back for a grass fire to the south.'

'So . . . you're saying I could wake up any night in the summertime and find my boat run aground because firemen have sucked all the water out of the slough?'

'You got a problem with that?'

'*So* many problems,' I said. 'When do the new things to worry about run out? I thought guns, rattlesnakes, black widows, wildfire, mudslides, and Lipton's tea was the full set.'

'That mouth,' said Molly, shaking her head. 'So anyway, I assume you know why I'm here?'

'Because a cop who bullies his wife is your buddy and a bullied wife looking for a sister should keep looking? What mouth, by the way?'

'You need a couple of "allegedly" in there, Ms Campbell. Slander is a crime. Like trespass—'

'I didn't trespass,' I said, interrupting. She loved *that*. 'I went on to the Flynns' property with permission from one of the householders to deliver something she wanted delivered. A message, in the form of a question with an added insult. No threat. Like you said.'

Molly pinched up her eyes and looked at me for a moment. 'That doesn't seem at all likely,' she said. 'A wife who fears her husband hardly ever goads him. But OK, if you say you had her permission, take me to her room and then if *she* says the delivery was made with her blessing, and not behind her back because you three chuckleheads thought it was a good plan . . .'

'Ah,' I said. 'Right. Well. Yes. So.'

Molly looked behind herself briefly. 'I thought someone was holding up flashcards,' she said, when she'd turned back to face me again.

I smiled. That was funny, for her, and also she'd given me thinking time. 'You can do that,' I said. 'That is certainly one option. Go and speak to Meera. Or you can *not* do that and I'll campaign for you to move in to the empty room. It's up to you.'

'Extortion!' said Molly. 'Nice.'

'We've got a healthcare professional on site.'

'On enforced personal leave.'

'Irrelevant. A certified therapist.'

'Certified in England.'

'Scotland. But OK then, *qualified* therapist.'

'The things I would rather do than tell you my private business.'

'And a laundromat, human companionship, a swimming pool, plus the chance to do more of your job than boring admin.'

'How so?'

'Because of the campaign of intimidation by one of two people. We can't work out which one, but maybe you'd be able to. With all your training'

'Subtle,' Molly said. 'I'm so skilfully reeled in on that line of subtle flattery, I don't even know it's happened.'

'Actually,' I said as the thought occurred to me, 'what admin work can you do from home anyway? Isn't everything confidential and not to be removed from the police station?'

'Everything what?' said Molly. 'You mean like cardboard files and boxes of evidence?'

'Yeah, exactly,' I said. 'Cold cases and what have you.'

'What have you been watching?' She shook her head. 'Thing is, we have this newfangled way of working now. We use these things called "computers".'

'But you can't do police stuff on your random old laptop hooked into a public Wi-Fi!' I said.

'Because of the confidentiality and the cyber-criminals waiting to pounce?'

'Yeah,' I said. 'Them.'

'Thing is we have this amazing thing we do to counteract that. It's called "Kaspersky".'

'Huh,' I said. 'Still, I bet you'd rather do detecting than . . .'

'Finish that sentence,' said Molly. 'Go on, tell me what you think a cop does when she's riding the desk. I need a laugh.'

I dug deep into every telly programme about police I had ever watched from *Morse* to *CSI*. If it wasn't cold cases, and it couldn't be uploading paperwork because she wouldn't have the paperwork, and it wasn't interviews of witnesses and suspects because surely that couldn't be done over the phone without the body language and facial expressions, then maybe it was . . .

'In-service training?' I said. 'Professional development to go with your new sergeant-hood.' Her scowl told me I'd cracked it. 'So you can do that,' I said, 'or you can move in and have a stake-out. Catch Scumspouse in the act on night three. Todd's got great snacks.'

'Cold cases and stake-outs,' she said. 'You'd be so disappointed if you ever took the badge.'

'Yeah, but I'll tell you what we really do have,' I said, as the clincher came to me, 'and that's a toilet-paper stockpile like you would not believe. I take it you've been following the news?'

I had her. Her eyes flared, then narrowed, and after a long pause she gave a sharp nod. And immediately started laying down the law. 'I'm not giving preferential treatment, or sharing information about this or any other case, or turning a blind eye to any unlawful behaviour.'

'I know. You've got be a cop to get *that* deal.'

'And I'll need to keep the financial angle with the Muntzes very clear and above board. I might have an allowance to spend but only if the receipts are scrupulously fair and square.'

'What exactly are you suggesting?' said Noleen, blatting open the office door behind us.

'I was going to ask y—' I began, but she wasn't talking to me.

'The gouging's already started down in the city,' Molly said, 'and Cuento PD can't be associated with any operation that—'

Noleen drew herself up and breathed in such a deep breath that her sweatshirt slogan grew pale as the fabric stretched over her chest. 'Annnnd thuuuuuuh horrrrse' it now seemed to say, on the top line, while 'you rode in on' stayed small and dark under her ribcage.

'Excuse me!' she said. 'But I never have and will never gouge prices. Nine/eleven, freak weather, derailments on the Amtrak or this clusterfuck right here. No matter. When that overgrown frat boy in the governor's mansion gets around to a mandate against rate hikes – which he will when he gathers all his brain cells in one place and counts them – there will be no change needed at the Last Ditch Motel.'

'What have you got against Gav the Gov?' I said.

'Nothing,' Noleen admitted, 'except he's not Jerry. Jerry is the one man I think could have turned me.' She sighed and went back into the office.

'I am not going to enjoy this,' said Molly. 'Buncha freaks.'

'Give it time,' I said. 'Give it taco night.'

Risking understatement, the installation of a law enforcement officer was not universally welcomed by our emerging big happy family. While Molly went home to pack her stuff, the supper table out front, now strung with fairy lights and bunting, was the scene of much loud grumbling in English and anxious muttering in Spanish. I got more sharp looks aimed at me than the time I'd worn a too-convincing faux-fur coat in Berkeley. (Todd had dressed me; it wasn't my usual style.)

'Look,' Noleen said. 'It's profit for the business because she's on expenses.'

'And she's not going to be taking chances,' I added, 'because of her health issues. Like I told you. She'll be on her best behaviour.'

'I wonder who gave her a kidney,' said Kathi. 'What a saint!'

'And no one here is planning to break any laws, are they?' said Todd.

'I'm not planning to get caught anyway,' said Barb.

'Not now it's legalized,' said Devin. This, I reckoned, was the truth of why he kept his own room on instead of moving lock, stock and barrel in with Della. He needed somewhere to smoke where Diego wouldn't be corrupted by him and Della wouldn't reconsider her choices.

'But we could get stuck with her no matter what she's like,' Arif added. 'If the governor passes an eviction ban.'

No one answered that.

José and Maria had finished their discussion and now he spread his arms as if to embrace us and said . . . something. My baby Spanish wasn't up to it.

'English,' said Maria, giving him a poke in the ribs. She turned and translated for us in a solemn voice, 'The bitterest struggle will not begin.'

'What?' said Barb. 'Della?'

'Uhhhhh, let's give it a go,' said Della. 'Basically.'

'Good,' said Blaine. 'I think I'll feel safer having a cop around. I wish it was a big, burly, guy cop, but this'll do.'

Everyone else turned to see how this had gone down with Meera, whose experience of the connection between safety and a big, burly, guy cop was different from what Blaine was imagining. Didn't Blaine know? Or was she too self-centred to care?

'Mama?' said Diego holding up his loaded fork. 'Are these really fingers?' That cut through the tension. I apologized once again for being British, agreed that they were fish *sticks*, reminded him that fish didn't *have* fingers, then said if he dipped the end in ketchup they'd look like severed ones. Then Joan started crying and Bob opened his lips and let his half-chewed mouthful thud back out on to his plate, which Salem took as permission to start spitting peas at everyone, and I decided to go to the boat and start drinking.

I didn't drink enough to sleep through a ruckus, which was good. But I did drink enough to wake up mid-ruckus pretty fuddled. When, sometime in the small hours, I felt the deck tip as someone boarded, my first thought was that Calfire were running a hose over my deck to fight a blaze. I staggered to my feet. This was partly because the boat was still rocking and partly because there isn't enough room in my midget fridge to store an opened bottle of wine and so I'd finished it. I headed along the corridor to the front, bouncing off the walls a bit.

It was only when the cold air hit me that I remembered Scumspouse – whichever one it was – and the intimidating-rising-to-threatening notes, and started to feel anxious. But I was too late. Whoever it was had hopped offboard again on the far side of the slough and was now making good progress through the scrub of bird cherry, willow and the odd spindly oleander. I squinted after the figure in the light of the half-waned moon and could see that it wasn't Command Presence Boy or Amazonian Wife rampaging through the undergrowth. So, while I wasn't thrilled that someone had breached what was supposed to become a quarantine whenever we hunkered down into Operation Cocker for real, I reckoned I could deal with it in the morning.

I went back to bed, plotting to install a fence on the southern bank (which I didn't actually own, but hopefully no one would notice) until gradually the thoughts turned into dreams and then into silence and when next I opened my eyes, my face was glued to the pillow with drool and my stomach was telling me I needed coffee right now and then a lot of fat and carbs and finally a supply of wine by the half-bottle so that this stopped happening.

But at least I had woken early enough to check the front fence for nasty signs on bedsheets before the rest of the Ditch got upset again. In the low, grey light of dawn I pulled my dressing gown on, shoved my feet into socks then Crocks and disembarked. As I struggled round the side of the motel building, reminding myself, like I did every day, to ask Noleen about

setting a pair of hedge trimmers on the encroaching branches,
I was busy plotting.

If our stunt on the driveways had worked, I told myself, there
would be no sign today. If it hadn't, then tonight I would
organize that stake-out in Todd's room. If Molly wanted to join
us, we would let her and—

Eugh. I spat and whipped my head aside as something I'd
thought was a cobweb turned out to be a human hair across my
cheek. It was just light enough to see it glinting. Then I was
finally at the front corner with my feet on asphalt and a clear
view of the car park and forecourt.

NO BITCH LEAVES ME. YOU WERE WARNED.

Scumspouse – whichever one it was – badly needed to work on
extending their repertoire, I thought, as I trudged over to the
fence to start taking everything down. They had used three whole
king-sized sheets for this one and it didn't add anything that
hadn't been covered the previous two mornings. But it was all
grist to the mill. I would fold it inwards very carefully and put
it somewhere safe until Noleen was up and about, then it could
join the other two in a black binbag as evidence of the campaign.

I wondered, as I worked on one corner knot, whether this
was intimidation or threat. It seemed nicely judged to stay on
the legal side of the line and that indicated the cop. But the
pointed use of the B word seemed to put Arif's horrible wife
in the frame too.

God, this paint stank. I hadn't noticed it on Sunday when I'd
taken Meera and then Arif to check the sheets in case they
recognized them. (They didn't.) But today my stomach was
rolling with the reek. And it wasn't a clean, chemical smell; it
was earthy and bitter. I couldn't imagine how anyone could
stand to use this paint inside their house. Or maybe it was
exterior, for those red barns you see everywhere. Actually, as
I looked more closely, it did seem to have dried to a rustier red
than the signs the first two days. Maybe Scumspouse had run
out of the good stuff and was using up leftovers from the garage.
Maybe it had gone off in storage and that's why it smelled so
bad as well as drying such a nasty colour. Like . . . Like . . .

I don't often throw my head back and scream out loud for real. Sometimes at Halloween, because this country is so good at it, but hardly ever out of actual, gut-wrenching terror like I did that morning at the Last Ditch fence when it finally pene-trated my hungover skull what liquid starts red and dries rust and smells bad and is perfect for the third instalment in an escalating series of messages intended to scare the bejesus out of someone.

Several doors banged open more or less at the same time, and people responded in line with their disposition.

'Shut *up*!' That was Noleen.

'Shut up, Noleen.' Kathi.

'Who let Jamie Lee Curtis in?' Todd. Obviously.

'Blood!' I shouted, pointing at the bedsheets. I tried to form a sentence, then gave up and said, '*Blood!*' again.

'Everyone stay calm.' That was Molly's contribution. It failed spectacularly.

Della started hammering on Meera's closed door, shouting 'Meera! Amiga! Cara! Estas ahi?'

And Devin took the stairs to Arif's room, thumped on his door, and shouted, 'You OK, bud?'

Then the babies started crying. It sounded like twenty but of course it was only five: Diego, Joan, Bob, Salem and Navy.

'She's OK!' Della sang out, wrapping her arms round Meera and ignoring the howls of alarm from her kids.

'He's good too,' Devin said, holding up one of Arif's arms like a boxing champ.

'Shush now,' Della said, hitching Diego higher on her hip and going back inside Meera's room with her to quiet the twins.

That left just two still screaming their heads off. I glanced over and saw that Blaine's door was closed. She might have slept through my performance but she couldn't be sleeping through the piercing squeals of little Navy and the lusty bellows Salem was giving out.

I took hold of Molly's arm as she got up beside me at the fence and nodded over to the closed door. 'Should I check if she's OK?'

Molly nodded, absent-mindedly. She was snapping photos

on her phone, zooming right in on the streaks and blobs forming the letters. I shuddered, very happy to go and hide in Blaine's room till the sign was bundled up and gone.

The children's cries rose in pitch and volume when I tapped on her door. 'Blaine?' I called. 'Are you all right?' I glanced up at the corner room she'd commandeered for dancing and/or eating PayDay bars. If she was practising with earbuds in, she might have missed the whole thing. But surely she wouldn't go up there and leave her kids locked in—

Not locked in. The handle turned as I tried it and the door swung open to reveal Navy purple-faced and sobbing in a travel cot just inside the door, Salem standing sweaty and hysterical in a high-sided playpen, and . . . blood. So much blood. It was all round the walls, dripping on to the floor, tainting the air.

I grabbed one kid under each arm and ran out to the car park, where my eyes lit on José and Maria, still stiff from sleep, who'd gamely toddled out in their nightie and pyjamas to see what was happening. I hustled over, handed Navy to José, Salem to Maria, and watched my hunch come good as each sweet little old person immediately started shooshing and stroking and rocking, and the babies stopped screaming and started grizzling, then stopped grizzling and started snuffling, and eventually stopped snuffling and plugged thumbs in mouths as they lay their damp little heads down on the pink cotton and blue striped shoulders and went limp.

Maria met my eyes over Salem's tousled head.

'It's bad,' I mouthed at her. 'Keep them away.'

When they had withdrawn into their room, I turned to face the music in the form of every other resident of the Ditch who had come up behind me like weeping angels when I wasn't looking. All except Molly, who was still taking pictures of the bedsheet.

'We might owe your other halfs an apology,' I mumbled to Arif and Meera through clumsy lips. 'I think those messages were for Blaine.'

'Where is she?' Meera said.

'There's no sign of her,' I said. 'At least, I hope not. But I think-I think-I think . . .'

I had never fainted before, so I didn't recognize the feeling that was washing over me. My head felt soft and my face went numb then it seemed as if the solid ground of the car park was lapping at me in little waves and the next thing I knew I was on the couch in Della's room, with a cold cloth on my forehead and Diego asking me if I wanted a juice box.

I did. And a cuddle and a bacon sandwich and a bucket of brain bleach that I could put my head in to sluice the sight of that blood-spattered bedroom away.

EIGHT

Tuesday 17 March

A nd it was human blood too. Molly was talking utter mince that we wouldn't get insider information on any cases. All we had to do was sit in Della's room with the window cracked and we heard all sorts of stuff. Human blood, no sign of forced entry, no sign of robbery, and – best of all – no mangled corpse of Blaine in the bathroom where I hadn't had time to look.

What else? The cops were calling it an abduction, not a murder. That was a surprise and I suppose they knew best, but if I'd had to say whether a woman could still be alive after losing enough blood to make that much mess of a motel room and provide the means of writing that long a message in such big letters, I'd have gone the other way.

'Oh no,' Todd said. 'Not necessarily. I once dropped a pint bag of blood when I was a resident and then I stomped on it, flailing around trying to catch it. It looked like a horror movie.'

'Heh heh heh,' said Noleen. 'I'd have paid to see that. Flubbing is always funny, but flubbing a bag of blood is next-*level* funny.'

'I live to serve,' Todd said.

Then we heard a voice from outside. 'We know that if we can hear you that means you can hear us.' It was Molly. 'Close this window or we'll clear the place.'

We closed the window. She was banging on the door within minutes anyway.

'Where's Mrs Muelenbelt?' I hadn't got used to Della's new name yet.

'In the Skweek with Diego,' Noleen said. 'Distracting him.'

'So,' Molly said, taking out a notebook. She still used a notebook? 'Do I need to split you all up and talk to you separately or will you cooperate?'

'Blaine Temple,' Todd said. 'Wife of Dr Philip Temple, mother of Salem and Navy Temple. I know.' Molly had quirked an eyebrow at the names. 'She moved in on Saturday to get her and the kids away from the family home so Phil could go in and out to work in the isolation unit without worrying about what he might be bringing home. Roger's there too.'

'In the COVID wards?' said Molly, and I'd have sworn her face paled. 'I thought Roger was a paediatrician. They've pulled him in already?'

'No, sorry,' said Todd. 'There the house, not there the unit. He's staying at Blaine and Phil's instead of here. Like you and . . .?'

'Cheyenne,' Molly said. Kathi and Noleen stared at the floor, concentrating very hard on not laughing. I was too astonished by Molly answering at all to react to the fact that her girlfriend sounded like she came straight from the Grand Ole Opry.

'Cheyenne MacAfee?' Todd said. 'APRN in the ICU?'

'Yup,' said Molly.

'And she's your honey?' said Todd. He had folded his arms and kind of wriggled himself comfy in his chair. All he needed was a cigarette and crossover pinny and he'd look like a 1950s housewife hearing snash about her neighbours at the back fence.

'So Blaine moved in on Saturday,' Molly said, in a voice that would make dry ice go 'brrrr'.

'And on Sunday morning, like I told you,' I took up the tale, 'there was a sign saying COME HOME, BITCH and the next day OR ELSE and this morning NO BITCH LEAVES ME. YOU WERE WARNED. Except we were wrong about who was doing it. Obviously.'

'So,' Molly said. She turned to Noleen, 'How'd he get in? I was sold this place as a gated haven. You forget to lock up last night?'

'That's not fair,' I said. 'What about Calfire and all that? Master keys. You said it yourself.'

'I locked up tight at ten p.m.,' Noleen said, 'including an extra chain and a new padlock. Fire season is months away,' she added as Molly started rumbling.

'So how *did* he get in?' Kathi said.

I shot upright in my seat as a flash lit my brain, then I had to grab the front of the vanity unit as the office chair I was on tipped backwards. What *is* it with these wheely chairs that tip backwards? What is the intended purpose of a chair seat that wibbles about like the head of a nodding dog on a country road?

'I saw him!' I said. 'Oh my God, I know how he got in. Well, I know how he got out. I saw it happen.'

'And you're mentioning it so soon?' said Molly.

'He didn't use the gate,' I said, ignoring her. 'He came in – well, he went out – across the slough and over the fields.'

'When was this?' Molly had her pencil poised over her notebook and a thought bubble poised over her head. I could see both of them equally clearly.

'Half one-ish,' I said.

'Around one thirty,' Todd translated.

'And you're saying he waded through the slough?' Molly said.

'No! I'm saying he hopped on board my boat and jumped off the other side,' I said. 'That's what woke me. I went out on to the porch and saw him thrashing off through the bushes. I knew it wasn't Meera's husband and I knew it wasn't Arif's wife – you know, from having seen Officer Flynn and Mrs Jafari when we dropped the signs off at the end of their drives earlier. Lucky we did that, eh?' Molly rolled her eyes, so I didn't push it.

'And what did you do?' she said. 'You call nine-one-one or the non-emergency? Who did you speak to?'

'Erm,' I said, 'I went back to bed. Like I said, I knew it wasn't either of the people we suspected so I reckoned it was just . . . someone else . . . so I went back to bed and back to sleep.'

It wasn't just Molly now. All four of them were looking at me in the same way. Or rather Noleen's face was a blank mask, Kathi's was squinched up, Todd's mouth was hanging open, and Molly was pulling at one of her eyebrows with her non-writing hand.

'In other words,' she said, 'if you hadn't harassed two innocent strangers earlier in the day, you would have suspected this boat-hopper of being a domestic abuser and called it in.'

'They're not innocent,' I said. 'There's no such thing as an innocent wife-beater. Or husband-beater.'

'My point stands,' said Molly.

'OK, fine!' I said. 'Your point doesn't stand because it's based on a pile of crap I just told you. It was nothing to do with who it was or wasn't. I only went back to bed because I was hammered. Happy?'

'Face hurts from grinning,' said Molly. 'Were you too hammered to see if it looked anything like Dr Temple?'

'I've never met him. Todd, what does he look like?'

'Ichabod Crane.'

'What does that mean?' I said.

'Peter Crouch,' said Noleen, whose bottomless love of all sport can sometimes help.

'Who?' said Kathi, who doesn't share it.

'Stephen Merchant,' I told her.

'Who?' said Todd, whose knowledge of non-Sunday-night British telly wouldn't get him through the first round of *Jeopardy*, whereas I can fling references to *Jeopardy* around with abandon.

'Ichabod Crane!' said Molly. She had actually pulled out an eyebrow hair now. She blew it off her fingers. 'Oh my God, how have you people not hacked each other to bloody lumps already?' Then she seemed to remember what had brought her in here to be bugged to death by us and cleared her throat.

'So did he look like Ichabod Crane and the rest of them?' she asked me.

'I don't think so,' I told her. 'Although it was dark and I was unfocused, like I said. But, thinking about it logically, I was sure it wasn't Officer Beefcake or Mrs Shotputter and so that might have been because he was too tall and skinny. I'd have said not, mind you. I'd have said average.'

'Of course you would,' said Molly. 'Everyone always does. But, since you're not saying Quasimodo, it doesn't sound like he was carrying his wife or his wife's body over one shoulder? Was he dragging anything?'

I screwed up my face and tried to remember. Surely that person wasn't carrying a Blaine-sized burden. I'd have noticed. Wouldn't I?

'If someone dragged someone else through the under-growth, they'd leave a hell of a trail,' I said. 'I didn't notice anything round the side of the oh! Wait, yes, I did. I had to pick a hair off my face this morning. I thought it was a cobweb.'

'Ew,' said Todd. I usually pretend there's no such thing as spiders around him.

'But it wasn't. It was a long human hair.'

'Ew,' said Kathi. She hadn't taken her eyes off Molly's plucked-out eyebrow hair since it hit the carpet, as if she was daring it to crawl away before she got the Hoover out.

'And I'm assuming Dr Temple doesn't have long hair,' said Molly.

'Actually,' said Todd, 'Phil Temple has a man bun with an undercut. He wears it in a top-knot, so I'm not sure how long it is.'

'A doctor with a man bun,' said Molly, in the blankest voice since the first generation of answerphones. 'OK,' she went on. 'Ms Campbell, you need to stay off your boat until we've swept for hairs, blood spots or any other evidence to back up your story. Meanwhile, we'll bring Dr Temple in anyway. In case your "lack of focus" averaged him out.'

I opened my mouth to argue but Todd beat me to the punch.

'Wait,' he said, as Molly unhooked her walkie-talkie from its holster. 'If you're going to pick up Phil, I need to call Roger, find out if he's home and tell him to get out of there.'

'What is it with you people?' Molly said. '*I* need *you* to not tip off Dr Temple before we can get a unit in there to pick him up,' Molly said. 'Put that phone away.'

'*A* unit?' said Todd. 'Pick him *up*? Are you kidding me? It's going to be six cars and twelve cops flightier than racehorses, armed to the teeth, charging in with a battering ram, all yelling their heads off and determined to bag a shoot-out and get them-selves a bit of paid leave.'

Molly was staring at him as if she'd like to start a little shoot-out of her own.

'Oh wait!' said Todd. 'Silly me. I forgot Philip Temple is whiter than Joe Biden's smile. It'll all be OK.'

Molly was still staring but she was frowning too. 'Yeah,' she said. 'But if the unit's not expecting Dr Kroger to be in there . . .'

'So phone someone and tell them he is,' I said.

Todd laughed. 'Right,' he said. 'Phone dispatch and tell them "another doctor" is in the house. That'll work.'

I looked at him, hard, and then at Molly. 'What am I missing?'

Kathi heaved a huge sigh and said, 'You're missing the part where the units hear there's a paediatric doctor in the Temple house and they bust in and see *Roger* and they think, "Oh that must be him". You're missing that, Lexy.'

Molly had her eyes trained on the floor as if pandas were learning to tumble there.

'Oh for God's sake,' I said. 'Tell them he's black then!'

'Can't,' said Molly, still watching the pandas tumbling about.

'Why the hell not?' I said. No one else said anything.

'Because our calls are taped and go on record if things turn bad,' she added, at last.

'So?' I said. 'So what? So people hear you trying to make sure nothing terrible happens to Roger. What's the . . . Oh. Yeah. Right.'

'So Blaine Temple arrived on Saturday,' Molly said, moving on for all the world as if she hadn't just casually confirmed it would be a bad idea for a great big black guy to be unexpectedly in a house when the cops rolled up on other business and the cops knew that and the only thing that bothered them about it was that, if they mentioned him specifically, everyone would *know* they knew. 'But she never gave any indication of thinking the messages were for her?'

'She played a blinder,' I said. 'Cool as a cuke. And she didn't make the mistake of pretending to be unbelievably happy either. You know? She complained about having to FaceTime Phil for the kids, and she was obviously enjoying a bit of space to loll about and eat crap when she should have been practising. She's a dancer.'

'Ummm,' said Todd.

'I'd hate to be as cynical as you, Lexy,' said Noleen, like a pot scolding a kettle. 'Sounds like she was unhappily married and you think that's normal. Happy and missing him would have been bogus?'

'Well, I do tend to meet couples once they've started making voodoo dolls,' I reminded her.

'Ummm,' said Todd.

Molly looked over at him. 'Are we interrupting your meditation?'

Todd stared right back. 'Are we just pretending that the question of my husband – who I am very happy with, by the way, Lexy – going down in a pigment-related hail of bullets has been addressed? Because it hasn't.'

Molly poked her tongue into her cheek, then chewed her lip, then took hold of one of her eyebrows again. Kathi moaned softly. 'Call him now,' she told Todd. 'Tell him nothing, just find out where he is. And don't *ever* say I told you to.'

Todd fumbled his phone out of his robe pocket. 'Babe? Where you at?' he said, after a pause. He mouthed *work* to Molly. 'Is Phil there?' he asked, making Molly start doing throat-slitting mimes at him. 'Oh, he's gone home? OK, OK. Well, stay there. Promise me you'll stay there. Stay in the lounge, sit outside at the picnic tables. Please, Roger! I can't tell you. Because I can't. I can't tell you why I can't tell you.' He held the phone out to Molly who shook her head and folded her arms. 'OK,' Todd said into the phone once it was back at his ear again. He spoke in a new voice, deeper and more sombre than I had ever heard him use. 'I am asking you in the name of Ken Horne to stay put till I call again. OK?' He waited. 'OK. Me too. Me more. I win.' He hung up the phone.

'Ken Horne?' said Noleen. 'Is that your skanky safe word? Ew.'

'Ken Horne was the first AIDS case in San Francisco,' Todd said. 'Sacred name.'

Molly was talking into her walkie-talkie. 'Need an address for a Philip Temple MD, Sacramento. Person of interest in the two-oh-seven at the Last Ditch.' She hung up. 'Sit tight,' she said to us. 'We will process the crime scenes as soon as

possible and turn them back to you. I need to go do this. And
I need to get CPS to come see those kids.'

She said that last bit half to herself on the way out the door
but it met with a wail of dissent. Kathi's was the loudest voice.
'You need to let Dr Temple say what happens to his kids. Even
if you think he killed their mama. Don't you?'

Molly shrugged it off and left us, banging the door after her
as if that was her way of getting the last word.

'Nobody move!' Kathi said, as soon as she was gone. 'I need
to vacuum up her hairs. What a . . . what's that word, Lexy?'

'Scutter?'

'What a scutter, yeah.'

We *tried* to sit tight and do nothing to get in Molly's way.
Honest, we did. Honour-bright, pinky-swear, cross my legs and
hope to burst. We held out for nearly forty minutes. Besides,
as Todd was phoning Roger after we finally cracked, Roger
phoned him first. Meaning that we were covered. One hundred
per cent guilt-free.

'Put him on speaker!' said Noleen.

'Lexy, lock the door,' said Kathi. 'Close the curtains.'

'Close the . . .?'

'Well, at least lock the door.'

'Shut up!' said Todd. 'Let me talk! Hi again, babe. Listen,
stuff's going down. Yeah, yeah, I know you did but I was dialling— Oh. Oh they have? Oh my God!'

'Put him on speaker,' said Noleen.

'Oh he did?' said Todd. 'Oh my God!'

'Speaker!' said Noleen. 'Now!'

'Oh he was?' said Todd. 'Oh my God!'

Noleen struggled up from where she was reclining on Della's
bed and went over to loom. 'Put. Him. On. Speaker,' she said.

Todd put the phone over his chest and filled us in. 'Cops
have got him,' he said. 'He used his phone call to call Roger,
to tell Roger to call us, to ask if we'll keep the kids.'

'That was dumb,' said Kathi. 'He shoulda called a lawyer.'

'Roger said Phil said he doesn't need a lawyer,' Todd relayed.

'Put him on speaker before I smack you,' said Noleen.

'He was on call last night and, because it was a rough night, he was physically there at the hospital from eight o'clock yesterday onwards. He got home just as the police rolled up. He wasn't alone for more than the time it took to pee either. So he doesn't need a lawyer; he needs to know his kids are safe.'

'That was smart,' said Kathi. 'Makes him look good. The jury's gonna love it.'

'And now,' Todd said, dinking the buttons, 'speakerphone.' I could hear Roger breathing down the line, as if he'd just run up a flight of stairs. 'I'm out on the balcony,' he said, 'so no one can overhear any of this. What the hell happened? Phil called and said the cops rolled up and arrested him, took him to the jail, mugshot, prints, one phone call, the whole enchilada.'

We filled Roger in: the sign, the blood, the crying children in an empty room, more blood, the on-site cop right there to start investigating . . .

'The what?'

'Molly moved in. Didn't Todd tell you?'

'Molly Rankinson is staying at the Last Ditch?' Roger said. 'Wow.'

'One kidney and her girlfriend's a nurse,' I said. 'Didn't Todd tell you?'

'Did you tell Taylor?' Todd said. 'Did you spend your phone time with your honey on third-hand gossip?'

'So how's Phil holding up, Roger?' I said. 'Could you tell?'

'Shattered,' Roger said. 'Shredded. I don't think they had the best marriage in the world . . .' He paused. The rest of us waited in silence, knowing that was the best way to make sure he carried on. At least, Noleen started to speak at one point but Todd lifted his phone, threatening to take it off speaker, and she subsided. 'Enh, it was probably nothing though,' Roger went on at last. 'Kids came along and took over. Blaine forgot she was a wife as well as a mommy.'

'How do you even know that much?' I said.

'We got kinda lit the first night,' Roger admitted, 'and Phil said more than he should have.'

'Oh he did?' said Todd. 'And he didn't mind that you didn't join in because you'd never dish dirt on me with someone else?'

'What dirt?' said Roger, which was masterful. 'I had to dream stuff up so he didn't feel bad. I told him you worked too hard and never took a day off from checking your business email.'

We all waited to see if that was far too much or if Todd would lap it up. 'That was kind of you,' he said. Lapping it was, then.

'Do you think they'll keep Phil in jail?' I said when the ripples of disbelief about how gullible Todd was had faded.

'I have no idea,' said Roger. 'I don't see how they can. He was here. And if there's no body . . .'

'But a whole lotta blood,' Kathi reminded him. It had to be killing her to think of one of the rooms being in the mess I'd seen. I wondered if she would have to take it back to the studs and refurbish it or if she would let us try to clean it first.

'If you speak to Phil again,' I said to Roger, 'tell him the kids are fine. They're with the old couple who moved in – José and Maria. Sweet people. Skilled at the grandparenting lark. They're having a bubble-bath with added singalong right now. Assure him they'll be fine till he can pick them up.'

'Yeah,' Roger said. 'See, he already went there. And I want to know what you make of it. If Phil gets out – cleared or bailed, either way – he says he needs to go back to work to keep from going crazy while they look for Blaine.'

'They won't let him back to work on bail though, will they?' I said.

'Not usually,' said Roger. 'They might right now.'

'Oh yeah,' Kathi said. 'Now.'

'And so,' Roger said, 'he wants you guys to keep the kids.'

'Uhhhh,' I said. 'His wife has been . . . let's call it abducted . . . and he wants his kids to stay in the place she disappeared from, looked after by people he doesn't know? I'm starting to think maybe his "too much of a mommy" setting is out of whack. And actually, I'd have said Blaine was at the other end of that sliding scale anyway.'

'Does anyone else think it's weird he had brain space to say all that in his first call from jail?' said Todd. 'He finds out his wife is gone and her room is covered in blood and his kids were left alone and he . . . he plays out his plan for if it *goes* well? That smells.'

'That stinks,' Noleen said. 'He shoulda said leave them here for now, then concentrated on being all broke up about Blaine. At least for the rest of the day.'

'You sound as if you think he's guilty of something,' Roger said. 'I keep telling you, he was in the hospital all night surrounded by co-workers.'

'Contract,' said Noleen and Kathi, together.

'He's as guilty as hell,' Noleen went on. 'He's getting it soooo wrong. He should be ripping off his man bun with worry about Blaine and he's not because he knows she's dead. Because he killed her.'

NINE

It's not that unusual for me to gnash my teeth about having clients all day, but it's unheard of for me to wish I didn't have to listen to people's problems, offer support and advise them about self-care because I want to offer an ear, a shoulder and a slice of advice to someone else. That was the score today. As I set off to shower in Todd's room, dress like an adult in whatever I could scrounge from Della and find some good tissues for my scratch consultation suite in Kathi's spare room (because of course my boat was still a crime scene), I was acutely aware of leaving Arif and Meera to the tender mercies of Todd and Kathi, with Noleen on top like a little mouldy cherry.

'It's not like it was mistaken identity,' Kathi was saying to Meera as I passed them on the forecourt where they were watching Joan and Bob chalking trains on to the ground. 'Blaine was definitely the intended target. There's no reason for you to worry.' To me, that was exactly like saying 'Hardly any movie popcorn has rat droppings in it' to someone who's never had the thought cross their minds in decades of guzzling with the lights down.

'You are so safe here now,' Todd was saying to Arif as they headed to the pool. 'There will be cops crawling all over for days and then drive-bys and Sergeant Rankinson. This is a good thing.' To me, that was like saying: you weren't safe before when I said you were and so you probably shouldn't listen to me.

I had thought my clients would balk at me meeting them by a locked gate, letting them in, taking them to a motel room and having our session there. Turns out I couldn't have been more wrong. When they heard that the gate was locked because we were gearing up to keep everyone out if the county entered into mandatory seclusion or whatever they were going to call it, half my clients started clamouring to join us. Of course, I couldn't

let them. The counsellor–client relationship would never survive
them seeing how much I drank and swore and how many tacos
I could inhale as long as I didn't put too much sour cream on
them. I had to tell a few of them about the abduction just to
get them off my back.

'Last night?' said my twelve o'clock, an impressively recovered addict who only needed the lightest of light hands on the
tiller as she horned in on ten years sober.

'He got away over my deck,' I said. 'The boat's a crime
scene. That's why we're in here.'

'Yikes,' she said. She had a deadpan delivery and so much
Botox that her face had little choice but to match it, so she
always chose hyperbolic words; they were her only avenue to
expressed emotion. 'So . . . will you be back in soon? Will this
room be free?'

I hauled in a deep breath. 'Are you in danger of relapse if
you stay at home? It's just you and your partner, isn't it?'

'Unless the governor closes the colleges and then it's
Armageddon,' she said. 'Nah, I'm just dreaming.' She paused.
'But will it?'

'I don't think so,' I said. 'I think it's going to be used as
overflow for a . . . family of . . .'

'Lexy,' she said. 'I'm kidding.' She really needed to try a
kboom-tsh on her punchlines if she couldn't crack a smile.

My one o'clock wasn't kidding. He suffered from relentless
severe anxiety and the news had him wound him up like Usain
Bolt on his blocks. Yet he couldn't stop watching.

'Pick a source,' I said. 'One source: Johns Hopkins, NPR,
Fox and Friends . . .'

'You're funny.' Since he didn't look the type for Botox – and
if he'd had it he was due a refund, because his forehead was
corduroy – I think this deadpan was from his anxiety tipping
him right over the edge into a freeze, like those Oliver Sacks
people whose tics got faster and faster until they were in rigid
stasis all the time. Poor them. Poor this guy too.

'I try,' I said. 'I can stop.'

'Don't. I like how you treat me as if I'm more than my
illness. My doctor never kids around.'

'So pick a source,' I said again, 'and check in once a day.

Get a friend to let you know if anything happens in between times. Take social off your phone. And log out of your laptop. Make it hard to keep grazing.'

'I'm working at home,' he said. Of course he was. He was a fund-raiser for a children's fostering charity and his job was mostly phoning people at the best of times. 'And I'm taking over a bit of the PR too so I can't log out.'

'OK,' I said, thinking. 'So keep social *on* your phone, take it all off your laptop, and lock your phone in your car. Have you got a landline?' He looked at me as if I'd asked him whether he had a buggy for rides out after church on Sundays. 'OK, *don't* lock your phone in your car. It's all one to me. Maybe just keep scrolling and checking and tweeting and posting and linking and commenting and see how it goes.'

'I could try drinking,' he said.

'Drinking's always a plan,' I agreed. 'Or pot.'

I hadn't got used to legal cannabis yet; it still felt very weird to recommend it for anxiety.

'Oh my God,' he said. 'You think I don't use "pot" every day of my life just to keep going without my head exploding? You really *are* funny.'

'And you really *did* lie on your intake form,' I said. 'Would you like to revisit it now you know me better?'

'Uhhh, sorry about that,' he said. 'Yeah, daily use but nothing stronger.'

'And how's your support system?' I asked. 'Do you have people you can call and vent to? Rant at? Cry with?'

'You tell me,' he said. 'Do I?'

We agreed on that: he wasn't moving in but he could call me whenever. Or text me. Or ping me. Or zazz me. Or dink me.

'How many of those did you just make up?' I asked him. But he only smiled and said he wasn't my Google. I'm not sure our relationship lands on the right side of the border that should separate a client/provider dyad from a couple of pals taking the mutual piss, but it seems to be helping him. His fingers used to bleed. These days his nails are still bitten but the skin around them is whole.

I had a late lunch in the room where Blaine was supposed to have practised, which Maria had turned into a crèche. All

five kids were there. Diego had scraped together his own
toys and everything from the lost property box in the back office
and put it into common ownership. Bob was playing with the
wooden fruit-cutting set, sawing away at the Velcro fasteners
in a sliced watermelon with the wrong end of the knife. Diego
was just about coping except for one fist clenching and releasing
as he watched.

'Maria,' I said. 'Look at that boy!'

'Abuelita Maria,' she said sternly. 'Y en Español?'

'Huh?' I said.

'Spanish immersion, baby!' said Meera. 'If we're gonna be
here we might as well make it work for us.'

'Oh, OK,' I said. 'Mirar el niño.'

Abuela Maria shook her head and corrected me, making
with her hand like she was conducting a choir. 'Mira a ese
muchacho,' she said.

After I'd said it three times and got the vowels right, she
patted my cheek and then shooed me off like a hen, to sit and
eat my tub of leftover taco fixings and watch the kids play. Joan
was mostly trying to scrape up Navy's three and a half downy
little head hairs into a ponytail, while Diego, Bob and Salem
organized the various trains, trucks, planes, 'copters, boats and
even tanks into the kind of integrated transport system
Switzerland could only dream of. As I chased the last little
beans round the bottom of my bowl with a plastic fork, they
were discussing flat-rate fares versus premiums for large teddy
bears and other out-of-scale passengers. They were going to be
fine. The whole of America was going to be fine if Diego
decided to go into public service one day.

Outside the door, José was sitting in a plastic chair with his
Rivercats cap pulled down over his eyes.

'Abuelo José?' I whispered.

'Sí,' he said, looking up.

'You can sit by the pool, you know. Under an umbrella. Or
in the shade by the office there. You shouldn't nap in the sun
like this.'

He pushed his hat back on his head and grinned at me. 'I
am a raisin!' he said. 'No! I am a currant. It's too late, cariña.'
And since the grin had made his face turn into basically a

bas-relief of Mother Teresa made of eucalyptus bark, it was hard to argue. 'Bueno,' he went on quietly, 'I'm not napping. I'm watching. Vigilando. Guardo.'

'Right,' I said. 'Do you still want to stay? After what happened?'

He jerked his head at the closed door, behind which I could hear Maria holding court, or laying down the law, or doing something anyway that lifted her voice in the pure joy of having a gaggle of little kids to be in charge of. I smiled at him and nodded. Message received and understood: it would take more than a bucket of blood and a missing person to winkle Maria out of here.

I stopped off next to ask Noleen if there were any spare keys for the new padlock but it was Della in Reception. Of course, there was no need for anyone to be in Reception, but maybe it would take a while for the habit to die.

'What are you doing?' I said. 'We don't need anyone on the desk.'

'I'm avoiding Devin.'

'Oh? That's new. Is the incarceration getting to you?'

She shook her head. 'I don't mind. I don't miss my job. I like Diego being home. I like having friends around.' That was what her words were saying. Her tone was saying she hated her life, her friends, her kid, her husband and the ground she trod on.

'Can I help?' I said, answering the tone not the words.

'Nope,' she said.

'Do you want to tell me?'

'Nope.'

'Is there anyone you can tell?'

'Nope.'

That was me out of ideas. 'The kids are enjoying José and Maria,' I tried next.

Della nodded. 'Kids,' she said. 'Plural.' Then she gasped.

'You OK?' I said. She nodded again. 'That sounded like a gasp of pain.'

She shook her head. 'Not pain,' she said. 'Dread.'

I nodded as if I understood but I didn't see why the thought of kids plural would cause a gasp of dread. *Until I did!*

'You're preg—' I shouted.

'SSShhhhhh!'

'—nant?' I whispered.

'I think so,' she said.

'Congratul— I can help you with any decisions,' I said, which wasn't the smoothest mid-sentence swerve I'd ever executed, it's true.

'No decisions to be made,' Della said. 'Just some coming to terms.'

'Can I help?'

'And some telling Devin.'

'Ah,' I said. 'Right. Well, you'd probably better do that on your own.'

Then I left her. I'm not sure she noticed I'd gone.

Round the back of the motel, there were still cops – three of them – on board my houseboat. What had they been doing for the last five hours? What they were doing now was sitting on the porch seats . . . folding my clean washing? As I got closer, I realized they were marking square evidence bags with Sharpies and stacking them in a box.

'You nearly done?' I said. 'Can I see my afternoon clients here or do I need to re-rent a room in the motel? Say, can I bill the city for that?'

'The PD,' said the youngest of the three cops. I hadn't met him before. The other two were old 'pals': Mills of God – the slowest man on two legs; and Soft Cop – who made Mr Stay-Puft look wiry. 'The form you need is number—'

'No way Noleen Muntz charged you for a room,' said Soft Cop.

'True,' I said. 'But if she did?'

'You could try,' said Soft Cop. 'But the paperwork would kill you dead.'

I hopped off the bank on to the bottom step and joined them in the fourth seat. 'So,' I said, 'how's it going? Did you find the long hair? Did you find any blood? Did you pick up the trail on the other bank?'

'We can't discuss matters like that with members of the public,' said the newbie. (I couldn't read his name tag.) 'If you'd like to attend one of Chief Pelletier's town halls, I can send you a link. What's your number?' (But let's call him Tigger.)

'I only ask because I want to know if I need to deep-clean,' I said.

'Uhhhhh,' Tigger said. 'Probably soap and water will be fine?'

That told me nothing but made sure I couldn't sue the PD if I caught hepatitis.

'And how about the Sacramento end?' I said, because nothing ventured nothing gained. 'Did they let Phil Temple out? Or keep him in? Did he confess?'

'Are you some kind of consultant?' Tigger said.

'Yes,' I told him, absolutely honestly.

'No!' said Soft and Mills.

'And just generally,' I said, 'have you found her body? She's dead, right? I think Molly said she was surely dead with all that blood lost.'

'Who's Molly?' said Tigger, bug-eyed from trying to keep up. Perhaps all that enthusiasm was to make up for profound stupidity.

'Sergeant Rankinson,' said Soft. 'And no way did she tell you we're starting to call this a homicide.'

I gave him a long look through narrowed eyes. If it had been Mills I'd have said he just gave it away. Mills isn't wily. But Soft Cop might conceivably be enough of a four-dimensional chess player to put the denial in *just* that way so I couldn't quite be sure how much of it he was actually denying.

'Uhhh, Stu?' said Mills of God, blowing the ploy completely. 'That's not what the sarge said at all.'

I gave Soft Cop a beaming smile. He came back with a deep scowl. Mills still hadn't caught up by the time the three of them left.

'Let us know if there's anything else we can do to support you in this difficult time, Ms Campbell,' said Tigger, from the bank. He'd definitely been on a course. He'd learn. Either that or his colleagues would lock him in a cupboard so they didn't have to listen to it.

'Who's the twink?' said Todd, arriving just after the cops had left.

'No!' I said. 'No way that's a thing you can still say.'

'Jeez,' said Todd, throwing himself down. 'Wokeness up the wazoo. OK. Here's what we know. Because of the alibi, Phil is back out. No booking. No arraignment. Back to work tomorrow, seething with microscopic bugs and general filth from the jail. I have told Roger to keep away from him. Can you imagine?'

'Viruses aren't bugs,' I said. 'Well, not the kind . . . Oh, whatever.'

'But the cops are looking into his financials and his phone records, so no way is he home clear.'

'They really *do* think he took out a contract on her?' I said. 'Phone and financials sounds like it.'

'I know. I don't know,' Todd said. 'But if he did, he's doing a fantastic job of making himself look innocent. Handed over his phone. Gave them all his PINs for the bank. And get this: he wants us to—'

'No,' I said.

'I haven't even—'

'There is no end to that sentence that's going to turn my no into a yes,' I said. 'Try me.'

'He wants us to keep the kids here.'

'We knew that already,' I said. 'You're lying.'

'OK! He wants us to scrape up some gunk from the crime scene and courier it over there because he has connections and Blaine had her 23andMe done. So at least we can find out if it's her blood.'

'Why the hell wouldn't it be her blood?' I said. 'Who the hell else's blood would it be?'

'Was the figure you saw through your drunken haze definitely a man?' Todd said.

I thought it over. 'Because it might have been Blaine running away after copy-catting a bedsheet note and leaving her kids locked in a blood-spattered motel room, all of which she could do because she'd gone out unwitnessed through a locked gate earlier in the evening to score a bag of random human blood on the street like something from *Buffy*?' I said.

'Exactly.'

'Look, Todd, I know she wasn't ever going to make the shortlist for Mummy of the Year but no one would do that. Why would anyone *do* that?'

'But you'll scrape the blood up?'

'Why me?' I said.

'Because not Kathi because blood and not me because flies because blood.'

'Right,' I said. I thought a minute. 'Well, I've got clients all afternoon but I'll do it tonight if you organize the courier.'

'Perfect,' said Todd. 'Except he's coming in an hour and you need to do it before Molly gets back. Plus your three o'clock is cancelled.'

'My three o'clock cancelled?'

'And there's one other thing,' said Todd, 'then I gotta go because Meera's polishing my T-zone. How did we ever limp on all this time without an in-house beauty therapist. I'm practically a make-up artist, as you know, but no concealer, contour, bronze and blush in the world can compete with the deep glow of healthy skin that's been professionally abraded.'

'I was with you,' I said, 'until so near the end of that. And circling back one more time: my three o'clock cancelled or my three o'clock *is* cancelled?'

'Lexy, I cancelled your three o'clock,' Todd said. I opened my mouth. 'And shifted her to five, which she said was much more convenient. And if *we* can wait a little longer for dinner without complaining, I don't see why you should have a problem. I'll even get started on the prep work for you, if you like.'

'So just let me check this,' I said. 'You went into my confidential online diary and made a last-minute appointment rescheduling for one of my clients, to free up my time to go and illegally scrape up blood to send to a possible murderer who might be using us as his cover story. Plus I've been volunteered to make dinner for seventeen people, many of whom mock my nation's cuisine relentlessly and mock my attempts to make anything from this nation's cuisine even more? Is that about the length of it?'

'And the county's told everyone over seventy-five to go home, go directly home, do not swing by Target and definitely do not collect a bunch of compadres.'

'That's news right enough,' I said. 'But it seems like a different category. I *meant*: is that everything you've done that's going to make a big dent or bulge in my day?'

'I'm getting there,' Todd said. 'So that's quite stressful, isn't it? Puts a burden on carers and leaves elderly people isolated.'

'Get there quicker.'

'Taylor's mom's moving in.'

'What?' I said. 'How? Why? How did you even . . .? Why would that . . .?'

'All very good questions,' said Todd. 'You had your phone off while you were in session and Taylor called the landline.'

'But *he* moved in with *her*! On Saturday. He was fine with it. He wanted to look after her. My God, if she's so hellish her own son can't take any more after three days, what makes you think we're going to be able to cope? How dare he off-load his mother on to us and . . . why are you looking at me like that? What have you done?'

'He would never leave his mother to the care of strangers,' Todd said. 'Surely you know him better than that? Don't you? Maybe not. Maybe you haven't had enough time together to learn who he is deep down. That's kinda sad.'

'Todd,' I said, 'are you telling me that you've just arranged for my new boyfriend to move in to the motel for some unspecified length of time when possibly neither one of us will be able to leave, depending on how strict this coming incarceration or whatever they're going to call it gets?' Somehow I had managed to say all of that and still feel as if I was holding my breath.

'No,' said Todd.

I let my breath go in a big shaky laugh.

'The motel's full with the old lady taking over Blaine's room,' he said. 'Taylor's going to be here on the boat with you.'

TEN

As I breathed deeply and tried not to shove Todd in the solar plexus, sending him over the side to drown in the slough, I realized I was standing in the exact same spot as the middle of the night, so I started trying to recreate the sight of that dark figure thrashing its way through the undergrowth.

'Where was he going?' I said, mostly to myself. 'I didn't hear a car start and it's a hike and a half to anywhere on foot.' Muelleverde, the next little town to the south, was at least five miles of tomatoes away. Five miles of nothing at this time of year.

'He might have parked at the edge of the field on the Old Cuento Road,' said Todd. 'It dead-ends but it's still there. Wanna go tracking?'

'Why not?' I said. 'I've got a free hour, thanks to you, and I only need five minutes of it to get a blood sample from Blaine's room.' I went down the porch steps and along to the end, then hopped off on to the far bank. I hardly ever came over here and I was surprised by how soft the ground was. In fact, if I didn't move soon I would sink over the tops of my clogs.

It was weirdly pleasant to pull against the strong suck of the bog and feel my foot come out with a loud liquid pop, then move on to the sticky gumbo and next the cobbles of grey earth and, as I burst out of the hedgerow into the field, finally the powdery dust. I looked down at my feet and saw that I was now wearing moonboots of mud with a moleskin finish. 'How the hell did he manage to run away?' I said. 'It would be like those nightmares except for real.'

Todd was beside me, barefoot. I pointed and frowned.

'My lo-tops are limited,' he said. It was a typical Todd sentence and, while I didn't know what it meant exactly, I could file it under fancy footwear. 'Maybe he had snowshoes on. Or galoshes and then he took them off. Or maybe scuba-diving flippers would work. We could try it.'

'We could learn the banjo and move to Nashville,' I said. 'But at least we know one thing for sure.' Todd raised his eyebrows. 'Even if I was too drunk to tell, there's no way he was carrying Blaine's body.'

'True. He would have sunk in up to his knees and still be there.'

'And he definitely didn't drag it,' I said, nodding at the flat field of undisturbed dust ahead of us.

'He must have gone along this way to the dead end,' Todd said, pointing. We set off, hugging the edge of the field, until we reached the crumbling tarmac where the amputated old road ran out in a depressing pile of binbags, burst pallets, condoms, and that one obligatory stained mattress without which un-official dumps don't really deserve the name.

'What exactly are we tracking?' I said.

'Uhhh, unusual tyre prints from where he turned around for a quick getaway?'

I looked at the ground for a minute and said, 'Let's go and scrape blood.'

'Fine by me,' said Todd. 'Tracking is hard.'

Even though my shoes were ruined already, I slipped them off when we got back to the slough. My bare feet made a lot less satisfying a pop in the mud but it felt fantastic.

'It's a shame Taylor's mom probably can't get around here safely,' Todd said once we were side by side on the bottom step, letting the cold slough water rinse off our feet, and watching my clogs bob around getting clean.

'Don't even,' I said. 'I haven't forgiven you for that yet. I'm not sure I ever will.'

'I thought you'd be pleased,' said Todd. 'Kathi and Noleen are pleased. Taylor sounded pleased.'

'Did you tell him why it is his mother can suddenly move into an empty room?' I asked.

'Oop! Your shoes are floating away,' Todd said, and leaned out right over the water to hook them back in again, hoping gratitude or maybe just the sight of his yoga stretch would distract me.

Except of course she couldn't actually move right in to Blaine's room. If I had any doubts, they would have been swept away as soon as I opened the door – capped, aproned, gloved, masked, booteed and holding up a sample jar like a cross to ward off vampires – and limboed in under the crime-scene tape. I don't know why I was surprised that the cops had made no difference to the abattoir-esque look of the place. I knew specialist crime-scene cleaning firms were only in business because cops did nothing.

Kathi was standing halfway back across the car park but still, inevitably, trying to run the show. 'Don't step in it, Lexy!' she called. 'Don't brush against anything! Scrape the jar over a hard surface, not the wallpaper!'

'Oh really?' I said. 'You honestly think you're going to be able to save this wallpaper?' It was worse than I remembered. Maybe the screaming babies had offset the screaming red blood but, now it was the star of the show, it was horrific. I hauled in a deep breath, unscrewed the cap of the sample jar and dragged it along the skirting board where a deep well of blood had settled in the moulding. The sight of it wrinkling and curling and finally plopping into the jar was not a highlight of my day. I stood up and shuddered.

'How bad are the crib and the travel crib?' Kathi called over. 'If they're unusable I need to get new ones before tonight.'

'Are you insane?' I said. 'They're . . .' But then I took a closer look. There wasn't a drop of blood anywhere on either the carrycot or the playpen. Not so much as a dot, like those fake freckles that spray off a flicked brush. 'Huh,' I said. 'That's weird. How could that be?'

'What?' shouted Kathi.

I went to the door. 'They're fine,' I called over. 'There's nothing on either. I don't understand.'

The door of 104 opened and Meera poked her head out. 'Hey, Lexy?' she said. 'I've just gotten Navy down for a nap. Could you maybe go over and tell Kathi close-up.'

'Prop the door,' I said, 'and come and see this. A quick look while Molly's away.'

Meera stepped up into the platform peep-toes that she'd shucked off just inside her door and came tottering out. I'd go barefoot whenever possible, I thought, if all my shoes were instruments of torture. When she was beside me at the open door of Room 102, I said, 'What do you make of the cots being so clean?'

'Oh my God!' Meera said. She put her hands over her face and looked around the room with wide eyes. 'I thought you meant a puddle. Or maybe a drip. Oh my God, look at this place!'

'Yeah, yeah, but look at the babies' beds too,' I said. 'How could that be?'

Meera looked and frowned. 'I see what you mean,' she said. 'Well, either he put the babies in the bathroom while he killed her – And she must be dead right? All that blood? She must be! – Or maybe he put blankets over the cots while he killed her.'

'And what would Blaine be doing while he was moving furniture?'

'Huh,' said Meera. 'Looks like I'm the expert here. Lucky me. At a guess he said he wanted to move the babies into the bathroom so he and Blaine could "snuggle".'

'Aw jeez,' I said. 'I'm sorry you know that.'

'Me too,' Meera said. 'If I ever get married again, one of the things I'm looking forward to is my heart not sinking when my hubs suggests the kids go to Grandma's.'

'And so it really does look like it was Phil,' I said. 'Who else would want to kill his wife but not want so much as a drop of blood to hit the children?'

'I dunno,' Kathi said. She had come a wee bit closer. She still couldn't see inside but she could join the conversation. 'Don't husbands usually take out everyone? Wife and kids together? Maybe whoever it was wanted them out of the way so they didn't make a noise and wake anyone?'

'This is hands-down the most morbid conversation I have ever had in my life,' I said. And suddenly I needed to get out of there, away from the splats of blood and the pristine cot and playpen, both full of pink and blue stuffed animals and fluffy blankies. I reeled out into the car park just in time to see Taylor's truck roll up to the locked gates. I waved and went to get the key from Noleen, in the office.

'Seriously?' she said, looking up. 'Is this what we're wearing? Did Gav do a presser?' I looked down at my bootees, plastic apron and gloves and then pulled my face mask down to explain while I wriggled out of the rest of it.

Noleen had blitzed the office, probably binning many crucial documents and much essential stationery if the past was anything to go by, and was now busy scrubbing down her ancient old desktop computer with some of the anti-bacterial wipes Kathi gets from her cousin in Costa Rica. After two breaths of them, I pulled my face mask back up again.

'I didn't want to leave my DNA in Blaine's room while I was getting hers,' I said. 'God knows how many laws I broke passing the crime-scene tape. Listen, Taylor's here with the old lady. Todd told you, right?' Noleen nodded. 'So where are we going to put her?' I said. 'Taylor's mum. She's blind and I don't want her upstairs but there's not much capacity down here except Blaine's and that's not a go-er.'

'Yep,' said Noleen. 'It's fine by the cops to leave crime-scene tape up till Christmas but it's not exactly convenient for us. Still, with Molly right here we can nag her to step it up and then the old lady can knock herself out. Blind is real handy.'

'You're kidding!' I said. 'Just because she can't see it doesn't mean she can live in the Amityville room. What would Taylor say?'

'Of course I'm kidding. Devin's moving up to the last spare, 201, and Mrs Aaronovitch is moving in to 101. What do you think I am, Lexy?'

'Right,' I said. 'Of course. Sorry.' I hated it when I thought I was losing my grip on irony. 'Can I have the padlock key to let them in the gate?' I asked, moving on. 'And the master key for the rooms?'

'Yes and no,' Noleen said. 'Padlock key no problem. Master key . . . problem. I can't find it.'

I looked around the office where, between blitzes, there was usually ample capacity to lose a key. Where – if I'm honest – a crack team of burglars, surprised in the act, would only have to stand still to go unnoticed. Today – clear surfaces, empty drawers, bare cupboards (no staples, lost bills, scrap paper a foolish daydream) – there was nowhere for it to be.

'Hence the scorched earth,' I said. Then, 'Hey! Did you tell Molly? Because that might be how he got in to Blaine's room, especially if it wasn't her husband, right?' Noleen was concentrating awfully hard on cleaning a monitor screen that was already sparkling. 'You did tell Molly, didn't you?'

'I will,' Noleen said at last, still not looking at me. 'Once I've broken it to Kathi that it's gone. Which I also will. Unless you'd rather do it?'

'So just the key to Room 101 then,' I said, holding out my hand.

'Here's Lexy,' Taylor sang out to his mother as I approached the gates. He was good at narrating what she couldn't see without bugging her. I was rubbish. I either left bits out or told her stuff she didn't care about. And she had her own special way of letting me know: she nipped me above the elbow, not hard enough to leave a mark but unerringly on the tendon that made my arm buzz all the way to my fingertips. If she wasn't ancient, the size of a clothes peg, and blind, I would flick her to teach her a lesson. As things stood, I just kept trying to learn what she needed to hear.

'You look lovely,' I said to her as I hauled the gate open and the truck rolled by.

She leaned out of the window to shout back at me. 'Wait till we park and I get down! Don't ambush me through the window like a gypsy selling roses!'

Right. Taylor was running away from a one-on-one quarantine with this woman and plopping her in a room at the motel while he scuttled off to live on a boat she couldn't get to . . . in case she felt isolated. That seemed true.

'Lexy,' he said, as he climbed out of the driver's seat and met me at the back of the truck on his way to open his mother's door for her. 'I don't know what to say.' He clutched my hands in his and beamed.

'Fine by me,' I said. '*I* know what to say; you can just listen.' But bugger me, if I didn't feel a smile spread over my face even as I tried to get stern with him. I liked this guy. I liked how he was beaming at me. I liked how he was an open book. I liked how he had never once tried to make me care about waterfowl in the month I'd known him.

'Put her down and come get me!' his mother snapped, leaning out of her window again. She was wearing, I saw as Taylor helped her out, a pair of gold-sequinned market boots that matched the stripes down the side of her purple lounge suit and picked up the clip-ins she wore in her white hair.

'So you're spitting on my shoe choice?' she said. 'And not too subtly.'

'Me?' I asked. 'Wha—?'

'You shout in my ear that I look nice waist-up then swallow your tongue when you see the rest?'

Taylor put his hands together as if in prayer and pulled up his eyebrows in a beseeching look he must have learned from a spaniel.

'Welcome to the Last Ditch, Mrs Aaronovitch,' I said. 'You look spiffy. We're all going to have to up our game to match your style.'

'Or just tell me you did,' she said.

'Good point!'

'No,' she said, shaking her tiny fist at me. 'Have you any idea how offensive it is to lie to blind people about what they can't see? Amaranth.'

'Amaranth?' I said. I had no idea if it was a curse or a drinks order.

'My name,' she said. 'I can't be Mrs Aaronovitch if I'm living with you.'

'Amaranth Aaronovitch?' I said. 'How glamorous.'

'Don't patronize me,' she said. 'Amaranth are beautiful flowers and I loved my husband, but put them together and it sounds like someone dubbed Popeye. Now where's my room. My Laxido just kicked in.'

We ushered her over to Room 101 and showed her where the bathroom was, then I prepared to hightail it out of there, since the Last Ditch internal doors are not that sturdy. Thankfully, I had a ready-made excuse; there was a small pile of boxes just inside the door with a note from Devin taped to the top one.

'Ran out of time. Gone on Target run with Diego for school supplies. Please ignore. Will tote up to new room today! Peace and bacon, D.'

'Yeah but we can't leave a pile of boxes here for my mom to trip over,' Taylor said. 'I'll take them now. You wait here and tell her—'

'I'll take them!' I said, quite loud and quite fast, with a look at the closed bathroom door. Before he had a chance to bargain, I grabbed the top one and fled.

'Have you got a spare key to Devin's new room?' I said to Noleen, leaning the box – heavy for its size – on the counter. 'He's left his crap in Amaranth's.'

'In what?' said Noleen.

'Amaranth Aaronovitch,' I said. Then Noleen said it. Then I said it again. It was irresistible. It knocked Shankar Vedantam right out the park.

With the spare key balanced on top of the box, I crossed the car park again, picking up Taylor and his two boxes on my way.

'She'll be a while,' he said. 'I can tell by the early sound effects.'

'You're a good son,' I told him.

'She wiped my ass till I was four,' he said. 'I got a-ways to go.'

'You're a nice man,' I told him. 'And it's starting to make me uneasy. Could you not just tell me what the catch is instead of letting me find out on my own and hit the ground hard?'

'Catch?' said Taylor.

'Kind, funny, solvent, honest, good to your mum, laidback, easy on the eye . . . The catch. You know, the catch. There has to be one.'

We were at the top of the steps now. 'How's this for a catch?' Taylor said. 'I can't open the door for you, because if I need to put these boxes down to take the key, I can either let 'em drop from where they are, or bend my back and make a noise like an old man so you never want to sleep with me again, or squat and fart.'

'Ha ha ha ha ha,' I said, only even more uncomfortably than that sounds. A month in, we weren't on farting terms to the best of my knowledge, although as to what happened when I was fast asleep after devilled eggs was anyone's guess. And now here he was moving into my tiny houseboat. But on the other hand, here he was broaching it first. 'You're lovely,' I said. 'I'll open the door.'

Big talker. I tried to turn the key, failed, jiggled it, tried again, failed again and was just about to take it out, breathe on it and rub it on the bum of my jeans when Taylor said, 'Maybe it's open.'

I tried the handle and tah-dah! The door swung wide.

'It's a bit stale,' I said as I set the box down on the breakfast table. 'You go back for more boxes and I'll open the bathroom window and crack this front one.' I watched him trot downstairs and I was still smiling when I went into the bathroom, which was as stale as mince pies by Easter. If stale was even the word for this. Any other motel and I'd have suspected the drains. But not here in Kathi's kingdom. I pushed the shower curtain aside.

'Blaine,' I whispered, quieter than breathing. Maybe not even as loud as that.

She was lying curled up in the dry bath, wrapped in a length of plastic sheeting – another shower curtain, I thought, looking at the edge where holes were punched through. Inside the plastic she wore her pale blue pyjamas with the sushi print still visible here and there, although most of the fabric was soaked through with blood. Her face was grotesque, pale grey behind the plates of silicone mask still stuck to it, looking more like fish scales than armour plating now.

I didn't need to touch her to check that she was gone. Now I knew what was causing it, the air was not so much 'stale' as noxious. I turned my face away and that's when I saw the key – the missing master key – sitting on the cistern with its outsize keyring and the message 'Noleen will END you if you don't return this', so ludicrously upbeat that it finally managed to jolt me into action. I walked backwards, pulling the door closed again.

Taylor was out on the walkway. 'I should have time for one more trip before my mom's good to go,' he said and took off before I could find any words to answer him. I moved all the boxes, one by one, off the table, set them down on the ground outside, locked the door, then slid down the wall until I was sitting on my haunches and started to cry.

ELEVEN

Wednesday 18 March

Fog is romantic: no one but a lamplighter abroad in London, footsteps passing and nothing to be seen; the quiet plink of water off the end of an oar as a small boat carries a prince out of harm's way; a loner walking away along the mean streets he's just made safe for lesser mortals.

So why, oh why, does California take every one of those luminescent droplets hanging with portent and mystery and call them 'the marine layer'? It sounds like something you wear between your sweatshirt and raincoat on a chilly morning.

'The mar—' Taylor began.

'Please don't call it that,' I told him.

'OK,' he said, a bit dejected. Then he perked up. 'I know! I'll call it a Scotch Mist!'

'Absolutely not,' I said. 'That's not a thing. Call it a haar.'

'A what?'

'A haar.'

'What is that sound you're making?'

'What sound? *Haar?* It's like "bar" with an H.'

'It's really not,' Taylor said, then did an impersonation of a heavy smoker swallowing a wasp.

'Wow,' I said. 'Call it a marine layer. And I don't mind it anyway.'

It was true. There was no chance of seeing a bird unless it came and perched on the sill of our hide, but I hadn't come for the birds. I had come for the endless, milky peace of the pale wetland reflecting the pearl-grey sky. I had come for the whisper of the reeds as a breeze blew through them, for the smell of dying grass going back to the earth. If I hadn't met Taylor a month ago, right now I'd have been standing on an overpass up in Cuento, looking at the clouds and trying not to hear the traffic. I was very glad to be here instead. The haar made it even better, as if we'd stolen away out of the world into a private limbo where no one would ever find us.

'Would you like a . . .?' Taylor said.

My irritation sprang up and I must have moaned out loud because he stopped talking. Good. Whatever he was going to offer – a hug, a head massage, a foot rub – if I could even manage to lug off my wellies in the confines of the hide – was an annoyance. I didn't want connection; I wanted to curl up and be invisible until it unhappened.

My fingers had been too numb to dial 911 and, even when I saw Molly cross the forecourt headed back to Room 102, I couldn't raise my voice enough to attract her attention. But cops, you know. She sensed an anomaly and started sweeping the parked cars, the motel-room doors and windows and finally the upper walkway, where she saw me slumped and no doubt whey-faced on the concrete. She took the stairs two at a time.

'Sup?' she said when she arrived at my side.

I held up the master key and nodded to the door. 'Blaine,' I said. ''s body.'

Molly looked at the key and then back at me. 'Where did that come from?'

'I found it on the cistern,' I said. My voice was returning. 'She's in the bathroom.'

Molly was rummaging in her jacket pockets. She found a Ziploc bag and carefully unfolded it over the key and keyring. Then she took out a paper bag and said gently, 'Can you slip your shoes off without touching the soles, Lexy?'

At some point she must have called for back-up. Maybe I zoned out. The next thing I knew there were more officers and several technicians on the walkway and Taylor was hoisting me up with his hands under my armpits and leading me away.

'What about your mum?' I said, when I realized he was taking me to the boat.

'She's fine,' he said. 'Maria stepped in. They're the same age and they're bonding over the delicate balancing of Laxido and Imodium when you're on seven kinds of blockers and thinners and the good pain meds for your knees. It'll run for hours.'

'She looked so small, Taylor,' I said. 'She wasn't small in

life. She was magnificent. A mane of hair and legs up to her
eyes, but lying in that bath, all wrapped in plastic, she looked
half the size. Oh God, and those stupid face mask things on
her, like plates on an armadillo. It's so undignified! They'll be
taking photos of her. They'll be sticking photos up on a board
in the precinct. They'll be drinking coffee and eating pastries
and laughing under great big pictures of her tacked to a
whiteboard.'

Taylor said nothing, but just handed me over the gap between
the bank and the steps and helped me up to the porch.

'Her kids!' I said, sinking down on to the swing seat. 'The
rest of their lives they're going to know that a man came and
killed their mum in the same room they were in. But they're
so small they won't remember her. And if it's their dad that did
it! Oh, Taylor. I hate this world sometimes. I hate everything
about it and everyone in it.'

'Not surprised,' Taylor said.

And because he hadn't argued and cajoled, because he hadn't
started listing things I didn't really hate, I added, 'Not you. I
don't hate you. I think I love you.'

'Don't say that,' he told me. 'I'm too old-fashioned to be
OK with you telling me first. So let's chalk that up to shock
and rewind, huh?'

'You're not helping,' I said, because of course I had thought
the better of it as soon as the word left my mouth, but him
having such a great come-back only made me love him more.

I hoped he wasn't flannelling me about his old blind mother
being fine with Maria for company, because he stayed glued to
my side while Molly and another detective put me through the
first lot of questioning. He had offered, and when I opened my
mouth to say no thanks I said yes please and started crying.

'So,' this other detective said. It was ages later, and both of
them looked exhausted. Molly was white everywhere except
pink round her eyes and this new detective – I hadn't caught
her name – had dark purple circles under *her* eyes that were
the opposite of bags. They were indented, making her sallow
cheeks appear puffy. 'You were asked to enter Room 201 via
a note from Mr Muelenbelt?'

'Devin, yes,' I said. 'Wait no. He had left his stuff behind in the room he was moving out of and the note said he'd pick it up later, but Mrs Aaronovitch is blind, you see? And she would need to acquaint herself with her new surroundings. A pile of boxes would stop her doing that. Right, Taylor?'

'So you decided to start to move the boxes yourself? Leaving the old blind lady alone in the room with the rest of the boxes?'

See now, this is why I really don't care for cops. The new one was worse than Molly. She was making trouble over absolutely nothing. By the time we got to the bit that mattered she'd have a lesser mortal scared to speak for fear of what twist she might put on it. 'No,' I said. 'Amaranth went to the loo and while she was in there we decided to make ourselves useful to her and to Devin.'

'Did you tell her? Or was she just supposed to pee, come out and wonder where you had gone, this poor old blind lady.' I usually enjoy sarcasm, but not today. This was tiresome.

'Shit,' I said. 'She didn't go for a pee. She went for a dump. And Taylor here, who knows her bowels well, reckoned we had time.'

'You know your mother's *bowels*?' said the sarky detective.

'They have been my constant companion these twenty years,' Taylor said, making Molly roll her eyes, Sarky-knickers frown, and me feel the first flicker of happiness for five hours. My boyfriend could quote Jane Austen.

'So I carried a box and Taylor carried two,' I said. My boyfriend could quote Jane Austen *and* carry boxes. 'And I tried to open the door with the spare key Noleen had given me, but it wouldn't open. So I wondered if it was already open and it was. So we went in and—'

'Slow down,' said Sarky. 'You found the door to Room 201 unlocked. You opened it and went in. Who was first?'

Taylor and I looked at each other. He shrugged. I tried to remember. 'You, I think,' I said. 'You were still holding your boxes and I put mine down to open up. So surely you went in first while I was picking my box up again?'

'Please don't speculate,' she said.

'OK,' I agreed. 'I can't remember.'

'You can't remember entering a room a few hours ago?' she said.

'Not to your satisfaction,' I said. Molly shifted in her seat, which was probably a warning to me not to get arsey. Or maybe it was a signal to her colleague to be a bit less arsey. 'To the best of my recollection, Mr Aaronovitch entered the room first.'

'And I—' said Taylor.

Sarky held up her hand like she must have done when she used to be on traffic duty. 'We hope to interview you later this evening,' she said. 'For the moment, you are here at our discretion to support Ms Campbell after her unpleasant discovery.' Except the way she said it, the withering tone and the iciness in her expression, it was better suited to someone testifying in an acrimonious divorce hearing. I concluded that it was Molly who'd let me have Taylor here and that Sarky Knickers would have had me in a windowless cell with a light shining in my eyes. I mouthed a thank you in Molly's direction while Sarky was looking at her notebook, but the flat gaze that came back acknowledged nothing.

'And then you entered?' Sarky said, looking up.

'I did.'

'And?' she said, with an enormous show of patience. What was wrong with this woman? First I was going too fast then too slow.

'And what? What did I do next? What were my impressions? What are you asking me?'

'Why did you send Mr Aaronovitch out of the room again while you remained?'

'This is nuts,' I said. 'I didn't send Taylor anywhere. I sniffed and said the air seemed foosty and I was going to open the bathroom window to freshen it up for Devin. And I said we could leave the front window open since the gate was padlocked. And I went to the bathroom.'

'And?'

'And the window is above the bath so I opened the shower curtain to step in and reach the latch and . . .' I snapped my eyes shut and swallowed hard. I could feel my hand growing slick inside Taylor's but he squeezed it anyway. '. . . there she was,' I said, opening my eyes again.

'Did you touch her?'

'No.'

'Are you sure?'

'Yes.'

'You didn't think to check if she was still breathing?'

'No.'

'You didn't think about trying to save her.'

'Fuck you,' said Taylor, swelling my . . . let's call it heart.

'I think what Mr Aaronovitch is trying to say,' I said, squeezing his hand back, 'is I've got steaks in my fridge I could bring back to life easier than Blaine and that was obvious as soon as I looked at her. She was wrapped in plastic, for God's sake. She was dead.'

'And you would swear to that under oath in a court of law?' said Sarky.

'No,' I said. 'I don't have any steaks in my fridge.'

'Do not,' said Sarky, 'get cute with me.'

Taylor stood up. 'And we're done,' he said. 'If you need to speak to Ms Campbell again, let us know what time she and her attorney need to present for interview. Or – and this would be my recommendation – go get that stick out of your ass and come back like a normal person.'

I love America. I'm sure if you spoke to a cop like that in Scotland they'd arrest you for something or other, but the first amendment is the dog's bollocks.

The only trouble was that Sarky Knickers' eyes had filled and her lip was wobbling and, as we watched, a tear splashed on to her notebook. She had no one to squeeze her hand either.

'Aw shit,' Taylor said.

'It's my first day—' she said.

'I'll take it from here,' said Molly, brisk even for her. 'What happened next, Lexy?'

'I turned to leave,' I said, as Sarky blew her nose with a huge comedy honk, 'and I saw the master key sitting on the cistern. Noleen had said it was missing.' Sarky sniffed and it didn't sound like the blowing had done much good. 'Listen,' I said. 'Don't be upset. Your job is so high stress and it must be difficult to do something like this for the first time with someone watching and at such an anxious time all round. Let's just . . . we're all professional women doing our best in the world. So let's just turn the page and start again, eh?'

Sarky glanced at Molly, who shrugged.

'OK,' she said. 'I'm Detective Akhtar and I'm here—'

'No!' said Taylor, Molly and me. 'I meant,' I went on, 'start again in terms of clean slate, no hard feelings. Not start again start again. This is *hard*. So. I picked up the master key, left the room, locked the door and then I was feeling a bit shaky – happens to us all, Detective Akhtar – so I sat down on the walkway and Sergeant Rankinson saw me there and came to see what was up. Right, Molly?'

'Final question,' Molly said to her colleague, ignoring me completely.

'Is there anything else you can think of that you'd like to mention?' Akhtar said. 'No matter how small or even if you think it might not be relevant.'

I opened my mouth to say no, but realized that there *was* something, just out of reach of my mind but still close enough to bother me. I squeezed my eyes shut and groped for it.

'Her silicon face-mask patches,' I said, opening them again. 'Those . . . you know; you saw her.'

'What about them?' Molly said. 'Freaky when you don't know what they are but it sounds like you do.'

'Yeah, Blaine wore them in bed at night,' I said.

'So . . .?' said Akhtar. 'She was killed at night in her jammies. And so she was wearing her night mask. Masks. Plural.'

'Aha!' I said, sitting bolt upright. 'That's it. Masks plural. Forehead, cheeks, under eyes and chin. She had them on wrong. She had three under-eye ones on each cheek and a cheek one on her forehead.'

Molly looked intrigued. 'She might have run out,' she said. 'And had to make do. We'll check the inventory from her room.'

'Hmmm,' I said. I would have to ask Todd but I was already three quarters sure it wasn't just the same stuff in different shapes. That wouldn't have been like the beauty industry at all. Not the foot cream, body lotion, hand cream, neck serum, day cream, night cream, eye cream, sun cream, after-sun cream beauty industry that Todd knew and loved and single-handedly supported.

But at least it had given Molly and Akhtar something to

move on to, which meant they finally let me go, which was lovely for about five minutes until the horror started to press in on me again and I had to go round to the motel to cleave to my friends and have them make me feel better. Even though that meant seeing all the cops and techs up on the walkway outside Room 201, which made me feel much worse.

And my friends couldn't help me anyway. When I found them all outside Reception, Kathi was having a meltdown about the filth of a murder, Todd was having a meltdown about Roger staying in the same house as the prime suspect, Meera and Arif were having meltdowns about escaping dire domestic situations for *this*, Della was having a meltdown because she was in the room next door and the rooms were identical and it could so easily have been her, and Devin was having a meltdown because Della was having one and she was the rock of the family. José and Maria . . . well, they weren't having meltdowns because that wasn't their style but they were looking after Salem and Navy, one on each lap, and the tears were pouring down their faces and plopping on the babies' heads.

'No kye!' Salem said, mopping José's cheeks with a tissue hankie.

'No llores,' said Maria, Spanish immersion surviving even this.

'No yoddet,' said Salem, which only made José cry even more.

Which was when I decided I needed to come down here to the wetlands with Taylor this morning, to look at haar and hazy water, gazing out and trying to see where one ended and the other began. And, because face-to-face therapy had been axed by Beteo County as the crackdown continued to ripple through the state, and the HMOs hadn't quite got their arses in gear to decide which platforms – phone, FaceTime, Skype or some new thing called Zoom – they would cover as legitimate counselling formats, I was free. So Taylor volunteered for an extra shift and we made a run for it before the sun was high enough to turn the marine layer lemon yellow. Only, now we were actually here, he was ruining it by trying to offer unneeded extras, and I was ruining it by biting his head off.

'Sorry,' I said. 'Would I like a what?' He was trying his best and doing a pretty good job, so I could surely thole a neck rub, or even a guided meditation, without being such a ratbag.

'Chocolate Hobnob,' Taylor said. 'I bought them at the ethnic food market and brought them down here in case you ever came. I got PG Tips too.'

'I don't love you,' I said, respecting his desires. 'But I must say, you are a very good boyfriend.'

'I should be,' he said. 'I studied hard.'

I'm not sure he was joking.

Once I had finished with the dunking tutorial and Taylor was getting good enough at it that he didn't need to count and concentrate, I started talking.

'It's got to be her husband, right?' I said. 'The signs, and the care taken not to frighten the babies. And the masklets.' I had learned they were called that from Todd last night, as he confirmed that of course they weren't interchangeable: the under-eye ones reduced puffiness, which would be terrible for cheeks, and the forehead ones had some kind of seaweed extract that the manufacturers pretended was like a natural Botox, which would also be terrible for cheeks in one as young as Blaine. 'Although,' Todd had said, looking at himself in his phone. 'It's coming to all of us.'

'The masklets?' Taylor said, through a mouthful of soggy, impeccably dunked Hobnob.

'She didn't put them on herself,' I said. 'Because they were wrong. So the killer had to be someone who knew she wore them,' I said. 'Who else but her husband?'

'Apart from everyone at the Last Ditch the last two days of her life who saw her in them?' Taylor said.

The hide didn't feel the same after that. All of a sudden, I wanted to go home and check no one had been arrested and hauled off. Or maybe it was just that the peace and quiet (and tea and biscuits) had done their work and I was ready to face the music again.

Of course, if I'd known what was happening in the Capitol, in the corridors of power, I would have stayed at the wetlands all day until it was dark, finished the Hobnobs and taken the slow road home.

'It looks different,' I said, as we came up under the tracks and approached the motel. 'What's changed?'

'Uhhhh, signs are down,' Taylor said. He was right. It still said Last Ditch Motel, because it was neon and would need an electrician to dismantle, but the other signs – 'Clean and Comfortable' and 'Free Continental Breakfast, Fast Wi-Fi, Bug Nets' – were gone. There was a new sign in their place. 'Private Property. No Admittance'.

Taylor beeped and Noleen came out to open up for us. 'Did you hear?' she said. 'Our county's closed. Us, Solano, Napa, Sutter, Yuba . . . it's happening. "Shelter at home" they decided to call it. So Operation Cocker is go.'

'What's Op—?' Taylor started to ask, but Kathi came out of the office wearing a paper jumpsuit with the hood up, surgical gloves and mask, a plastic face shield on top, and a mob cap. She was carrying a disinfectant spray.

'Where have you been?' she said.

'The sanctuary,' I told her. 'You know that.'

'Where else?'

'Nowhere,' Taylor said.

'Where did you eat lunch?'

'In the hide,' I said.

'Sandwiches we made here and cookies I bought three weeks ago,' Taylor said. Three weeks ago? A week into our dating life he had stashed Hobnobs in his bird hide? I'd gone out with men who didn't have my name in their phones after a week and were still answering my calls and texts with a 'Who dis?' Hell, I'd married one.

'OK,' Kathi said. 'I've put a plastic sack on the boat steps. Take your clothes off and put them inside. Tie it shut. Todd is going to launder everything from outside tomorrow. Did you give her the key?' she added, to Noleen.

'I hadn't gotten around to mentioning that,' Noleen said.

'The key to what?' I asked, looking between one and the other.

Noleen handed me a little shiny padlock key. It looked brand new. 'It's not just the virus,' she said. 'It's the murder. It's the murderer getting away across the deck of your boat. If you're not happy you can move in here. Todd said maybe he could give you his spare. Or Kathi might.'

'Or Todd,' Kathi said.

'I'll get back to you,' I told them. I walked round the side of the motel, not looking forward to what I was about to see.

'So there are two more empty rooms, huh?' Taylor said. 'So when you said to Todd that I had to move in with you, you were just being keen?' I was leaning against the wall with my head back, feeling the good hard nibs of the harling digging into my scalp. Taylor came and fitted himself over me, stooping to kiss me quite thoroughly, totally misreading the moment.

'What is it you call this bobbly stuff on walls?' I said. Pub Quiz trivia is a good way to distract him, I had already learned.

'What? Popcorn paint?' he said, lifting his head.

'That's such a great name. I love that. It sounds so much nicer than pebbledash.'

'No way,' Taylor said. 'Pebbledash sounds like a *Paw Patrol* character.'

'It's also what we call sick that's soaked into a carpet. And sorry, but no there aren't free rooms. Todd's got a bolthole for if he finds an insect in his real room, and Kathi's got a room to keep clean while she messes up the room she's living in. Except she's already given that up and moved back into the owner's apartment, which freaks her out a bit because it's too big to clean every day.'

'Is that what's wrong with you?' Taylor said. 'Right now, I mean. As well as everything and finding the body and all that? You're worried that Todd and Kathi might lose it because of the epidemic?'

'Pandemic,' I said. 'No, it's not that. It's the fact that I think Noleen's blocked off the motel with a gate. I mean, she's given me a key, and that's lovely, but it's symbolic, you know? I'm outside the city palisades.'

'Yep, yep, I get that,' said Taylor. 'Well, we could move round to a room – Mom would like it.' Briefly we both considered being that close to Amaranth.

'Let's sleep on it,' Taylor said. 'On the boat.'

I nodded and pushed myself up off the wall, bracing for the sight of a locked gate blocking the way to the riverbank. But there was no such thing. When I saw what there *was*, I stopped moving and felt my eyes fill with tears. Someone – and God knows who, because when I cast my mind over the possibles, none of them was even a remotely plausible – had got some rolls of barbed-wire mesh from somewhere and strung it like Christmas lights all the way from the Last Ditch boundary fence on one side, out to the boat, along the far deck and back to the boundary fence on the other side, gathering my little floating home into the fold with the rest of them and telling murderers, marauders and anyone else who fancied it that there was no welcome here. I heard a sound at my side and turned to see Noleen's, Todd's and Della's heads in a row looking out of Della's high bathroom window.

'OK?' Noleen said.

'What's the key for?' I asked her.

'We couldn't get one roll long enough,' she said. 'We had to join it with a chain halfway along. Then we reckoned that was probably just as well, in case there's a heavy rain and the slough floods. So you can undo the wire if the boat rises and the paint's getting scraped on the barbs. OK?'

'I love you,' I said. If I wasn't allowed to tell Taylor, I needed to let it out somewhere.

'OK, Katy Perry,' Noleen said. 'Don't lose your blob.'

I was so happy I hardly regretted teaching her the phrase at all.

TWELVE

A ll that love and Persian lamb too. Arif had brought a tandoor with him, or had nipped out and bought one before the Gov banged his gavel. Either way, dinner in the forecourt that evening was lamb with olives and peanuts, pomegranate seeds sprinkled on top, and gravy so rich and lustrous it was a heartbreak to choose between mopping it up with torn hunks of charred flatbread – delicious but filling – or spooning it into your face like soup – also delicious and less filling, so you could keep going longer, but you missed the bread.

'So we're in,' Kathi said, when the plates were scraped clean, the kids were playing under the table and Arif had lit a cigarette that smelled so good I'm sure I wasn't the only one tempted to try and bum one. 'We are now sheltering at home. No one out. No one in after Molly gets here with the rest of her stuff. Groceries ordered online and delivered to Noleen, who will triage them. Leave the ambient items for seventy-two hours in the storeroom, scrub and sanitize the packaged goods and things like apples and bananas, store perishables like lettuce in a quarantine refrigerator.' She was sitting at the head of the table and she swept a gaze down one side and up the other like the chairman of the board. 'Do not order anything without telling us. It will be destroyed on arrival. Inform Noleen, me or Todd of what you need and we will take care of it.'

'What if we need something—?' Devin started.

'Condoms included,' said Kathi.

Devin cleared his throat and looked at his feet. Della looked at hers too. She had obviously not yet told him she was pregnant if he was still thinking about condoms. My God, he was going to be mad when he realized he could have been using them all to make water balloons.

'If anyone needs to go out,' Kathi said, 'for emergency doctor appointments or emergency dentist appointments, the deal is you wear a mask and gloves and you hand over outerwear when you come back, shower, and isolate – that's no shared meals, or close proximity for . . . what's the latest?'

'Seven days,' Noleen said. 'But the CDC says masks—'

'Todd,' said Kathi.

'Yeah, see, thing is,' Todd said, 'the CDC's only saying that so people don't panic-buy and make the hospitals run out. When they've gotten the stocks up they'll change their tune. So we might as well get ahead of the curve.'

'But if they're worrying about stocks running out,' said Meera. 'My husband is a first responder and I wouldn't like to think of him not having what he needs.'

'Your husband should pray he only gets the 'rona,' said Della. 'Dying on a ventilator is too good for him.'

It seemed a little extreme but when Meera didn't argue I concluded that they'd kept on with their heart-to-hearts and Della now knew even more about the thin blue line of abuse that ran through Meera's home.

'So we're going to have ourselves a good old-fashioned sewing bee,' said Noleen. 'Starting tomorrow, in the Skweek, anyone who can thread a machine or do a backstitch by hand. Nine a.m. until the elastic runs out. We have a shit ton of cotton and wadding but Jo-Ann's was rationing elastic already this afternoon and they weren't open to bribes.'

'I can teach you how to put sliding hitches in tape,' Taylor said. 'Shoelaces or what have you.'

'That's my boy,' said Amaranth.

'And *my* boy will take care of adding sequins,' said Barb. 'Right, honey?'

'No sequins,' Kathi said. 'These masks need to be washable at sixty.'

'No sequins?' said Todd, putting the back of his hand against his forehead. 'Oh well, we'll just have to make do with boas.'

'Next,' said Kathi, 'mail. If you look at the front gate you'll see a mailbox there. We attached it earlier today and we'll tell our carrier that it's now the only place where mail is to be left. No more coming in for a coffee and a pastry while he hands over the fliers and other junk. Those days are done. If anyone sees him with a package, come get Noleen, Todd or me. We will not be going to the post office to stand in line and pick them up. OK?'

'I won't be getting mail,' Arif said. 'No one knows I'm here.'

'Uhhh,' said Todd, 'I might have this and that coming.'

'Yes,' said Kathi. 'Your toiletries alone are enough to expose whoever picked them up to dangerous levels of viral load.'

'It was the worst day of my life when he moved out and took it all with him,' Barb said. 'I aged a year in a month.'

'You used my skincare regimen elements?' said Todd. 'When I lived at home? When you still smoked and drank whisky? Oh Mom. That's like . . . making hash with filet mignon.'

'So,' said Kathi sternly, 'we need to be sure that someone meets Dan the mailman and catches the parcels when he . . . Lexy?'

'Hoys them over the dyke,' I said. Kathi had laughed so hard the first time she'd heard that particular bit of linguistic colour that I'd had to thump her on the back, and since then she had it on hard rotation, but only if I said it to get the authentic sound. It was amazing how often she could bring a conversation round to something getting lobbed over the top of something else.

'Once mail is delivered,' Kathi said, 'postmarks will be checked by Noleen, Todd or me.' She kept saying that. I caught Della's eye to find out if she was beginning to feel like chopped liver, same as I was. 'Local mail postmarked a day previous will be left for twenty-four hours. Mail two days in transit will be opened by a gloved and masked operative and the contents emptied out on to a clean surface in the open air. It can then be dealt with in the normal way. Envelopes, packaging and junk mail will be discarded in the recycling dumpster, which is not to be opened except by—'

'You, Noleen or Todd?' I said. 'Just taking a wild guess, you know. What did Della, Devin, and me do to get side-lined?'

Kathi stared at me. 'Side-lined?' she said. 'Are you kidding me? We're protecting you. Della and Devin need to be healthy to look after Diego and share in the care of Salem and Navy. And you need to be healthy because – call me crazy, but I think therapists are going to be seeing a lot of action for a while. So I'm designating you an essential worker, Lexy. You'd be missed if you went down.'

'Ha!' said Barb. 'Missed! That's right, Lexy – you'd be *Scotch mis*—'

'Don't! Finish that sentence, Barb,' I said. 'I am not a fictitious drink or an irrelevant egg. Or a chili in a hat, or anything else.'

'You know,' said Noleen, 'you wouldn't have to deal with being an egg or a drink or a chili if you'd just admit you're basically English.'

'And finally,' Kathi said, 'enforcement.'

Noleen stood and stretched. 'Kathi had me draw up agreements to abide by the letter, spirit and intent of Operation Cocker. I'll get them and you can all sign them now. They're not legally enforceable but they'll help us if anyone goes to the press after we kick their ungrateful asses out for putting the rest of us in harm's way.'

'It's getting quite Gilead-y quite quickly,' I said, as Noleen walked away.

'No!' Maria had been quiet over dinner. I reckoned it was tiredness, because she was not young and she had suddenly been catapulted into a new living arrangement and a job as a Spanish immersion nursery teacher slash professional grandma. But however draining her new role and all the upheaval had left her, she was fired up now. '*Handmaid's Tale*?' she said. 'That was for bad. This is for good. There is the difference.'

It was hard to dispute, if a little Dr Seuss-y, and I dipped my head in apology.

'Mi petarda,' said José, leaning over Navy's sleeping body to chuck Maria's cheek.

'What does that mean?' I said.

'Firecracker,' said Bob, from under the table.

'Correct,' said Diego. 'Firework.'

'Petarda,' said Joan. 'Firework.'

We all waited but Salem said nothing. Then Noleen was back with a sheaf of printed, stapled documents and enough pens for everyone. I bent my head and started reading. The agreement was big on 'loyalty to OC' and came down hard on 'covering up others' flaunting of the rules'.

'Flouting,' I said. 'Page two, second item, third sentence. You mean "flouting" not "flaunting".'

'Show-off,' said Todd. 'Persnickety Brit.'

I didn't tell him he meant pernickety, which was *huge* of me. 'If we're signing this,' I said instead, 'such things matter. If I vow not to hide someone flaunting, then I hide someone flouting, I can't be thrown in the piranha tank. You can't be the Stasi and a bunch of laidback hippies at the same time.'

'The Stasi?' said Amaranth. 'You think these kind people converting their business into a sanctuary for us deserve to be called the Stasi?'

'Oh for f—' I began before I remembered that this was my boyfriend's mother and made do with rolling my eyes.

'Look,' Arif said, 'we're all tense, for various reasons. And Lexy is probably still in a state of shock after finding Blaine's body. We should take a beat, take a breath, go round the table and each say something kind. Name something you're grateful for right now.'

Uh-oh. He'd hidden it well up till now, but if that was Arif's jam then being banged up with him until Big Gav had built a new hospital might not be the piece of cake his lamb stew had made it seem.

'Esta bebé,' said José, holding up Navy to show us how cute she was fast asleep.

'Mi esposo,' said Maria. I managed not to make puke noises.

'I'm grateful for bleach,' Kathi said, like she always did.

'I'm grateful for Raid,' said Todd, like *he* always did. Between the two of them they could really put a crimp on a Thanksgiving round-up. This was no different.

'Working from home,' Della said.

'Hulu,' said Devin.

'Hulu?' said Barb. 'Oh, I was a ninja with them when I was a girl. If I can't get to the gym I should take it up again. Can I borrow yours?'

'Sure,' Devin said, mystified.

'The pandemic,' said Meera. Then added, 'Don't look at me like that. I am grateful for the pandemic because it got me out of that house. A revolution or alien invasion would have been cool too. Any kind of nudge.'

'I get that,' said Arif. 'Yeah, me too.'

'Federal funding for wildlife protection,' said Taylor. I reckoned it was his bleach/Raid equivalent. If we were still together in November I would see.

That left me. I ran over the options – being seven thousand miles from my mother, stretch denim, Mandy Patinkin – but I could feel it coming, unstoppable as a burp. 'You,' I said. 'All of you. This. I don't even know myself any more but that's the truth.'

'Will we do the kids?' said Devin. 'Hey, dudelet!' He bent and looked under the table. 'What are you grateful for?'

'Huh?' said Diego. 'Leave me alone, I'm busy. And I *am* careful. Get a grip.'

'Well OK then,' Devin said, straightening up again.

'So,' said Kathi, 'now that the ground rules have been agreed, we can move on to urgent business.' She drew a big breath. 'Phil Temple, we now think, came here in the night, broke into a room, killed Blaine, got into another room with a stolen master key, I now hear,' Noleen dipped her head but said nothing, 'dumped a body and ran away. Which gives us a huge problem.'

'Uhhhh, is it OK for the kids to be in on this?' I said.

'Bueno,' said José, standing up and cuddling Navy in tight to his chest. 'Hora de acostarse, niños!'

From the chorus of groans under the table it sounded like, somehow, Bob, Joan and Salem had already learned that meant bedtime, or maybe Diego started the chorus and they were so clued in to him being the ringleader that they took it up without delay. I kind of hoped it was that; I wanted to see Diego cool and obnoxious. It would be cute. And watching Della crush it back out of him would be a lot of fun too.

'What problem?' said Arif, when they were gone. 'Security? We've upped it. And there's a cop living here. And . . . I don't want to be mean but it was personal. So it's over. The only urgent business now is healing.'

Oh God. Gratitude *and* healing? I caught Todd's eye and we shared a long conversation of tooth-sucking and hmph-hmphing, like two old ladies on a bus bench. All without saying a word.

'*This* problem,' Kathi said, but before she could go any further a car drew up outside the padlocked gate, shining its headlamps straight at us through the chain-link. The horn bibbed, as if we couldn't all see already that someone wanted in, as if we weren't all shading our eyes from the dazzle of the headlamp beam. 'Two problems actually,' Kathi said hurriedly, as Noleen was getting to her feet and picking over her bunch of gaoler's keys. 'And one of them is that Molly doesn't believe Phil did it.'

'How do you know?' I said.

'Wait and see,' said Kathi.

I had never seen Molly driving anything but a police car, either an actual cruiser or an unmarked sedan bristling with extra antenna and looking hardly less conspicuous, but this was evidently her own personal choice of motorized conveyance. I only wished I knew more about cars and/or Americans so I could parse it like Todd and the rest of them were.

'No way,' was what Todd said, to go along with Devin's snort, Della's chuckle, Noleen's whistle and Kathi's 'Wow' as a vintage red Chrysler pick-up with wooden sides pulled into the check-in bay and Molly stepped down.

'Happy Holidays!' Todd called over to her, making her scowl. I knew he was needling her but had no idea how.

'I'm off the clock,' she said. 'And ready to turn in. I'll text you all slots for interview tomorrow. We'll have Detective Akhtar on video-link.'

'What?' I said. 'Why do you need us again?'

Molly regarded me steadily for a while before she answered. 'Right,' she said. 'Sure. Wall-to-wall innocence. OK.' Then she left us, climbing the stairs to her room, then closing and locking the door and drawing the curtains, shutting herself in and the rest of us out like she really meant it.

'See what I mean?' said Kathi. 'That's how she was on the phone too. She suspects one of us of something.'

'What a pooper,' Barb said. And she was right; the party was stone dead.

Taylor led Amaranth off. Barb followed, muttering about beauty sleep and Netflix. Then it was just us again. Plus Arif and Meera, who didn't look like they were going anywhere and might be helpful with the inside track on domestic strife.

It was still a lovely night – Molly couldn't stop that – warmish and purple-skied, the stars a bit smudged and yellow so it felt

as if we were in a Van Gogh painting, even if it was only dust
from them starting to till the fields. Noleen had strung lights
from old basketball hoops and they were reflected in the dappled
surface of the swimming pool. And there's something about a
messy table with crumpled napkins and finished drinks that
always makes me feel happy. I'd rather it was a white tablecloth
with linen napkins to match and that the empty glasses had
stems and people were sipping espresso and cracking walnuts.
But even this – plastic cloth, beer bottles and Todd sucking a
Red Vine (still coasting on Roger's absence, although the crash
was surely coming) – this would do. I almost didn't want to
spoil it with talk of murder. But Kathi was fit to pop.

'So what makes you so sure Phil did it?' I said.

'It's not me that's sure,' said Kathi. 'It's Roger. Tell 'em,
Todd.'

'He doesn't see him at work,' Todd said, 'but they're
commuting together and living together and Roger says there's
definitely something going on with the guy.'

'Of course there's something going on!' I said. 'He's a doctor
in the middle of a healthcare emergency and his wife moved
out and took the kids with her and what was that other thing?
Oh yeah: she got murdered. If he was the same as ever, that
would be weird.'

'As I was trying to say,' said Todd, 'there's something going
on with the guy because he's not in shock, not weeping, not
grieving, sleeping like a baby – snoring for hours – and pretty
much absolutely fine.'

'Yeah but . . .' I said, planning to point out that grief takes
everyone differently until I realized I'd be completely contra-
dicting myself.

'And not wanting his kids back is so weird it's creepy,' Todd
said. 'Plus choosing to keep working. He should be on condol-
ence leave at least until after her funeral. Why doesn't he want
to be with his kids?'

'Saviour complex,' I said. 'You know doctors.'

Todd scowled. 'And,' he said, 'the most damning thing of
all: motive.' He paused to see if we would bite. 'Philip Temple
has one,' he went on, when no one did. 'The usual one too,
when a husband offs his wife.'

'He has wife number two lined up?' Noleen said. 'Rat bastard.'

'How does Roger know that?' Meera said. 'If Phil's sneaking out to see her or sneaking her into the house, Roger shouldn't be there. It's not safe.'

'No, no, they're not meeting,' said Todd. 'No doubt they'll have to be careful not to see each other for a while until the case is cold. But remember how fine he was about handing over his phone to the cops?' He paused again, waiting for someone to nod. Arif obliged. 'That's because he has two.'

'Eugh,' said Noleen. 'Two phones. Seals the deal for me.'

'But hang on,' I said. 'Of course, he's got another phone *now*. He probably ordered one as soon as he realized he was going to have to give his old one to the cops. Why does Roger think he had two at the same time?'

'Because the cops took his phone away when they hauled him in for questioning and when they brought him back four hours later another phone rang. He answered this phone and had a long conversation with whoever was on the line. And he hadn't been to the phone store and nothing had been delivered.'

'Maybe . . .' I said, 'they kept a burner in the house in case of a lost phone and he'd emailed his contacts to tell them his new number.'

'Do people do that?' said Noleen.

'Some people keep new toothbrushes in case of unexpected guests,' I said. 'And some people without pets keep dog, cat, hamster and fish food in the house, in case they suddenly need them.'

'Who does that?' said Kathi. 'Why would you set yourself up to babysit vermin?'

'Seriously,' I said. 'Epi-pens, kitten milk, champagne in the fridge door, sympathy cards . . .'

'Are you talking about a client?' said Noleen. 'Can I remind you that your clients are all nutjobs?'

'I keep Naloxone *and* Epi-pens,' said Arif. 'And formula and diapers. And booze, even though I don't drink. And coffee-creamer though I take it black.'

'Do you keep a burner phone and an emailable list of contacts to tell your new number to?' said Todd.

'Well, no,' said Arif. 'Because that's just weird. If you lose your phone you need to grieve, shop, curse the app store and cull your contacts. How would any of us ever get rid of people we hate unless we shed them when we change phones?'

'Exactly,' said Todd. 'I believe Roger. Phil Temple had two phones.'

'Philly Two Phones,' Noleen said. 'Sounds like a bad dude, you ask me.'

'OK,' I said. 'I'm not the guy's sister. I'm not trying to get him into heaven. I give in.' I thought it over. 'And that's good, isn't it? Blaine's husband killed her; nothing to do with us here, no need for us to worry.'

'Yeah there is!' said Todd, just as Kathi said, '*Huge* reason to worry!' Then they stared at each other. 'You go first,' Kathi said.

'No reason to worry,' said Todd, 'except he's living with my husband and he's a murderer. Apart from that tiny detail, sure. Plus the fact that Molly has someone here in her sights again for some reason. Or else why would she reinterview everyone? So we need to knock *that* on the head. And my vote is to do it with some old-school detective work.'

Meera and Arif, as well they might, looked a bit perturbed by this declaration.

'We should explain, maybe,' I said. 'You know I'm a therapist, right? But did you know that Todd is a make-over qu— specialist? And Kathi's a de-cluttering consultant?'

Meera and Arif shook their heads and glanced at one another.

'That doesn't actually explain anything,' Della said, obviously deciding that the newbies were too polite to point it out.

'Right,' I said. 'No, you're right.'

Taylor had finished settling his mum for the night and was coming back across the forecourt. He had added a sleeveless puffy jacket and a bobble-hat to his pocket pants, against the chill of advancing evening.

'So what are we talking about?' he said, as he sat down beside me and put an arm across the back of my chair.

'The evolution of Trinity,' I said. 'From counselling, to personal attention, to household management and then to investigations.'

'Investigations of what?' said Arif.

'Don't you ever read the *Cuento Voyager*?' Todd said. 'Crime. Investigations of crime.'

'I'm the investigator,' Kathi said. 'I'm working towards my PI licence.'

'But,' Meera said, 'that's like lost dogs and insurance fraud and divorce work, isn't it?'

'You would think,' Todd said. 'And mostly yes, but when someone takes *another* way out of marriage . . .'

'But who's your client?' said Taylor. 'An investigation agency doesn't just . . . Or how do you make your money?'

'That's what I've been trying to tell you,' Kathi said. 'Remember? *Two* huge problems, I said. One being that Molly suspects us. The other being the fact that . . . our client is Dr Philip Temple.'

'The killer,' Noleen added, in case anyone had forgotten.

'He asked Roger to ask us if we'd take the job,' said Todd, 'and, since we need to get Molly off our backs anyway, two thirds of Trinity, including the actual detective, made an executive decision when the other third was off feeding ducks.'

'So . . .' Devin said, 'you're going to fake-search for a fictitious killer because the real killer is paying you to?'

'No,' said Kathi. 'We're going to clear ourselves of suspicion by finding evidence that will put Philly Two Phones away.'

'Then bill him for it,' said Todd. 'Bleed him see-through. And it couldn't happen to a nicer guy.'

THIRTEEN

Thursday 19 March

My bed is small. My boat is small, which means the rooms in it are small, which means the things in the rooms are small, and my bed is a thing in a room in my boat. It had never bothered me before when Taylor stayed over, but I woke up on Thursday morning trapped on the inside with my knees hard up against the panelling and Taylor's hot breath making my hair stick to my neck, and I felt the sudden urge to move into an industrial loft.

I inched my legs straight and shuffled on to my back, then began to ease my way up to sitting, hoping I could step over him without waking him up.

His eyes snapped open.

'Hi,' he said. 'Would you be offended if I took the spare room across the passageway for actually sleeping. Not to avoid you. Just to get a night's sleep? I'll stay here until you drop off. Until you're feeling better about . . . you know . . . finding Blaine.'

He really was shaping up to be well-nigh perfect, I was thinking, when his phone rang and he answered it and it was his mother asking him to come and remind her how the shower worked.

'Ten minutes, Mom,' he said, and dropped his phone on the floor.

I felt the slight shift in the boat as someone came on deck. It was about the right time for Todd to bring my coffee but he wouldn't be doing that any more, now that Taylor was here. Surely.

Todd strolled in. 'Oh great. You're awake. I wasn't sure whether this would change things. Your coffee, Lexy. Taylor, I got you a black Americano but you can have my latte if you'd rather. Tell me what you want tomorrow and going forward.'

'Tell you,' said Taylor, 'what kind of coffee I want you to

be holding when you burst into my bedroom unannounced at the crack of dawn?'

'Yu-huh,' said Todd, whose mind was already on other things. He sat down on my little chair and took the lid off his cup.

'Todd,' I said, 'how did you get Cocker-compliant coffee?'

'Double-gloved barista dropped it off in exchange for free laundry. So obviously,' he went on without breathing, 'there are a lot of complications with our new assignment. Lexy needs to work, I'm in the Skweek and Kathi is dealing with a significant uptick in anxiety, although the shelter-in-place order is helping with that.'

'How is the order helping Kathi?' said Taylor, sitting up and taking a sip. He had decided to go with it, the whole Todd in his bedroom thing.

'*So* many ways,' Todd said. 'Kathi would have chosen a set of people, locked them in and told the rest of the world to beat it years ago if she could.' He was eyeing Taylor's unkempt chest hair with an avid enough expression on his face to make Taylor pull the covers up and clamp them under his armpits. Of course, that untucked them at the bottom and made Todd shift his attention to Taylor's superlatively unlovely bare feet. 'But anyway,' he said, with a sort of a shake that was not quite a shudder, 'there are still things we can do. First – well, after dark – a re-enactment. We find out how tall Phil is exactly, find someone about the same size, if we can, and have them run through the bushes with you watching, Lexy. Find out what he weighs and get someone the same weight to run across the boat. See what you think.'

'How's Roger going to find out how much his room-mate weighs?' I said.

'Oh he couldn't. He'd blow it,' said Todd. 'I've put you down for that. You can either bring the conversation round to it while you're showing him live footage of his kids, or you could maybe pretend you're puzzled by BMI guidelines.'

'Right,' I said. That was just Todd's way of killing two birds with one jab. He thought I was obese because my thighs met when I stood with my feet together. (He couldn't stand with his feet together, because of his calf muscles.)

'What Roger *can* do and has just about agreed to do,' Todd

said, 'is pretend that he's happy to be away from me. Can you imagine? Talk up marriage problems, see if he can get Roger to share his own.'

'Which he surely won't if he's just killed his wife,' said Taylor. 'He'd be a fool.'

'Au contraire, mon frère,' said Todd. 'He'd be a fool to pretend to be happy if there's any evidence to the contrary. Which there must be. So I'm going to pull on every string I can find the end of – all my Sacramento contacts – to find who's ever been in the same bar, restaurant, benefit dinner, spin class, theatre, coffee shop or nail salon as either one of them – ideally both – and seen or heard anything. No marriage dies privately. My mom taught me that.'

'I'm going to get you on the couch one day if it kills me,' I said.

'Meanwhile Kathi's on a deep dive into techniques to interview toddlers,' Todd said. 'It's maddening.'

'What's "maddening"?' Taylor said. I could hear the quote marks. So could Todd and he scowled.

'We settled on that word between the three of us,' I said, 'because Kathi can't pronounce "exasperating" any way that doesn't drive me nuts, and me saying "off-pissing" annoys Todd because it reminds him of how I corrected his pronunciation of "off-piste" one time and he called me a pedant and I corrected his pronunciation of that too. Then Todd took up "irksome" just to aggravate both of us. So we agreed on "maddening" and I'm trying really hard to pretend he doesn't say it like he's in Tennessee Williams, because it'll all start again.'

Taylor said nothing with his mouth. His eyes asked me if this was really where we were at the *start* of sheltering in place together for God knows how long, and there was a follow-up question with his brows about whether he'd made the right choice in becoming a part of it.

'What's "maddening",' said Todd, in a voice that would let him walk on in an underskirt, opposite Paul Newman, and have no one miss Liz Taylor, 'is that there are two witnesses to what happened in Blaine's room that night and it's going to be no stroll in the park to shake it out of them.'

'Navy is a tiny little baby,' I said.

'OK, one witness,' said Todd. 'But still. So Kathi's on that and we'll see if we can get anything useful out of Salem without, you know . . .'

'Putting him through any further distress by reminding him of a recent trauma?' I said.

'Still talking about Salem?' said Todd, with his head on one side. It was a fair question and very irritating. I got up and went for a pee without answering.

I was in the shower when Taylor sidled in.

'Quick!' I said. 'Close the door!' My shower room is too small to have the door ajar when the water's running without it leaking out and wrecking the varnish on the passageway floorboards.

'Do you mind if I pee?' Taylor said.

'In the loo? No,' I told him. 'Did Todd leave and let you get up and put those shorts on or did you have to flash him to get rid of him?'

'I know he's your friend,' Taylor said, peeing pure coffee and making me regret the permission, 'but he's pretty predatory, isn't he?'

'What the hell did he do?' I said, peeking round the curtain. Taylor had peeled his shorts right off, obviously planning to join me. I wasn't going to say no. I'd be a good sport and let him discover for himself that my shower is too small for shenanigans.

'You didn't notice? I would call it undressing me with his eyes except I was naked, so it was more like exfoliating me with his eyes. Coffee or no coffee, I don't think I can be cool with that.'

'For God's sake,' I said, handing him the soap and then twisting myself round to rinse my hair, banging my elbow off the flyscreen in the open window. If that had loosened the net and I got mozzies, I was sending Taylor to Deuce Hardware to get a replacement. Mosquitoes hated him, something to do with his natural oils or lack of natural oils, and they loved me with my thin northern skin and my rubbish mosquito-slapping game that I'd only been at for a year. 'He wasn't exfoliating you with his eyes. He was waxing you and trimming your cuticles. It was make-over ogling, Taylor, not recruitment.'

'I don't think so,' Taylor said. He had soaped the top half of his body, working up a lather that was now flying off in ropes and landing on my cistern, my washbasin, my floor and my walls. I was going to have rinse the whole place with the hose attachment of the shower head and then use a squeegee on it. I hate the noise those things make. 'At least he never said anything about making me over.'

'Huh,' I said. That was weird, actually. He had piled right in on Arif. 'Thanks for not freaking out when he burst into our bedroom, why ever it was he did it.'

'*Your* bedroom,' said Taylor. 'Remember? I'm going across the passageway to stretch out.'

'Oh yeah,' I said, and I must not have hidden my ambivalence because he followed up with:

'With lots of visits though. And now, are you done? This shower is too small for two so, after today and unless you need me close, bathroom rota?' He rinsed his face and flicked his wet hair back. It sprayed the window. 'And I need to get all this soap off of everywhere. Say, do you have one of those things they use to clean your windshield at the intersections?'

'Under the sink,' I said. And that was all I said. Which was a bloody miracle, because I really and truly more every day *loved* this guy. And I wouldn't start loving him any less if Todd tamed his chest hair and took a chainsaw to his toenails.

I went to look in on the crèche once I was dressed. Three reasons. First, gazing at the babies was the best way to keep the vision of Blaine in the bath out of my head. It was still there whenever I didn't strain to resist it.

Also I wanted to see what Meera and Maria had pulled together by way of lessons for Bob, Joan and Diego, because I was going to have to switch to online with my clients when the insurance paperwork came through and I needed to shame myself out of deciding it was too hard and shutting up shop until they could come to my boat again.

It worked. Meera, looking like a porn-star playing a school-teacher in a micro-mini-kilt and a blouse that somehow managed to be low cut and have a peter pan collar at the same time, had scared up a whiteboard from somewhere and was teaching the three of them to spell each other's names. They were having more fun learning to write than I ever had.

The third reason to lurk in the crèche was to get a bit of news to give to Phil, so I had an excuse to phone him. When Salem asked for story-time and picked his baby sister up off her playmat to cradle her in his crossed legs, I reckoned that was the photo-opportunity of the day, clicked it, and went out on to the balcony.

Noleen and Kathi had been busy: there was a gazebo set up in the far corner of the forecourt, currently with the side flaps rolled down and evidently with a lot of electrical equipment inside, judging by the thick rope of cables that snaked out of the office window and was taped across the tarmac until it disappeared under one of the tent's sturdy white sides. Maybe it was a screening room. Or maybe Della and Meera had set up a mini-spa in there. But was there enough business among the dozen of us to make that worthwhile? Even if one of us was Todd?

I shifted my attention back to my phone. 'The scene right now,' I typed. 'Story-time in the motel kindergarten. He's a good big brother. Call me when you get a minute. Lexy (Part of Trinity. Counsellor. It was me that sent the film the other day.)' Then I realized that Phil had surrendered his phone and I had no way to get this bait photo to him anyway. But someone must have his new number. His kids were here, weird as that was, and we surely had a way of getting in touch with Daddy.

I set off to the office to ask Noleen, but didn't get very far. Molly opened the door of Room 203 as I was passing and said: 'Might as well start with you. Are you free right now, for an interview?'

'That would be fine,' I said. 'Actually, you could help me out. Have you got Phil Temple's phone number?'

'We have his whole phone,' Molly said. 'Why?'

I followed her into the room, feeling the slight vertigo I always felt whenever I saw an identical layout to Todd and Roger's, Devin and Della's, and saw the wrong knick-knacks and different detritus lying around. I had half-expected lots of monitors and an outsize corkboard covered in distressing photographs here, but Room 203 was as neat as an army barracks,

with both queen beds made and every piece of china and glass-
ware drying upside down on spread sheets of kitchen roll beside
the sink.

'Huh,' I said. 'So this isn't the incident room then?'

Molly gave me a look of pity and puzzlement. I used to get
that look every day, whenever I asked what a Cinnabon was,
or a groupon or an easement (which is not as creepy as it
sounds, by the way).

'You . . . didn't spot the incident room?' she said. 'With your
eagle eye, part therapist part detective?'

'Ah,' I said. 'The white tent? Right. Of course. I thought that
was ours.'

'You thought the tent we put up yesterday was what now?'

'Really?' I said. 'That was there last night?' I willed myself
not to blush and, Molly having all her windows thrown wide
open in this north-facing room on this chilly March morning,
meant I was cold enough to stop the colour climbing my neck
and warming my face from the inside. 'And what's the other
one? In the row of parked cars?'

'The other white tent in the row of parked cars?' Molly said.
'You mean the tent we put over Blaine's minivan until it's
processed?'

'Of course,' I said. 'Silly me.'

She stared at me. 'You waiting for me to disagree?'

I smiled. 'So,' I said. 'Interview?'

Molly nodded, just once, more like a heel click with her head
than a gesture of concurrence, and I wondered if it was bothering her to be conducting interviews in her bedroom. I'd lived
in and then behind the motel for long enough, close friends
with its permanent residents, that it had come to seem normal
to me. It couldn't yet feel normal to Molly.

And, when she had finally got her video-link software set up
– Zoom was a misnomer, the way Molly did it – her colleague
didn't help. 'Yo, Mike! Where's your stuffie?' The voice came
out of the laptop monitor loud enough to make the speaker
crackle. 'Mike' was a precinct nickname based on Molly's
sexuality, which struck me as harassment it must be possible
to have addressed by HR. Or maybe I didn't know cops. For
whatever reason, she put up with it instead of dealing with it

the way she dealt with anything *I* ever did that displeased her. It was just one of the mysteries of Molly Rankinson.

'Interview of Ms Lexy – L-E-A-G-S-A-I-D-H – Campbell – C-A-M-P-B-E-L-L – Thursday March 19, 2020, at 09.13 a.m. Present are Sergeant M.R. Rankinson and Officer D.E. Huang. Talk me through your dealings with Blaine Temple.'

There was no kind of pause or segue at all and so it took me a minute to realize the interview had started.

'Officer Huang?' I said. 'Before we settle in, I need to make something clear between you and me. I won't stand by and witness homophobic bullying. If it happens again, I'll be leaving the interview and lodging a complaint.'

Molly scowled. We'd had beef on sight, she and I, and nothing about Todd, Kathi and me sticking our nebs into police business on three occasions since had de-beefed matters any. Me suddenly weighing in on an outrage she had decided to swallow, for her own reasons, took that beef and flash-froze it like a liquid-hydrogen-flavoured ice-pop. She wasn't pleased.

Officer Huang was none too chuffed either. His face on the grainy Zoom grew puckered and off-set as he ground his teeth and frowned at the same time.

'Glad we got that straight,' I said. 'Now then, what specifically is it you'd like me to tell you?'

Molly tried to psych me out, by looking over her notes in silence. But it's only at work that I let silences stretch without filling them.

'Okay,' I said. 'While you're gathering your thoughts, can I ask something?'

'No.'

'Did she suffer?'

Molly had her lip ready-curled, all set to blow off whatever my question turned out to be, but she's a human being underneath . . . a lot of other stuff. 'The autopsy hasn't been scheduled yet,' she said. 'Budgets. But from first look at her neck, it was a clean cu—'

I must have whimpered.

'—it looked instantaneous.'

'And, as I said, I want you to describe the conversations you had with Blaine Temple while she was here at the motel,' said Molly. 'In your own words.'

'OK,' I said. 'I suggested she move to a ground-floor room. We chatted about eating habits. I talked to her about family-style dinners out front and what she would cook when it was her turn. Hey, are you in for the dinners, Molly? What's your speciality?'

'Anything else?'

'Umm, we had a short conversation about me filming her kids to send the footage to their dad. Oh, by the way, don't let me go without you telling me Phil's new number. I've got a pic of the kids from just now to send to him.'

'This is not a two-way street, Lexy,' Molly said, 'This is an official police interview. So keep talking.'

'I think that's it,' I said. 'Met when she was moving in, introduced ourselves. We talked about snooty doctors' wives giving her a hard time . . . Wait, that's weird. Yeah, we talked about the über-mommies giving her a hard time about junk food and then, when we were talking about family dinners, she was all about . . . oh, you know, kale and clean chicken and stuff. Then I caught her eating a bar of chocolate when she was supposed to be practising. None of that adds up.'

'Adds up to dancer, ya ask me,' said Officer Huang from the laptop.

'And what else?' said Molly.

'Nothing. She said she was hacked off with having to FaceTime Phil, which was why she was happy for me to film the kids and send it instead.'

'Let's dig down into that a little deeper,' Molly said, in a light and breezy voice which could not have sounded more ominous if there was background shark music.

'This *is* to do with the murder investigation, isn't it?' I said.

'Duh,' said Molly, despite having just reminded me quite prissily that it was an official police interview.

'So . . . it's not Meera complaining that I filmed her kids then?' I said.

'"She was "hacked off" with having to FaceTime Phil, so she was happy for me to film the kids and send it instead",' Molly said, reading off her notebook.

'Close enough,' I said. 'But what are you getting at?'

'Wouldn't it be more accurate to say that you told her she had to FaceTime her husband and when she understandably told you to butt out, you made the pretty passive-aggressive move of filming her kids and sending the film to their dad to make her look bad?'

'No,' I said. Then I upped it a bit. 'No! That wasn't what happened at all. Where is *this* coming from?'

'You thought it was A-OK that she didn't want to let the children speak to their father when she suddenly moved them out of their home?'

'No,' I said, 'I thought it was mean and weird.'

'Mean to her husband?'

'And her kids,' I said. 'But she was pretty off-hand with her kids most of the time, I think.'

'And you told her that,' said Molly. It wasn't a question. 'Speaking professionally, although she wasn't a client and hadn't asked for your advice.'

'No!' I said again. 'What *is* this?'

'So you never – at any point in the time Mrs Temple was here with her children – offered any advice about her parenting or her marriage.'

'No,' I said. 'Well, I pointed out that having them in an upstairs room wasn't great and I might have looked at her funny when she put them on the bed to bounce. But that was about the springs, not the kids.'

'And nothing about her marriage at all?'

'Not a— Oh! Well, she was complaining about Phil expecting her to hang out with other doctors' wives, and I agreed that it was out of order.'

'She said she was unhappy with her marriage and you confirmed that she had cause to be?' Molly said.

It was true and it was harmless-sounding: the sort of thing I might have said to a woman on the bus, or a check-out girl. But Blaine was dead and everyone knew her husband had killed her and so whatever Molly was building here, I didn't want one of the bricks to be me discussing Blaine's marriage.

'I wouldn't put it like that,' I said.

'Neither would I,' Molly said. 'Neither did Blaine.'

'What do you mean?' I said.

Molly smiled very sweetly. 'Interview terminated at 09.23 a.m.' She clicked a switch on her laptop. 'Free to go, Lexy,' she said. 'Thank you.'

'Thank you for what?' I said. 'What just happened?'

'You seem anxious,' said Officer Huang. 'Mi-olly, I gotta admit I thought you were blowing smoke but this is a lotta nerves for someone with nothing to hide.'

'What do you mean "neither did Blaine"?' I said again.

Molly got up and held the door open for me. 'If you see anyone else, send 'em in,' she said. 'I need to speak to everyone in light of what we've learned.'

'Would you like a white cat?' I said. 'Or some organ music?'

Molly just smiled.

'Anyone else like who?' I said. 'Who else do you want to talk to?'

'Not the Bernals,' Molly said.

'The what?'

'José and Maria Bernal. Not Mrs Truman. And not Mr and Mrs Aaronovitch.'

'So you want to speak to Todd, Kathi, Noleen, Della, Devin, Arif and Meera?' I said.

'Not the Muelenbelts, actually,' she said. She seemed pretty sure that Della had given up 'Salinas'. 'They slipped my mind.'

'I bet,' I said. 'Della's not nearly as prominent in the minds of law enforcement these days, she tells me.'

At last, I'd got to her. Her brows lowered. 'I didn't deserve that,' she said. 'What did I ever do?'

The true answer was 'plenty' but all of it so subtle that I'd sound daft if I started to list things. 'I'll let the rest of them know you're waiting,' I said, hoping someone would have more of a clue than me what she was up to.

FOURTEEN

Outside, the Last Ditch had taken a step towards the bizarre: Arif's creepy stalker wife was here. (Damn the *Cuento Voyager*! Wasn't there enough going on without them doxxing abuse victims?) She had set herself up on the far side of the chain-link along with an a cappella group all dressed in tuxes, a lot of gold lamé about them. As I watched, they started singing 'I will always love you', presumably to Arif, now that she knew where he was living.

'What the hell?' said Todd, appearing beside me in a paper suit and with his mask on and shield down. He must have started in the Skweek on Kathi's terms already.

'Molly wants to talk to you,' I said. 'See if you can work out what she's driving at because I'm stumped.'

'OK,' said Todd. 'But can you go wait for the first delivery of laundry over the fence then? We're doing our soft opening today.'

'Soft opening,' I said. I wasn't asking a question. I wasn't even mocking him. I've found it sometimes helps just to repeat the bulletins from Planet Todd until they stop bothering me.

'OK then "dry run",' he said. 'Jeez.'

The a cappella group were still droning away and thumping themselves.

Molly's door blatted open behind me. 'What the good god damn?' she said.

'That,' I said, pointing, 'is Arif's wife, that I wanted to get a restraining order for, if you remember, come to harass him like I knew she would. What are you going to do?'

Molly listened for a while. 'That's not harassment,' she said at last. I rolled my eyes. 'I tell you what it is though.' She lifted her voice. 'Mrs Jafari!' Creepy Stalker Scumspouse looked up. 'Are you paying those people to sing for you?'

'What's it to you?' Arif's wife shouted back, once again displaying that fabulous American lack of giving a monkey's about pissing off cops.

'Is she?' Molly asked the leader of the group. He was easily identified since he had a whole gold tux and everyone else had a plain tux and gold just on their waistcoats and bowties.

'Yeah, why?' he called back.

'Gotcha,' said Molly softly with a smirk only I could see. 'They're giving a professional public performance of a copyrighted Dolly Parton song. And Dolly don't do that. This is going to be an expensive morning.'

'Why Sergeant Rankinson,' I said, 'I thought I knew you. I had no idea you could be so awesomely petty.'

'You think that's petty?' Molly said. 'When this case is closed, if you're cleared, I'll show you petty.'

'What do you mean "if I'm cleared"?'

'Yeah, what the hell. Even if you're not,' Molly said. 'I'll visit you in lock-up and tell you there.'

And, no matter how closely I looked into her eyes, I couldn't tell if she was serious or messing with me, so I hooked it.

I had to turn my head away from Room 201 as I made for the stairs. Even still, the sight of Blaine's body wrapped in that cloudy plastic flared up behind my eyes again. Maybe I was going to need some professional help to get over finding her.

Or maybe not. After five hours on hold with the four main mental healthcare insurers in the state, trying to untangle the ball of string they called 'a simple adjustment to encompass virtual provision', I was close to weeping. No way was I going to do this as a patient as well as a provider. I would drink my cares away. Or eat chocolate. Or stay in bed with Taylor. Or all three.

So, of course, the first thing I saw when I went back round to the motel was a reminder that Taylor wasn't free to stay in bed with me all day. Amaranth was sitting in the doorway of Maria and José's room, crocheting happily in the watery sunshine. 'Hi,' I said. 'What you making?'

'Sshhhh,' she replied, 'I can only do it if I count. See you at dinner.'

'Is Taylor back?' I whispered. I hadn't seen him since the shower, although he'd been texting me encouraging little texts – plus some goose news – all day, until about an hour ago. Either he was driving now or the goose action had intensified.

Amaranth said something so quietly I couldn't hear it.

I bent my head close. 'What was that?'

'Don't they have numbers where you come from?' she said. 'I told you I'm counting and Taylor's *forty-six*. How should I know where he is and why would I care?'

Since I couldn't ask for clearer evidence that she was fine and I wasn't needed, I took myself off. All the other doors were closed and there was a hum of busyness from behind Della's; I assumed Devin was working in there until the crime-scene tape came off Room 201. Next door to Della, the crime-scene tape was still on Room 102 as well. I hurried past with my eyes down and, when I looked up again, Noleen was beckoning me from the office doorway.

'You been mollied yet?' she said when I got close.

'This morning,' I said. 'You too?'

She drew me into the office and closed the door. 'You work out what it was about?'

'Not even nearly,' I said. 'What did she say to you?'

'She wanted to know what I'd said to Blaine and what Blaine had said to me.' I nodded to show her same here. 'Which shoulda taken two minutes. "Hi, hi. That sweatshirt is offensive, your kids' names are dumb, I ain't cooking squat, well, you ain't eating either then." But she wouldn't let up. I was in there for half an hour and I still don't know why.'

'Well, where was she pushing you to go?' I said. '*Was* she pushing you to go somewhere? Because she was pushing me towards Blaine and Phil's marriage all the time. I talked about the kids, food, dancing, safety . . . and Molly was determined to keep bringing it back to marriage, marriage, marriage.'

'Well, duh,' said Noleen. 'You're a marriage therapist, Lexy. Like I own a motel and so Molly – you're dead right, by the way; she did – kept trying to get me to talk about what Blaine might have said regarding the motel.'

'I suppose,' I said, then let a big breath go. 'Yeah, I suppose so. That must be it. Not very imaginative, is it? I mean, we could have talked about anything. Look at the stuff you and I talk about sometimes. Motels and marriages barely get a look-in.' In fact, once last autumn Devin had gone in a mysterious huff with Noleen and me, flouncing off from Game Night and locking his door. It turned out that our innocent conversation about why watch-chains had survived so much longer than monocles had convinced him we'd got our hands on some really great weed and weren't sharing.

Maybe because life was so uncertain then – that day especially as the state shut down – we grabbed on to this likely explanation. We would have stuck with it too if Kathi hadn't been just about to burst in and blow our theory sky-high.

'Wow,' she said, standing and stripping off her paper suit, plastic face shield, surgical mask, latex gloves, bootees, polo shirt, jeans and socks and grabbing Noleen's nap blanket off the office chair to wrap herself up in; it was a bit too fresh to stand in a bra and pants even if there was no chance of customers coming in and wondering what kind of place they'd decided to break their journey. 'Molly's . . . I don't even know. I hope she's drunk, but she's on duty and there was another cop on video-link so probably not. But then I don't know *what's* up with her.'

'You did your interview?' I said. Noleen had gone for a binbag and was holding it open, while Kathi picked up her garments with the toes of one foot and dropped them in. When the bag was knotted shut, she put her disposable garments into the bin the same way and Noleen knotted that bag shut too. 'You've got fantastic balance,' I added, as Kathi stood on one leg and scrubbed her grabbing toes with a Clorox wipe. 'You should do yoga.'

'Why, if I already have such great balance?' Kathi said.

'To show off and make the yummies feel inadequate,' I said. 'Why else?'

'So what happened?' said Noleen.

'She grabbed me,' Kathi said, 'and forced me into her disgusting room. I wish we had put in all the stuff I wanted to put in the contract about housekeeping.' She turned to me. 'Noleen reckoned there was so much about personal hygiene we couldn't really add more, but I didn't think I'd ever see a Last Ditch room looking like that.'

I cast my mind back over the tight corners on the sheets and the clean dishes draining on paper then I shook the question away; there was no way of guessing what minuscule or imaginary infraction Kathi was reacting to by stripping to her scanties and – she was doing this right now – buffing every bit of her exposed skin with anti-bacterial wipes.

'And?' Noleen said.

'And she started peppering me with insane questions about Blaine's clothes.'

'Her clothes?' I said.

'Did she ask you all that stuff too?' said Kathi. 'Wasn't it weird?'

'No, she asked me about her marriage, not her laundry,' I said. 'But it makes sense. Nolly reckons—'

'Who said anything about laundry?' Kathi said. She had finished wiping her face, neck and ears and she was now wiping the outside of the tub of wipes where she had touched it. Ordinarily it would have made me feel sad, but truth to tell I was watching her for tips. We were all Kathi now. 'This was about her practice clothes – I never *saw* her in her practice clothes! – and her nightwear – I told Molly I couldn't have said she had sushi pyjamas with a gun to my head. It was just weird.'

'Talk me through it,' I said.

'She wanted me to guess how many conversations I'd had with Blaine while she was here,' Kathi began. So far, so the same as Noleen and me. 'I said none and it wasn't a guess. Then she goes "But hadn't I complimented Blaine on her clothes?" So I go "nope". Because of course I didn't. I don't care what the chick was wearing. Why would I? But she wouldn't leave it. Where did I sit and where did she sit at the dinners those first two nights? Did she listen to me talking? Did I listen to her? And – again – what was she wearing? Did she get changed to practise once she'd gotten to Room 202 or did she change in her own room and go upstairs already in her . . . some word I don't even know.'

'Tutu?' I said. Kathi snorted. 'Legwarmers, wrap, blocks?' Kathi gave me a look of deep pity. 'Leotard?' I said, because it was the only other dancewear word I could think of.

'That's it. What the hell's a leotard?'

'How can you not know wh—?'

'I thought it was a kind of possum,' Kathi said. 'So I told Molly I had no idea what she wore or where she changed or why Molly was asking.'

She looked to Noleen and then to me for enlightenment, but we had nothing. 'Is she just messing?' I said at last. 'Is she pretending there's digging to do here so she gets to stay here, like she wants to?'

'She's already squared it away that she's sheltering here,' said Noleen. 'I got an expense payment claim form faxed through from the city this morning.'

'Faxed?' I said. 'Wow.'

'Or,' said Noleen, 'is it maybe that a desk job is paid less than active investigating and so she's investigating really actively?'

'Hm,' I said. 'Could be. How would we find out?'

'But would Molly do something that shabby?' Kathi asked. 'She's no angel – she's trashed her room and remember how she used to issue veiled threats to Della before she was married and legal, but she has that . . . you know . . . that cop thing?'

'Ostentatious adherence to the letter of the law that makes you want to smack her?' I suggested.

'That's the one,' said Kathi.

'Enh, but it's business,' Noleen said. 'We can't turn it away.'

'Not while Todd tanks the Skweek,' Kathi said. 'I can't believe I didn't see it coming.'

'What did he do?' I said, already laughing. But before she could answer Todd himself arrived, throwing open the door and standing there framed in a dramatic pose.

'I've just been violated,' he said, in that voice that makes me unable to believe he's never had actor-training. 'I think.'

'You *think*?' said Noleen.

'That's why psychological abuse is so much worse than a straightforward fist to the nose,' Todd said. 'Gaslighting and trolling are pernicious. I'll teach you how to drape a serape, by the way, Kathi. If you'd like me to.'

'It's Noleen's nap blanket, you moron,' said Kathi. 'That straightforward enough for you?'

'But who's been doling out psychological abuse and gaslighting and trolling?' I said. Then I answered myself and Noleen and Kathi joined in too.

'Molly!'

'Typical!' said Todd. 'You three knew all about these tendencies and didn't tell me? What is that, sisterhood? Because I'm a better sister than that little bee-yotch any day. What is this, time's up? Me too? Did you know that an out gay man is five times more likely to experience—'

'No,' I said, counting off his questions. 'And no, and no, and no.'

'Aw, Le-xy!' said Noleen. 'You know I love it when Todd pulls a statistic out of his ass. You spoiled my fun.'

'You can't say ass to a gay man,' said Todd. 'It's targeted harassment and all the more painful when I've just told you about my ordeal already today.'

'Look,' I said. 'I'm pretty sure we know roughly what you've been through because so have we. Comparable but different weird shit from Molly. So how about you take a deep breath, allow yourself to be grateful that it was nothing personal, go and lock up the Skweek, Kathi go and put some clothes on, Noleen make margaritas, and we'll meet on board in fifteen minutes to compare notes. I'll just try and find Taylor and tell him to stay away.'

'Why?' said Todd.

'Business meeting,' I said. 'Official Trinity business.'

''At's me off the hook,' said Noleen. 'Make your own margaritas.'

'Who's to say Taylor doesn't have his own horror story to share anyway,' said Kathi.

'After me,' Todd put in.

'He doesn't,' I said. 'Molly told me this morning she wanted to talk to us four, Arif and Meera and no one else. Not Taylor or his mum or the Bernals or Barb. So, no Taylor.'

Kathi shook her head and sucked her teeth. It was a bold effort at haughtiness for someone barefoot and wrapped in a fleece knee-blanket. 'What?' I demanded.

'I knew this would happen,' she said. 'I knew as soon as I saw Taylor that you'd never see past the pocket protector and the utility belt to the man below. Lexy, he's great! He's good and kind and funny. He's perfect for you and you're trashing it.'

'What the hell are you talking about?' I said. 'How am I trashing it? What have you ever seen me do?'

'Exactly!' Kathi said. 'You've done nothing. *We* had to move him in here. You were just gonna let him stay up there in the suburbs with his mom and not set eyes on him until all this was over. And that's after . . .' She folded her lips together.

'After what?' I said.

'After being so cold and indifferent and hands-off and so . . . blank!'

'What the hell are you talking about?' I said again. I could feel my face starting to get hot. 'Has he said something to you? What did he say to you? Because he's lying. I told him I loved him. First!'

'Oh no, you should never do that.' Noleen had gone back to her paperwork but she looked at me over her glasses as she shared that unhelpful little offering.

'He doesn't *need* to say anything,' Kathi said. 'You only have to look at him.'

'I have no idea what you're getting at,' I told her. I glanced at Todd to see if he had a clue.

'He's still wearing cargo shorts!' Kathi said. 'And not even shorts! Shants! He's still brushing his hair flat to dry. He still has sweaters with zippers. You're not even trying!'

'What?' I said. 'Since when did you tell Noleen to torch the obnoxious sweatshirts? Since when did Roger tell—' Todd cleared his throat. 'OK, forget that. You can't improve on perfection, but still. And anyway why look at me? I never dreamed I'd get to have a say in what Taylor wore or how he did his hair or what his glasses were like. It's *Todd* who hasn't lifted a finger. How could I have guessed it would be left to me, with Mr Boundaries over there?' I frowned and turned to Todd full face on. 'Actually, why haven't you gone steaming in on Taylor already? Arif's reeling from your attentions. Maria told me you want her to cut her hair short and throw away her black dye. So why am I getting a hard time for indifference when even *you* don't care? You saw his chest hair and toenails and you said squat!'

'Lexy,' Todd said, in a smarmy voice with a hand over his heart, 'how can you speak these painful words? What greater evidence could there be of how *much* I care?' He gave me a patient look, as if he was waiting for an answer to a real question. 'I think Taylor is the one,' he said at last. 'So I don't want to blow it.'

'Todd,' I said, 'you have no idea what it means to me to hear you say that. Now, if you could just generalize from Taylor to everyone? If you can see that *Taylor* might not welcome you interfering and might run away from me to get away from you, can't you just go that one extra step and accept that no one, *no one* – not Maria, not Arif, not that poor Uber driver that time . . .'

'Not my laundromat customers,' Kathi chipped in.

'. . . No one,' I repeated, thinking we'd circle back to whatever was wrong with Kathi, 'wants to be told that their hair or clothes or posture aren't to your liking.'

Todd was grinning at me. 'Maniac,' he said. 'I didn't mean that. Why wouldn't someone want the benefit of my obvious experience? Look at me: I'm gorgeous. Different if I was Edith Head – out from under my bridge to tell someone else *they* weren't making the grade. Different if I was Anna Wintour telling some other chick her bangs were too heavy. Different if I was Donatella—'

'We get it,' said Noleen, which was a shame because I kind of wanted to hear the end of that one.

'No,' Todd said. 'My thing was: imagine if I fixed Taylor and you didn't like which way I went with him. If I did him dapper or rugged or Euro or preppy and you wanted K-pop.'

'I can guarantee I don't want you to turn Taylor dapper, preppy or K-pop,' I said.

'OK,' said Todd. 'Euro with a rugged edge. I'll get started.'

'Please don't,' I said. 'He's a man of— Huh.' It had gone past me at the time but now it went home. Amaranth had said he was forty-six. A month ago, Taylor had told me he was forty-four. At last I had found something wrong with the guy! I felt my heart swell as that little bit of vanity and bullshit brought him down to earth where I lived and made me love him even more. 'A man of mature years,' I said. 'He can pick out his own clothes.'

'The evidence is against you,' said Todd. Kathi and Noleen

both snorted, which was rich coming from Mrs and Mrs Fleece
Goes Anywhere.

'So what did you do at the Skweek?' I said, partly to stop
them all laughing at Taylor and partly because I wanted to
know.

'I offered an extra service,' Todd said. 'For no extra charge.'

'You graded their clothes!' said Kathi. 'You stalked them on
social media to find out their age and shape and you separated
their laundry into yeses and nos.'

'I did no such thing,' said Todd. 'There were no outright
yeses. I sorted the laundry into "Well, OK then if you must"
and "Girl, please".'

'Even the nuns!' said Kathi. 'Nuns!'

'All I said was if they're going to wear such high necks they
need to buy better bras.'

'Lexy,' said Kathi, turning to me with her hands out,
beseeching me to do something. I had lost count of the number
of times she had beseeched me to do something about Todd,
while he looked on blithely, not even entertaining the idea that
there was a problem.

'You can't talk to nuns about their bras,' I told him.

'And another thing,' said Todd, rebuffing it all as I knew he
would, 'are we ready to do the re-enactment? Have you asked
Phil Temple how much he weighs and how tall he is?'

'I can't,' I said. 'I haven't got his new number.'

Todd clicked his fingers for my phone and keyed it into my
contacts.

'You get it from Roger?' I said.

'Molly,' said Todd. I had to smile. She might be the boss of
me but she was no match for him.

'He's probably busy,' I said, as it was ringing. But he
answered. 'Oh, hi. The kids are fine. They're really remarkably
fine. It's a testament to you both how resilient and flexible they
are. Are you getting some FaceTime with them though? I know
that wasn't quite settled before . . . before.'

'So if that's all,' Phil said. He sounded beyond distracted.
'Or is this a client briefing?'

There was a lot of background noise and I could picture him
rushing about corridors with machines on casters and shouting

terse instructions to nurses. I should let him go, since he was a doctor. But I should keep him on the line, since I thought he was a murderer. But on the other hand I should do what he was asking, since he was a paying client. This case was very confusing.

'Neither,' I said. 'What height and weight are you?'

'Six-five, one-eighty,' he said, without hesitation, as would anyone if that was the true answer. 'Why?' he added, which is what most people would lead with. Most doughy, shrimpy people like me anyway.

'Because we've got a witness who saw someone who was here on the night . . . on the night.'

'A witness who saw *me*?' Phil said.

'No,' I said, again being as straightforward as it was possible to be. 'A witness who felt someone jump on and off a houseboat and then saw them run off through the bushes, in the dark.'

'A houseboat?' said Phil. 'At the motel?' If it was an innocent act it was a good one. 'And this witness thinks it was me?'

'Not even nearly,' I said. 'We want to prove to the cops that it couldn't have been you so we need to be able to eliminate you.' Because being straightforward had its limits.

'Well, I'm six foot five and I weigh one hundred and eighty pounds except after Christmas.'

I told him I'd phone back tomorrow, we said our goodbyes, and I hung up.

Noleen was sucking her teeth and shaking her head. 'Subtle,' she said.

'It worked,' I told her. 'He's one metre ninety-five and he weighs twelve stone twelve.' I only did it to bug them and it didn't even work anymore because they had all cracked the code.

'Perfect,' said Todd. 'I can stand in for him.'

'Uhhhhhh,' I said. I loved Todd but I loved objective reality too.

'In platform cork wedges and carrying a sack of flour in my backpack,' Todd said. 'My God, one-eighty? If I ever get to one-eighty you have my permission to staple my stomach with a craft gun. Go straight through my belly skin and shut that sucker down.'

At which unfortunately violent-sounding moment, the office door opened to admit Arif and Meera. They walked as if in a daze, eyes wide and faces stark. They even stumbled a little. And, while Meera might well stumble in her stilettos and second-skin pencil skirt, Arif was in Timbies and he stumbled too.

'Can we talk to you?' Arif said. 'I know we don't know you that well, but can we trust you?'

'We need to talk to someone,' said Meera, a tight frown drawing her face into lines.

'Ahhhh,' I said. 'Yes, come in. Or rather come to the boat. And tell us everything. I know that look. You've just been mollied, haven't you?'

FIFTEEN

'Can we really just disappear round to the boat, though?' Kathi said. 'All of us?'

'Amaranth is napping,' said Meera. 'José has crooned all the babies into a hundred-years-in-a-castle nap too. They're lying on the floor like seals on a beach. The man's a genius. Maria is cooking for tonight. I think she might be cooking every night if we don't stop her, because she doesn't think much of anyone else's food. Della and Devin are . . . I think they're . . . resting.'

'I gotcha,' Noleen said. 'A little afternoon delight while Diego's off their hands.'

'And that other woman,' Meera added, 'is swimming.'

'My mom,' said Todd. 'I can tell from your tone that she's wearing a bikini. Just be glad she has both halves on.'

It was Meera and Arif's first time aboard and, despite everything going on, I still managed to feel proud of my dinky little pad. I put a match to the stack of twigs and crumpled paper in the woodstove then laid an apple log on top, leaving the door open so we could all hear the crackle and smell the deliciousness. I loved that there were enough seats without anyone having to perch on a dining chair. Luckily, since I didn't have any dining chairs, because my dining room was my office. (I really would need to get to grips with the insurers and my growing wait-list of online clients. Tomorrow.)

'Who's going first?' I said. 'Or will we wait for Noleen and the margaritas?'

'I'll go,' Arif said. 'It's really weird but that cop is not willing to believe I spent three nights close to Blaine and didn't swear some kind of a blood oath. She wouldn't let me go, even after I told her everything I knew. She was like a dog with a bone. On and on and on.'

'Talk us through it, baby,' Todd said. 'All the way through.'

'I told her I met Blaine at dinner the night we all moved in.

I admired the kids, because they *are* cute for one thing and also
. . . moms, you know.' He darted a quick look at Meera, who
shrugged as if to say it was true. 'Then we talked about sourdough for a bit the next day.' Because of course they did because
we were only ninety minutes from San Francisco, well within
range. 'I brought my starter with me,' Arif went on. Because
of course he did. No one who grew heirloom tomatoes in his
front garden would ever leave home without his sourdough
starter. Except I didn't know they were heirloom tomatoes.
Except I did. 'And that was it,' he said. 'That was the entirety
of my relationship with Blaine Temple. I'm sorry she's dead
and if she hadn't died we might have gotten closer, but we
didn't. Only try telling that to crazy cop lady!'

'Go on,' said Todd. 'Give us the deets.'

'Did I say to her that those mean signs were from her
husband, not my wife? Did I accuse her of telling my wife
where I was? Did I tell her I had heard her husband had an
affair with three different women at his clinic, two moms and a
nursing assistant? All complete garbage. I mean, really and
truly garbage. Not a grain of truth in any of it. I wouldn't have
known she was married if I didn't know from Todd that his
hubs was staying with hers. I never mentioned her husband. I
didn't know his name until after she died. And I certainly never
mentioned my wife. I had only just met Blaine and, first impressions, I didn't much like her, if I'm honest. Why would I go
spilling my guts about my wife, or my job, or the tread on my
tyres? It's nuts. It's bananas. But it was scary the way that cop
kept pushing it. It's hard to explain, but trust me.'

'Oh we don't have to trust you,' I said. 'We know. She did
the same to everyone.' I turned to Meera. 'How about you?'

'Yep, same deal,' she said.

Noleen arrived with the margarita jug and a smaller pitcher
she set down next to Arif. 'Elderflower cordial with mint and
lime,' she said. 'I brought a little hipflask in case you only
"don't drink" when the what's-he-called's watching. The
rabbi?'

'Imam,' said Arif. Noleen clicked her tongue. 'No, I really
don't drink.' He turned to me. 'Cliché, huh? Not like you, Lexy.'

'Eh?' I said. He had a point, but had he really known me

long enough to say I was permanently trolleyed, like most of my countrymen?

'Drinking margaritas,' he said. 'Instead of S—'

'Don't!' said Todd. 'Don't get her started on allegedly fictitious drinks.'

'Nothing alleged about it,' I said. 'The Scotch Mist doesn't exist in actual Scotland.'

'I was going to say Stag's Breath,' said Arif. 'That's real. Or do you call it a Rusty Nail?'

'What the hell's a Rusty Nail?' said Noleen.

'A Stag's Breath with cheaper whisky,' I said.

'Or a Black and Tan,' said Arif. He certainly knew a lot of drinks for a teetotaller.

'They're Irish,' I said. 'But two out of three? I'll forgive you.'

Noleen had finished serving and let herself drop into a chair with a hearty sigh that was halfway to a groan. It never ceased to amaze me how she could do that with a brimming drink and not spill a drop. Even when it was martinis and margaritas, in the sloppiest glasses ever blown. 'So where we at?' she said.

'Meera's up,' said Kathi.

'And my story starts the same way,' Meera said. She took a huge glug of margarita and her eyes popped wide open. Noleen has no truck with syrup; her margaritas are basically half lime juice and half booze. 'What conversations did I have with Blaine? So I told her. We talked about whether all this would last long enough to home school or if we would just give all the kids a holiday.'

'*All* the kids?' I said. 'Her kids? Salem isn't three yet and Navy can't sit up.'

Meera flushed and it wasn't just the tequila hitting her bloodstream. 'Oh no!' she said. 'I do that all the time. I thought we were talking about *our* kids and it turns out I was just blabbering on about mine. I need to stop that. If you hear me doing it, please tell me.'

We all waited to see who was going to speak. Or so I thought. In fact, the rest of them were looking at me, some of them pretty hard, and one of them – Noleen – with that look that's drawn as a thick, black, dotted line in comics. And I suppose I am a therapist, so I can hardly complain.

'Meera,' I said. 'Honey, you need to stop doing that thing you just did, OK?' She frowned. 'You were repeating a pile of mean crap your pig of a husband made you believe about yourself. Don't.'

She took a couple of beats but at last she smiled. 'You're kind,' she said.

'I'm not,' I countered.

'She really isn't,' Todd added.

'Never,' said Kathi. 'It's a policy.'

'A day without bitching is a day wasted,' Noleen said.

Arif hadn't said anything yet, but when he saw Meera still wavering, he said: 'My wife said I smelled like burnt wax. That's how they do it, Meer. They make it so specific you can't believe it's invented. Because who smells like wax? What does wax even smell like? I made an appointment to have my sweat glands frozen and then, on the way to the clinic, I suddenly realized how badly she had played me. I pulled off and went to a brothel. Paid a girl a fifty to tell me what I smelled like.'

'What did she say?' Meera asked.

'Irish Spring and Colgate,' said Arif. 'On the nose. She could get work in the wine trade.'

'That was an inspired idea,' I said. 'Arif, can I use that with my clients?'

'If it comes up,' Arif said. He was such an innocent, in some ways. *If* body dysmorphia 'came up' in counselling?

'Oh it will,' I said. 'It does. And I keep trying to find new ways to counter it. So thank you. What else, Meera?'

'Not much,' she said. 'We talked about chlorine in the pool for like a minute the next day, because your mom was swimming underwater, Todd, and we thought her hair might go green. We were bigging ourselves up for having natural dos, I think. No! Wait! I was and she was just joining in to be— Sorry! And she spoke to me a little about the second note on the fence. She said, "Can't accuse him of indifference!" like it was a joke or something. But I didn't answer her, so it wasn't even a conversation.'

'Was she annoyed?' I said. 'When you didn't answer.' Because this was the first hint within a million miles of actual aggro. And even *it* was a stretch.

'I don't think she noticed,' Meera said. 'No one clueless enough to say that would notice how hurtful it was, would they? My mom's just the same. "He loves you," she says. "He loves you so much! He's obsessed with you. If he didn't love you, he wouldn't" . . .' She had sounded OK but suddenly she let out a sob and had to stop talking.

'Wouldn't hire an a cappella choir and stand outside your home like creepy John Cusack,' said Arif. 'For instance.' He leaned over and grabbed the only bit of Meera he could reach, which was her shoulder, squeezing it gently. It's hard to squeeze a shoulder and not have it go a bit Vulcan death-grip, but Meera looked up and smiled.

'But that crazy cop wouldn't have it,' she went on. 'It was just like you said, Arif. She kept poking and digging and baiting me. What else? When did we meet? Where did we meet? What did we talk about? I kept telling her we met out front and at dinner, never alone except for watching your mom in the pool and worrying about her hair. But that cop didn't believe me. She asked me what I had said when Blaine told me how much she was missing her husband. Which was nothing, because she didn't, because she wasn't. Then she – the cop – asked if I was missing *my* husband. Didn't seem relevant. Asked if I was jealous of Blaine. I said she meant envious. Ho, she didn't like that, but I said of course I was envious of someone with a happy marriage. And then she goes "to a doctor", like that was the main difference between Blaine and me. So I told her no way, and that I was proud of being married to a cop. I even got a sticker for the back window of my car – don't hate me. Then things changed and I saw that it was a terrible thing to be married to a bad guy who was a cop because who do you call?'

'And how did that go down?' I asked.

'Like a cement soufflé,' said Meera. 'But it didn't put her off her stride. She kept pressing, asking if I had ever taken Bob or Joan to Phil Temple's paediatric office. Like I wouldn't have mentioned it? And even after I'd said no, she said how often did I take them to the doctor, and what reasons had I taken them in for. So I was having this bizarre conversation with a cop, about why I take my kids to their doctor in Cuento – strep throat, pink eye, vomiting bug, shots – because the husband of the dead woman does the same job in a hospital in Sacramento. I mean. How weird is that?'

'That is, indeed, very weird,' said Todd. 'Does anyone have a clue what could be behind it?'

I shrugged. Everyone shrugged.

'Let's press on,' I said. 'Maybe it'll make sense once we hear what she said to you, Todd.'

'OK then,' Todd said. He dipped his pinkie in his margarita, used it to smooth his eyebrows, and dabbed the last drops behind his ears. 'I'm ready,' he went on. 'Here's what happened to me. Same start: when did I talk to Blaine and what did I say? Not often and not much was the answer. General hellos, the tiniest little briefing about the importance of insect control, and an attempt – a failed attempt, mind you – to bond over husbands who work together. That went nowhere.'

'And what did Molly home in on?' I asked. 'Maybe yours is the last piece of the puzzle that makes it all make sense. Marriage in general, motels, clothes, Phil's infidelity, Meera's doctor-fixation. What was it with you, Todd?'

'Tattoos,' Todd said. He paused to enjoy our befuddlement. 'She asked me if I had any. I told her nothing an inkster could add to my body would be an improvement. Which,' he turned to Meera and Arif, 'isn't as snotty as it sounds, is it Lexy?'

'Um,' I said. 'Well, I think everyone should consider what they add to their body more than some people seem to. You know? Millennia of evolution to get you as you are and then one night in Atlantic City to add a Tweetie-pie to your left bum cheek.' I bit my lip. 'Unless either of you two have got a Tweetie-pie on your left bum cheek, obviously.'

'It's haram,' said Arif. 'Also, I'm a coward.'

'It would be a little too much,' said Meera. 'What with Yosemite Sam on the right one.'

'But getting back to Molly and Todd,' Kathi said.

'Then she asked me if I had seen *Blaine*'s tattoos,' Todd said. 'And I was like "Uh, unless she had love and hate on her knuckles or tear drops from her jailhouse kills, how exactly would I have seen her tattoos in three days at the chilly end of spring?" Wasn't that a weird thing to ask?'

'It would be in most cases,' I said, carefully. The first time
Todd had seen me in my underwear was two days after we met.
And it wasn't even really *my* underwear; he had bought it for
me because he didn't think my old underwear was good enough.
Me and the nuns.

'So then she moved on to ask if Blaine had *told* me about
her tattoos and if we had discussed tattoo removal or blocking.'

'Roger's got blocked tatts,' I said. 'Maybe he talked to Phil
about that and Phil talked to Blaine and . . . yeah nah, that
doesn't work, does it?'

'And she ended up,' said Todd, 'asking me if I would be
willing to sign an affidavit swearing that I had never discussed
tattoos of any kind with Blaine.'

'Seriously?' I said. I had finished my margarita and I got up
to take the jug round again, seeing that I wasn't the only one.
'She never mentioned affidavits to me. Did she to anyone else?'

'Yeah,' said Kathi, sounding sorrowful. 'They came up. What
do Todd and me got that nobody else does?'

Of course when she put it that way, what Todd and Kathi
had that no one else did were onerous psychological burdens.
But Molly hadn't asked them anything about germs or insects.
And besides, Meera and Arif had their problems too – inevitably,
after being in abusive marriages. I looked around the gathering
and thought it was coming to something when Noleen and I
were the normal ones.

'Tattoos, clothing, the motel business, marriage in general,
infidelity in particular and . . . whatever it is Meera's supposed
to have done with her kids and their doctor. It sounded as if
Molly was accusing you of Munchausen's, the more I think of
it,' I said. 'Which makes no sense on its own and even less
added to the rest. What's she up to?'

Todd drew a huge breath as if he was going to share something momentous. 'Dunno,' he said. 'Why don't we try the
re-enactment?'

'The what?' said Arif, drawing back and even lifting his feet
off the floor to crunch up into a protective ball.

'Of the suspect bouncing over my boat and making off across
the fields,' I said. 'Not of the . . . anything that happened inside
Blaine's room.'

'Oh,' Arif said, putting his feet back down again and clearing his throat hard as if that would mean we hadn't noticed. 'What does that entail?'

'Everyone will have to get off,' I said. 'I'll unlock the barbed-wire perimeter then lie down in bed. Then Todd with twenty pounds of flour in a backpack – so he weighs the same as Phil Temple – is going to bound over the deck and I'm going to watch him run away.'

'At great risk to my ankles,' said Todd. 'Because I'll need to do it in platforms to be the same height as Dr T.' He stood. 'So,' he said, looking round the rest of them like a gracious host, suggesting the party move to the dining room, 'shall we? Lexy, are you going to slug half a bottle of grog down to make it identical, or is that going too far?'

'I had slept myself sober anyway,' I said, 'so I'm good. But after we've done it, can everyone come back, please?'

'If you do a quick sweep,' said Kathi. I looked around my perfectly tidy living room, then nodded. It's an oddity of Kathi's neat freakery that she prefers a nasty shock to what she calls 'flagged filth'. That is, much as she dislikes walking blind into a room that could have coffee-cups with scum, tissues in the bin or even shoes under the couch, she can take it. If she knows the details of a 'disgusting' room she's coming back into, though, she can really get into trouble, with a tight chest and a raised pulse, cold sweats sometimes.

'Why do you want us back anyway?' she said.

'I need to brainstorm what to say to Phil about it all when I call him tomorrow. I promised I would.'

'He's off like last week's mackerel, isn't he?' Noleen said, hauling herself to her feet. 'His wife was killed. He leaves his kids where she died. He stays at work. He's not on the phone all day every day to check they're OK. He hires a detective to investigate the murder, like he doesn't trust the police. It's just . . . hinky.'

'Maybe,' Meera said. 'But now is a hinky time. I'm doing things I never thought I'd do and I'm planning to do even more.'

Arif didn't look at her, but he didn't look at her so hard that tendons stood out on his neck. And everyone saw that because everyone else looked at him. Which was all so very awkward and adorable at the same time that it got everyone out of their chairs and off the boat, still clutching glasses of cocktail and cordial. I took the dregs of mine through to my bed to finish it off there once I had undone the padlock and bent the wire back to make a gateway.

I knew I would have time to drain my glass, because I knew Todd. If he was changing his shoes and adding a backpack, he'd have to change the rest of his outfit too, and possibly tone his jewellery down a bit, taking out the diamond studs and putting in some gold hoops. And if he changed his nose-stud to plain gold too he'd be looking at his face in the mirror long enough to want a general touch-up. I probably had time to call Taylor after checking my inbox.

'Hey,' I said, once the inbox was empty.

'Hey. You sound like you're lying down. Is this a sex call?'

'I'm propped up far enough to sip a cocktail, so you never know. It could be. Where are you?'

'Just a leather vest and a pair of silk— Oh!' he said. 'That's not what I thought you were going to ask.'

'Don't make me laugh,' I said. 'I'll spill my tequila. And please don't ever wear a leather vest.'

'OK,' he said. 'I'm still at the reserve and I can't make myself leave. It's the same as ever down here. You wouldn't know anything was happening. But driving down was eerie. There's no one on the roads and nothing open. I didn't like it and I'm not looking forward to driving back. I don't blame you for going to bed and starting drinking.'

I laughed and explained what I was really doing, then I tried to apologize for what was bothering me. 'I've hardly seen your mum all day,' I said. 'I hope she's OK.'

'She's never been better and she loves you, Lexy.'

'But I haven't—'

'Because you've left her alone and not patronized her and treated her like a kid. She's been so bored and lonely since her sight failed. Truly, this is the most fun she's had in years. Friends her own age, kids to spoil, and . . . Barb.'

'Yeah, Barb can be pretty entertaining,' I said. 'And impossible to offend too, so whatever made you pause there— Uh-oh!' I had felt the boat tip. 'Here we go! Todd's just leapt on-board.

And yes, that feels pretty much the same. A good rock but not enough to slam me against the walls. And now he's gone again. Right, I need to go and see him plunge off into the bushes.'

I scrambled out of bed and jogged along the passageway to the porch, just in time to see Todd dash between two of the closest toyons and thrash his way through the tall stalks of yellow grass. 'Wow!' I said.

'What? What?' Taylor's voice was tinny and sharp in my phone. Instinctively, I raised it not to my ear but up in front of my face and took a photo. It flashed as Taylor kept squawking.

'Lexy! What's happening?'

I put him on speaker. 'He nailed it!' I said. 'He looked exactly the same as the guy on Monday night. Felt the same too. Six-five, one-eighty. So it was definitely Phil Temple who killed his wife, then. Or someone else the same size and weight as him. But that's not likely. God almighty, Taylor. You know what this means.'

I was working on the shot I'd taken of Todd running off, zooming and sharpening, lightening and darkening.

'Roger's rooming with a murderer,' Taylor said.

'Exactly.' Then I drew back into the shadow of the living room doorway and clicked my phone screen to black. 'There's someone coming,' I whispered.

And they were coming at a fair old clip. The light was low and I couldn't tell who it was until he had bounded up the porch steps, making the boat rock hard enough to set me staggering.

'Todd?' I said. He was panting from the weight of the back-pack full of flour and he loomed over me in his cork wedges.

'Lexy!' he said, dragging his breaths. 'What are you doing standing there? You're ruining it!'

'What's happening?' said Taylor.

'Todd, do me a favour,' I said, 'and jump off the boat on the other side. Take a path between those two toyons with the berries still on.'

'Well, duh!' Todd said. 'You mean like I was going to? But you were supposed to be in your bed, waiting for me to make the earth move.'

'What?' said Taylor.

Todd jumped off the deck on to the bank and again the deck

walloped up and back to the accompaniment of a lot of sloshing. Once I had regained my balance, I watched him go, busting through between the bushes, his feet splatting on the wet ground and then thumping on the dry.

'Come back!' I called out to him. 'That's far enough.'

'Someone's been here before me!' he shouted, turning round.

'I know,' I shouted. 'Come back! I don't know where they are! And just come back anyway, because no way was it someone the size and weight of you.'

'What is going *on*?' Taylor shouted out of my phone.

'Nothing good,' I said, lifting the phone to my ear and holding my hand out to Todd to help him back on board.

That's when we heard the screaming.

SIXTEEN

I t was Amaranth. Taylor knew his mother's voice even down a phone and over the sound of me dashing straight round there to see if she was hurt, my feet braver than the rest of me. He knew it even over the added sound of Todd puffing and stamping along behind, twenty pounds of flour on his back and the same amount of mud on his wedges.

'Oh God, oh God, oh God,' Taylor said, as I took the corner by Reception and powered my way into Amaranth's room through the open door; I was braced for horror, the memory of Blaine stark in my mind.

'She's fine,' I said, stopping and trying to switch the call to video so he could see for himself. Amaranth was standing in the middle of the floor with a golf club in both hands like a baseball bat, swinging it wildly and still screaming her head off.

'Amaranth!' I said. 'It's me. It's Lexy. Put the golf club down!'

'Mom!' Taylor bellowed from my phone.

'What is it?' Kathi had arrived, also doing a fairly decent Babe Ruth impersonation, but with an actual baseball bat.

'Cara, cara, cara,' said Maria, beetling into the room and walking straight up to the old lady, even though Amaranth was still swinging the golf club about fast enough to make it whistle. Maria dodged its arc like she'd trained the stuntmen for *The Matrix*.

Amaranth let Maria take the club out of her hands and lay it down but she didn't submit to the hug that followed. She struggled free and turned to me. 'Check the bathroom and under the bed,' she said. 'Someone's in here! I heard them.'

'I know,' I said. 'I heard them too. But I think they've gone.' She lunged for the club – of course she knew where it was. 'No! Wait!' I said. 'They've *definitely* gone.' Maria got the golf club back again while I was shouting and rolled it under the bed. 'I think . . .' I said. 'No! I don't think; I know. I know they absolutely no question ran away across the slough.'

'But there's *something* different,' Amaranth said. Her fingers were twitching and I knew that if she had a clue where Maria had put the club this time she would have grabbed it and held on harder.

'Uh, yeah something's different,' Todd said.

'You're taller,' said Amaranth. 'But it's not that.'

'Heels,' said Todd. 'But also the connecting door is open to Blaine's room. How did that happen?'

I turned to where he was pointing. I always forget about these connecting doors between the rooms. Noleen doesn't encourage their use – she says it attracts partying teens who can get sloppy, and extended families who can argue all night – but they're there. And now the door between Amaranth and the downstairs crime scene was lying open, its lock buckled and the latch on the door jamb splintered and useless. My blood drained at the thought of what lay behind it.

'Someone kicked it in,' I said.

'Noleen's going to need blood for that,' said Kathi.

'Did someone open that connecting door?' Molly's voice behind us was low and grim. 'I didn't tell you amateur gumshoes not to tamper with my crime scene. I didn't think I had to. But if someone has been in there . . .'

'Of course, no one's been in there!' I said, since she didn't mean the time I broke in and scraped up some spare blood no one else wanted. She meant tonight. 'Well, none of *us* has. But someone else has definitely been in there, and I wouldn't swear to it but I'd put a tenner on it, it was the killer. Because they just ran away across my boat. Again. And I saw everything and it was the same person.'

'Through the barbed wire?' said Molly. 'Cool. We might get some DNA.'

'Ah,' said Todd. 'Well, no. We had unlocked the wire, you see, to do a little experiment.'

Now he mentioned it, that was very unfortunate timing.

'What kind of experiment?' Molly said. 'And what the hell are you wearing?' Then she flicked her hand at him. 'Never mind.' She turned to me. 'You're telling me the killer came back? And broke into the crime scene?'

'Why would he do that?' I said.

Molly's eyes flashed. 'To retrieve something left behind,' she said. 'But why would anyone imagine that stuff would still be there for the taking, instead of tagged, bagged and locked in the evidence room? What you're saying makes no sense. Ergo it wasn't the killer.'

'Is that what "ergo" means?' said Taylor, but I had taken him off speaker so no one heard him except me. Probably just as well.

Molly had strolled towards the connecting door, to take a look at the state of the lock, I think, and see if it could be made secure. I certainly hoped so. We were running out of capacity, and if Amaranth had to shift, something would have to give. Such as Todd. Or Kathi.

I looked round at them, to bestow a smile of encouragement, and was disappointed to see them both edging towards the outside door. And doing it pretty furtively too. Even Molly's voice didn't stop them. And it could have stopped a runaway bull. Possibly a runaway train.

'What the hell is this I am looking at in here?' she said.

I felt my blood sink down my legs into my feet and drain out of me. What *was* she looking at?

'Is . . .?' I managed to say, though my mouth was sandpaper. Molly poked the door wide open with her elbow. 'Oh,' I added, when I got a view.

The bloodstained carpet was gone, replaced with a new one in a slightly darker shade. The bloodstained walls had been painted over in brilliant white. The furniture was still there, although the bed-frame might have been sanded and repolished. There was a new mattress in a wrapper sitting on top of it and new curtains, starched and stiff, at the window.

'Did another detective sign off on my crime scene?' Molly said, still in the bull-stopping, train-stopping, possibly tornado-stopping voice.

'Maybe we jumped the gun a little,' said Todd. 'But in our defence—'

'When did you *do this*?' I said. 'And where did you get the stuff? What's the point of Operation Cocker and all the agreements we signed if you two are going to go shopping?'

'Operation what?' said Molly.

'We did it last night, when we couldn't sleep for thinking about the mess,' Todd said. 'Blood, Lexy. Going bad. Attracting . . . what blood going bad attracts.'

'And of course we didn't go shopping,' said Kathi. 'It's stock. Use your eyes. It's the same rug and drapes. How could we go out to downtown Cuento and pick up trade furnishings like take-out?'

'Stock?' I said.

'Have you never wondered what we store in the store, behind the apartment?' Kathi said.

I never had. I didn't even know there *was* a store. I didn't know how far back into the corner below the Skweek the owners' apartment went because I had never been in it because Kathi had never allowed me to set foot over the door.

Molly had entered the pristine Room 102 by this time, ignoring Kathi's squeak of distress. She opened the front door and started snatching the crime-scene tape off the frame. 'Kinda pointless now,' she said. 'Even if you didn't cross it and I can't get you on criminal trespass.'

'Uh, Molly,' I said. 'Shouldn't you be doing another round of seeing if there's physical evidence left behind, instead of trampling all over it and letting the dust blow in off the forecourt?'

'What are you talking about?' Molly said.

'The killer? Kicking the door in? Maybe leaving more DNA in here? If there's a hair or a flake of skin,' Kathi moaned, 'and it's the same as a hair or a flake of skin from before then you've got him, haven't you?'

'Wait,' said Molly. 'Let me get this straight.' She turned to face Todd and Kathi. 'Are you saying you didn't kung-fu this door in to move mattresses?'

'Of course not,' Kathi said.

'Of course not,' Amaranth said too. 'You think just because I'm old and blind I wouldn't notice two people carrying drop cloths and rolled-up rugs through my room? Painting all night through an open doorway.'

'So you *did* cross crime-scene tape?' Molly said. Like she fully intended to arrest Kathi and Todd and make them go to a filthy, roach-infested jail cell.

'No,' Kathi said. She widened her stance until her feet were planted a yard apart. 'We got in through Della's room on the other side.'

'That door was locked on this side,' Molly said. 'You couldn't have.'

'It wasn't,' said Kathi. 'We did.'

They faced off for another few seconds. Maybe as long as half a minute. Molly blinked first. She deflated and turned away with a long sigh. 'Yeah, I can believe Huang tried the door, found it locked, and left it at that,' she said. 'But anyways . . .' She pulled the door closed as far as it would go and then started to reattach the crime-scene tape to block off access from Amaranth's room. 'Just until we do check for forensics,' she said. 'It won't take long, in an empty room.'

'Speaking of,' I said. 'Last time, did you—?'

'Excuse me,' Amaranth said. 'Can you have your little coffee klatch somewhere else, please? I need to use my bathroom and I don't want you all out here listening to me.'

She didn't have to tell me twice and Maria beat a retreat too. Molly lingered but not for long. 'When you get to my age,' Amaranth was saying as I passed out of earshot, 'with the pills and the vitamins and the eggs and the bran . . .'

'Well, you take care now, Ms Aaronovitch,' Molly said, backing away.

I saw my chance. She might answer my nosy questions just to make sure the subject was well and truly changed. 'So did you find any unaccounted-for DNA in there before, that you could match new stuff to now?' I asked her.

'We did,' said Molly. She turned to Kathi. 'Although, Mrs Muntz, the boys said they had never found less crud in a motel room in all their years of blacklights and sample scraping. All they got was the victim's hair, the kids' hair, and one other lot of hair. Just one. They were suspicious, until I explained the cleaning regime to them. So, professionally and personally, thank you, Kathi.' She turned to me. 'And thanks for the heads-up about the person of interest absconding over your deck again.' She turned to Maria. 'Mrs Bernal, we owe you one for—'

'What's she saying?' Taylor asked in my ear. I'd forgotten he was there.

'If you would stay here where you belong, you wouldn't find out everything second-hand. You'd be on the spot. I mean it's literally wild geese with you, isn't it?'

Molly swung round to face me. 'Don't push it,' she said. 'You are still of interest to this investigation. And it's very far from being wild geese. I have the kind of solid, swear-it-in evidence you rarely, if ever, get in a case of murder.'

I opened my mouth to explain, but Todd cut me off. 'Solid evidence about the motel business, tattoos, paediatrics, therapy, marriage, infidelity and wardrobe choices?'

'And I will find out which one leads to the killer,' said Molly.

'Or,' I said, 'you could just go after the killer.' She did a bit of eyebrow work. 'Ergo or not ergo, he went south over the fields. About ten minutes ago. I'm pretty sure he did anyway.'

I saw her reaction. It was another eye-flash, as plain as day. But I couldn't tell what she was reacting to.

Todd had caught it though. 'So you catch him, Sergeant Rankinson,' he said. 'And we'll stay out of your way.'

Molly reacted again and I still didn't know what to.

'Or,' said Kathi, 'stay home, Molly. Swim, read stories to the kids, eat Maria's cooking. Let the Sacramento PD pick him up.'

And another reaction and still I had no clue.

'Yeah, you stay safe here,' Kathi went on. 'Keep Arif's wife from stalking him. Stop Meera's husband if he ever decides to roll up too. You need to think about yourself. How can you even *be* a cop if you've had a kidney transplant?'

'Who said I had a kidney transplant?' Molly demanded.

'Or, you know, kidney disease and lost one,' Kathi said.

'Who said I had a disease?'

'Lexy told us you—' Todd began.

'I have one kidney because I donated the other one,' Molly said. 'I've never been sick a day in my life and I don't intend to start now. So go fuss over someone else, why don't you?'

She turned on her heel and marched off to the bottom of the steps, up them, along the balcony and, after an extensive fumble with her keys, into her room.

'This place sucks for dramatic exits,' I said. 'Especially in crêpe-soled shoes.' They both nodded but absently. And I knew why. Todd adored knowing something I didn't know. Kathi didn't hate it. 'What?' I said.

'You mean you didn't work it out?' said Todd, pressing his hand to his heart as if undone by shock.

'Sod off,' I told him. 'What have I missed?'

'Come on, Lexy,' Kathi said. 'I double-checked. Did you miss that too?'

I scrutinized both of them, trying to make completely sure they weren't messing with me. They weren't messing with me. They both wore identical looks of smug superiority.

'But tell me round on the boat,' I said. 'We should relock the wire before it's dark.'

Amaranth was back outside her door again, wearing a bathing dress – it really did demand more of a label than 'swimsuit' – of great antiquity and little elasticity. She had her scant hair covered in a cap made like a bunch of chrysanthemums, and a towel rolled under her arm.

'Maria is taking me swimming,' she said, as we passed. 'Taylor is such an old fuss budget about me swimming.'

I stopped. 'But you'll wait till Maria comes to fetch you, right?' I said. 'You won't jump in on your own? Right?'

'You're a perfect match,' Amaranth said. 'Taylor and you.'

I walked on a few steps but I was determined not to go round the corner until I was sure.

'I can hear you loitering,' Amaranth said. 'Fuss budget. You wait till you're my age and see how you like being treated like a toddler.'

'How old *are* you, Amaranth?' I said. It had only just occurred to me that whichever of Taylor's two ages was true, it would put his mother down in her seventies somewhere.

'Why?'

'Because Taylor said he was forty-four and—'

'Ha,' she said. 'Forty-four? And you believed him? He bribed me with Audible credits to get me to say "forty-six" to you.'

I stood staring at her, trying to clear my mind of all preconceptions. What age of woman was this standing here before me, with her knotted veins and turtle spine? Eighty-five? Oh my God, ninety? And how old would that make my boyfriend

exactly? If she had bought that swimming cap when it was new
. . . But she couldn't have. It must be reproduction.

'I love kitschy vintage too,' I said, sending it up like a test
balloon.

'You love what?' Amaranth snapped.

Shit.

Thankfully, before I was forced to summon all my courage
and ask her straight out, Maria and Barb appeared in their
respective doorways. Barb was wearing a bikini that was mostly
gold chains and only three tiny triangles of Lycra. Maria wore
a pair of José's long silky shorts and one of his basketball tops,
like old ladies in California should be required to, by law. She
had her hair scraped up into a Croydon facelift, suggesting that
she was also planning to swim as old ladies should, with her
head sticking up like a periscope.

'Who's looking after the kids?' I said. I was just making
conversation, but all three of them rounded on me as if I'd
started something serious.

'Why?' said Maria.

'Oh, so we're not allowed any me-time,' said Barb.

'Drill sergeant,' said Amaranth.

I put my hands up and backed away. 'Jeez, sorry. Don't
shoot. Wow.'

'José and Arif are taking a turn,' Barb said. 'Young people
are supposed to get that men can look after kids and women
can change tyres, ain't they?'

'Thanks, Barb,' I said, even though there was no way she
would know what for, and went to join Todd and Kathi.

'Whoever invented this stuff,' Todd was saying, trying to
bend wire with his thumbs and forefingers like a Southern
debutante eating fried chicken on a picnic, 'has a sadistic
streak. Ow!'

'Oh for God's sake,' said Kathi. 'Hold it firmly between the
barbs and show it who's boss.'

'*It's* boss,' said Todd. 'Owie.'

'So,' I said, 'I wished aloud that I'd caught him. Todd told
Molly to follow him across the fields so she could catch him.
Then, Kathi, you told her to let the Sac cops catch him. And
she totally failed to keep her poker face. Is that it?'

'Congratulations for getting there in the end,' Todd said.

'Make her say it in case she's bluffing,' said Kathi, as she snapped the padlock shut on the repositioned wire.

'Good point,' said Todd. 'Spell it out, Lex.' He stood with his hands on his hips and stared me down. It was disconcerting having him loom like that.

'Can you take those ridiculous shoes off?' I said. 'Why do you even own them? Cork wedges?'

'For a bathing beauty pageant,' Todd said, like that was an explanation. I didn't have the energy to enquire further, though, because he'd reminded me of Amaranth's swimming cap and ropy veins, wrecked digestion, and total blindness, and once again I was consumed with panic about how old Taylor was.

'There's no "him" to catch,' I said. 'The DNA left in Blaine's room – the stuff that wasn't Blaine's, that is – belonged to a woman.'

'Well done,' said Todd. 'Slow and steady but you made it.' He sank on to the swing seat and started unbuckling the ludicrous wedges. 'But we don't think they've actually had time to get DNA back yet, do we Kathi? Even our back-room rush job that Phil's doing isn't back yet. But think about what Molly said: hair. Two lots of adult hair and two lots of kids' hair. She said nothing about skin flakes – sorry, Kathi – or secretions – sorry, Kathi. Just hair. Which is naked-eye stuff, right? Even I could tell baby hair from toddler hair from adult hair.'

'But male hair versus female hair?' I said.

'Probably long hairs, coloured and well-conditioned,' said Todd. 'Something like that. Let's not quibble. The killer – Detective Rankinson has just revealed, although she doesn't know it – was a woman.'

'And that's great, isn't it?' I said. 'It means our client isn't a murderer. It means Roger isn't rooming with a murderer.' I took a moment to let this welcome reality sink in. 'Wait though. Are there female hitmen?'

'Are there even hitmen?' said Todd. 'In real life? In Cuento?'

'Google it,' I said.

'Uh, no,' said Todd. 'With cops sniffing around us and the

possibility of search warrants, I am not googling for a hitman. You google it.'

'Arse,' I said. 'I meant google the stats on Wikipedia, not "Hey, Alexa, contract killers near me".'

Kathi had beaten us both to it. 'Two per cent,' she said, looking up from her phone.

'Of hitmen are women?'

'Of murderers are contracted out. Worldwide.'

'And surely nearly all of them are men,' I said. 'So we'd be looking at a tiny fraction of a two per cent chance that it was a hit Phil Temple paid for? I reckon we could say he's innocent, don't you?'

'Does eliminating him help us any?' said Kathi.

'It means we can trust what he tells us,' Todd said. 'For a start. And we stop worrying about Roger when he's at home, if not when he's at work. And we look for women with a motive to kill Blaine.'

'Which presumably is what Molly thought she was doing when she chewed us all out,' said Kathi. 'Right? You, me, Noleen, Meera.'

'But she chewed out Arif and me too,' said Todd. 'Covering her tracks?'

'But not Della, Barb, or Maria,' I added. 'So maybe not, eh?'

'Hey, you don't think . . .' Todd began, sitting up very straight, as if he'd just been tasered, if tasered made you sit up straight rather than fall to the floor. But before he could finish the thought, Kathi held up one finger and cocked her head, listening.

And now I could hear it too. Someone was creeping through the undergrowth on the far bank, edging slowly towards to the boat.

'Sssshhhh,' breathed Kathi, and the three of us waited with held breath as the rustling came closer and closer. Then there was a pause and a clattering thump as someone tried to leap on to the deck and got tangled in the wire hidden by the deep shadowed darkness.

'Fuck!' The cry rang out clear and sharp in the stillness. Clear, sharp, *and* high-pitched. It was definitely a woman.

SEVENTEEN

Friday 20 March

I woke before Taylor the next morning and lay looking at him with new eyes. Had I stopped him going through to the other bed last night just so I'd have this chance in cold daylight to stare and stare, without him asking me what I was looking at? Could be.

Of course, everyone looks young flat on their back after eight hours' sleep. I nuzzled in closer to peer at the fine lines around his eyes and the creases either side of his mouth. If he was older than forty-six he must have got into Korean skincare as an early adopter, because there *weren't* any lines and creases worth the name. Maybe he was forty-seven, but that birthday had felt like a continental divide, and he was enjoying this wee trip back to the other side of it.

And even if he was forty-eight. Did I care?

I did not.

But I cared a great deal about the fact he hadn't told me.

I was in that exclusive club of second wives who had emigrated from home to marry a man who was only marrying them to make a point to his first wife, and who barely paused in the re-wooing and re-bedding of that ex-wife for his honeymoon with his new wife, and who did some of that bedding right there in the brand-new marital bed. So, like all members of that club, I was now one of honesty's biggest fans. Finding out Taylor was lying had floored me.

I refocused my attention on his neck and tried to have a serious think to myself about the concept of *white* lies. Lying about your age is not the same as lying about knocking off your ex. And maybe Taylor could get special dispensation. His neck had no crêpe swags, no plucked chicken, no turkey wattle, nothing. Maybe if I asked him straight out and he told me without pausing, I could let it go. But if I asked him and he waffled then, despite everything, we might be history.

There was no more time to plan my attack, because his eyeballs were moving under his eyelids, and his lashes were fluttering, and his eyes were open, and he turned his head and smiled at me.

'How old was your mum when she had you?' I said, because crapping out of a straight question was different from crapping out of a straight answer.

He took his sweet time saying anything back but, when he had gathered his nerve he took my nearest hand in his and said: 'I'm glad you asked me.'

'Don't play for time.'

'OK.'

'So?'

'I really am glad you asked me,' he said. 'The truth is I don't know.'

I lifted myself up to climb over him and escape. And get this: he thought I was climbing on to him to stay a while.

'Heyyyy,' he said, in the cheesiest voice I had ever heard come out of him. He gripped my hips. Briefly, until he saw my face.

'What's up?' he said.

'You "don't know"?' I said. 'You "*don't know*"? Because lying about your age runs in your family and your mum would no more tell you how old she is than you would tell me how old you are?'

'What have you heard?' he asked. 'What did she say?'

'That's right,' I said. 'That's what every innocent person always says. "What have you heard." Jesus, Taylor. You know what Bran did to me. You must know that being straight with me is more important than anything else and yet . . .' I was struggling into some clothes and trying to do it without letting him see any of my body, which is not easy in a small room with two mirrors. '. . . and here we are stuck together for God knows how many more weeks until this house arrest or whatever we're calling it is over. Thanks very much.'

'Look, Lexy,' he said, sitting up and letting the covers fall to his waist. Bastard. If he hadn't lied to me about it I wouldn't have cared how old he was, because he was in fantastic shape.

Sitting there all naked and— No! I was going to be strong. This was not going to happen to me again.

'Look what?' I demanded.

'You're probably still rattled from last night,' he said.

Of course, dumping him would go better if he kept making it this easy. 'I'm "rattled" from last night?' I said. Something in my voice made him clutch the covers up to his chest. 'I've had the kind of shock we women aren't really built for and it'll take me a few days of bland food and light reading to settle down again?'

'Um,' he said.

I had enough clothes on my body to be decent, and plenty more clutched in my hands to form an actual outfit. I gave him a cold look and stalked off.

But the truth was, as I got to the front door and out on to my porch, I did have a short flashback to the night before and it was unpleasant enough to make me shudder.

After that single high-pitched 'fuck', Todd, Kathi and I had frozen in a tableau of utter panic. She was back! The person – woman – who had killed Blaine, made her getaway over my deck, returned to boot in the connecting door, and once again high-tailed it off across my boat, was back.

But this time the wire had caught her. We could all hear her scuffling and struggling like a trapped rat, halfway up the side of the narrow deck.

'Call nine-one-one,' Todd breathed.

'No,' said Kathi even softer. 'I'll call Molly.'

'What if she gets away?' I said. I would have sworn I was just as quiet as them but, as I spoke, the scuffling stopped.

Todd shot me a hell of a look and then stood up, signalling for Kathi and me to flank him. He squared himself and stepped round the corner of the living-room wall so he was facing the side deck. I peeped round his left shoulder. I could see a bulge where there should have been only the sleek line of the deck rail. A bulge. A crumpled, curled-up, person-sized bulge. Blaine in the dry bath was back behind my eyelids again and my palms were sweating.

'Why are you back?' said Todd in a voice I didn't know he had in him.

The bulge said nothing.

'What do you want?' I could feel his voice through my feet. The bulge whimpered but no more.

'The cops are coming,' said Kathi. 'It's over.'

'The cops?' said the bulge at last. 'No, please don't call the cops. I'm sorry.'

'You're . . . sorry?' I said. '*Sorry?*'

'I was desperate,' said the bulge. 'Oh please, Lexy. I can explain. Todd, please, you don't know what it's like. Kathi, please, I thought you understood.'

'You know us?' said Todd. 'You know our names?'

'What?' said the bulge.

And at last Kathi switched on her phone light.

'Meera?' I said as the beam lit up her pale, tear-stained face. 'What the hell are you doing?'

'I'm stuck on this freaking wire,' she said. 'Please help me. And don't call the cops on me. I was careful. Please.'

'Just one question though,' said Todd. 'Did you kill Blaine?'

'*What?*' Meera said. 'Why would you say that to me? Why would I kill a total stranger? What the hell are you talking about?'

'OK, OK, OK,' I said. 'Stop struggling. You'll only hurt yourself even more. Where's it sticking in you?' I went over and switched my own phone light on too. She was caught in the wire by both legs and one arm like a cat's cradle. But that wasn't the weirdest thing. She seemed to have puffed up since the last time I saw her. 'What the hell happened to you?' I said. 'Are you having some kind of allergic reaction?'

'No,' Meera said. 'I'm wearing three pairs of yoga pants and a pair of jeans and three shirts and two jackets. So it's not sticking in me anywhere but I can't bend my limbs enough to get free.'

'Why?' said Todd. He didn't actually laugh but, as he started plucking the barbs out of the top layer of Meera's clothing, his eyes were dancing.

'In case anyone saw me,' Meera said. 'I couldn't walk back in with bags of shopping.'

'You've been clothes shopping?' said Kathi.

'I was desperate!'

'You betrayed Operation Cocker to go clothes shopping?' said Todd. 'I mean I knew you were a bit of a—'

I shushed him, because Meera had started silently weeping. 'I'm not a bit of an anything,' she said. 'I couldn't stand wearing those clothes he picked out for me and forced me into. Not any more. I saw you all looking and judging. So I went to Target for sweats. Sorry.'

'Meera,' I said, 'you've no idea what trouble you caused. When you bounded across the deck earlier I truly thought you were the killer. You're the same shape and weight as the killer. Well, not right now but usually.'

'I didn't bound across the deck earlier,' Meera said. 'I went out the front way.'

'Without being seen?' said Kathi. 'Jeez, our security is Swiss cheese.'

'I didn't stroll out, waving to everyone,' said Meera. 'Barb ordered food and got the key from Noleen to open the front gate. Amaranth kept Noleen talking. Maria was asking you about borrowing an iron, Kathi. So I slipped out when no one was looking and I said I would come back in this way when it was dark.'

'Wearing it all,' I said. 'Like Heidi.'

'Who?' said Meera.

'She says random British stuff like that just to bug us,' Todd said. 'We ignore it now.'

'Heidi is Swiss,' I said.

'Random Euro stuff,' Todd said.

'Shirley Temple played her in the movie,' I said. 'Wait.' I turned back to Meera, and the matter in hand. Todd had just prised open the last piece of wire scissoring her into immobility and now she twisted free and landed on the deck with a very muffled thump, three sets of sweats breaking her fall. 'If that wasn't you, then you were lucky it was only barbed wire caught you. You could have run into the killer too. Because *someone* bounded across the boat and set off into the fields.'

That freaked her out enough for her to insist we take her back to her room and check it over before she went in alone. (Bob and Joan were spending the night with their new grandparents. In fact, we could all hear José's voice singing a lullaby through his open window as we came round the corner.)

'Hey!' Barb shouted from the pool. 'What happened to our deal?'

'The plan went wrong!' Meera shouted back.

'What was the plan?' said Kathi.

'I was going to wave from here and Amaranth was going to pretend to drown, to cause a distraction. When everyone was at the pool I was going to waddle to my room unseen.'

'And how is that a "deal"?' Todd said.

'Barb was going to make a rope out of her bikini to tow Amaranth to safety.'

'Ah,' said Todd.

'How is *that* a deal?' I said.

'Oh God, Lexy,' said Todd. 'You know my mom. Have you never heard her bit on the amazing silky luxury of free swimming?'

'Mmmmmm,' came Barb's voice from the deep end of the pool. 'There is nothing like the feeling of warm water coursing over your skin unimpeded. You have no idea . . .'

'Unless you've ever had . . . a bath!' said Todd. He had one hand over his eyes.

'I'm keeping up my end of the bargain!' shouted Barb.

I didn't have Todd's problems and I watched in awe and admiration as Barb floated flat on her back, legs and arms starfished and naked body gleaming in the security lights.

'What the—?' said Molly's voice as she came out on to the walkway and looked down. 'Oh God,' she said, and scurried back inside again, just as Amaranth's bathing dress, newly removed from her body, began to whip around like a propeller, spraying water over everyone.

'Yeee-hawwww!' she said. 'Barb, you're dead right. This feels great!'

And of course it was then that Taylor's truck rolled up to be let in. Noleen opened the gate. He drove to a parking space, climbed down, looked at the scene in the pool for a moment, chewing on his lip, and then shook his head and walked away.

'Two days,' he said. 'She's been here two days. What the hell's she going to do for a big blow-out on Saturday night?' He kissed me. 'Hey, Lex,' he said.

'Hey, *Tay*,' I said. I wanted him to ask why I was being sarcastic when all he had said was hello. Then I would tell him I didn't like games. Such as lying about your age and getting your poor old mum to help you. And he'd either fold or play a new one. Unfortunately, random sarcasm being my default setting, it barely registered.

'I'm going to get changed,' Meera said. 'It's kind of hot with all this on.'

'Can I ask what you've done with your old clothes?' said Todd. He was still hiding his eyes. 'You didn't cut them into pieces or put them in a burn barrel or anything, did you?'

'Do you want them?' Meera said. 'Are you going to make the world's tackiest quilt? Or are you thinking ahead to Halloween?'

'Not that old things are necessarily tacky,' I said. 'Old can be good.'

Todd gave me a look and so did Meera, but still nothing from Taylor.

'No quilts, no costumes,' said Todd. 'Trust me.' He grinned at her then took his hand away from his eyes as his phone started ringing. 'Roger,' he said, and answered. 'You OK? You sick? What's wrong? What's up? Is Phil—?'

At which point I assume Roger finally got a word in.

'What?' said Todd after a pause. 'Are you serious? When? Last night? Just once?' He opened his eyes wide just in time to see Barb haul herself out of the pool. 'Oh gack!' he said. 'Not you. Mom's swimming in the nude again. But are you actually serious?'

'What's up?' I said.

'I won't,' said Todd into the phone. 'I promise I won't. No one. Of course I mean it. I swear. I'll call you back when I can talk, OK?'

Then he hung up the phone. 'You will not believe what Roger—'

'Stop!' I said. 'Were you just about to tell us what you swore you wouldn't tell us?'

'Oh, phooey,' said Todd. 'You'll never guess what he—'

'No!' I said. 'Todd, for God's sake. Stop. We all just heard you promise your husband that you would not betray this confidence. So don't.'

'Well,' said Todd. '*Who's* been on an ethics course?'

'Get lost,' I said. 'It's not that, it's just that I've had a recent reminder of how crucial trust is in a relationship. Trust and honesty.'

Todd flicked a look at Taylor with his eyebrows up. 'Say, Lexy,' he said. 'I'm just spit-balling here, but is there a chance that you're not entirely talking about Roger and me?'

'What did you do?' Kathi asked Taylor. Then she turned to me. 'That straight-talking enough for you?' Next she turned to Todd. 'Is it anything to do with the case?'

'Nope,' Todd said. 'It's just Roger flipping out.'

'So don't tell us,' she said. She turned back to Taylor. 'And don't be a dick to Lexy, OK?'

'Wasn't planning to,' Taylor said. I kind of loved him sticking up for himself, even though I hated him for lying to me about his age. I've folded when Kathi was having a go at me, and more than once. They stared at each other some more. Then Taylor stared at Todd for a bit. Finally he turned to me. 'I could stay in my mom's room tonight if you like,' he said. 'I've never been interested in a foursome.'

'No need to overreact,' I said. 'I'll see you later and maybe we can talk this through.'

'Tell me what *it* is and I'll talk all night.' And with that he left.

'Damn,' said Todd, watching him go. He got three syllables out of it.

'Oops,' said Kathi. 'Sorry, Lex. I was messing with him for shits and giggles. But that looked serious. What did he lie to you about?'

'His age,' I said.

'Oh come on!' said Todd. 'How old can he be? He doesn't look any older than you.'

Amaranth was now headed back to her room, leaning on Barb's arm. They had towels on, thank God, but still. I nodded towards them. 'That,' I said, 'is his mum. So you tell me.'

Todd whistled and Kathi opened her eyes wide and nodded slowly.

'See what I mean?' I said. 'If forty-four was a lie and forty-six was the next lie, where's it going to end? How old does Amaranth look to you? How old would that make Taylor?'

'In a skimpy towel,' said Todd, 'with her hair plastered down and right next to a woman pushing sixty, for comparison . . . I'm afraid to say, Lexy, Taylor could be AARP.'

It's one of the more annoying things about people here that they try to tell you ages in ways impossible to understand. 'Middle school,' they say when you ask how old their kid is. 'Ninth grade,' they add, as if that helps, when you point out that 'middle school' isn't a number. AARP wasn't a number either.

'How old is AARP?' I said.

'Don't tell her,' Kathi said.

'Oh,' I said. 'That old, eh?'

Of course, I could have googled it, but the truth is I didn't really want to know. I wanted Taylor back, smiling at me, choosing to sleep in my tiny spare bed or even my tiny *own* bed, instead of threatening to move to the other queen in Amaranth's room, through the flimsy bathroom door from her digestive adventures. (How could I not have realized how bloody ancient she was before now?)

Then I told myself there was more going on than one short relationship having its first wobble and I should direct my attention elsewhere. I went to join him on the boat, repeating to myself that there was the case to think about. There was the virus to be taken into consideration. There was the brand-new community finding its feet here at the Last Ditch, challenged only by Target runs, naked swimming, and the pressure of finding a dinner menu everyone liked night after night after night in a row.

He met me in the passageway, wearing only his boxers and damp from the fastest shower even an ecological warrior ever took. 'Talk?' he said, pointing at the living room. So he *did* care that something was bugging me then. 'Sleep?' he added, pointing his chin to the spare room where he could stretch out and let me stretch out in my room across the way. 'Or . . .?' he said, pushing open the door to my cramped little bedroom and smiling at me.

No contest.

'Good!' said Todd, the next morning, as I met him and Kathi on the forecourt. 'You got over yourself and stopped obsessing about an arbitrary number.'

'How can you tell . . . Never mind!' I said. 'Yes. I did make the most of the evening as it happens. Then, this morning, I tried to do some of that boring relationship crap I'm always recommending.'

'Wow,' said Kathi. 'I know it's not ideal to take your work home with you, but you can go too far the other way.'

'And it got worse!' I said. 'He's still lying about his age, but now he's doubled down and started lying about Amaranth's too. Well, fudging. Right now, in bed, he wriggled and slithered and blustered and bullshat. And you know, after what happened with Bran . . .'

'That's not fair,' said Kathi. 'The new guy can't pay for what the last guy did. Todd, tell her.'

'No time,' Todd said. 'We've got a mission. The Skweeky-Kleen's inaugural no-contact laundry drop. With a little something extra. Let's go!'

The streets were deserted. We saw a couple walking a small dog on the edge of downtown and a young man with a baby in a sling who was obviously just walking up and down his block trying to get it to go to sleep. There was a postie dropping off mail and, most disturbing of all, there were three squad cars gliding about the residential areas, rolling from stop sign to stop sign with a cop looking out each open window.

'Thank God for the decal,' Todd said. He had slapped the 'Skweeky-Kleen' name and washtub logo on the side of his Jeep before we set off.

'This is unreal,' I said. 'What are they looking for?'

'People out when they should be in,' said Todd. He shivered. 'I've only ever seen this after a shooting before. This quiet and cops on the prowl.'

'A shooting? In Cuento?'

'Sac,' he said, shaking his head. 'Years ago.'

'Do you think this'll work?' I asked him. I was clutching a bundle of Meera's clothes, trying not to let them get tangled.

'I really do,' Todd said. 'Look at the state she was in, and Arif was in, at the start of the week. Of course it'll work. It's going to look fantastic. It's art and activism, justice and mayhem all rolled into one. We need to make sure and get some good clear shots of it once it's up. Put it online.'

'We can't put it on our professional website,' I said. It still bugged me that 'we' even had a website. I certainly didn't want it to turn into the kind of carnival Todd was going for. But we had just taken the corner on to Meera's street and Todd was slowing down at the end of her driveway.

'God bless Google Earth,' he said. 'There is the handy hackberry tree and there on the other side of the lot is the handy eucalyptus, just like we saw. Perfect. You ready?'

'As I'll ever be,' I said and hopped down.

It looked fantastic when we were done and we were done in a minute flat. Working late into the night, Todd had turned every one of Meera's obnoxious degrading micro-mini dresses, low-cut blouses, transparent nighties and shortie shorts into covers for huge cardboard letters that he then stapled to a rope just the right length to fill her house's front garden from one corner to the other.

I MADE MY WIFE WEAR CLOTHES THAT BARELY COVERED HER BRUISES, it said. Todd took two photographs of the bunting alone and then made me take two of him standing sternly pointing at it. He texted all four to the *Cuento Voyager* as we were driving away.

'Not that we need them,' he said. 'Look.' At houses on either side and opposite, neighbours were already out on their front lawns with phones aloft, snapping away. 'Everyone's home,' he said. 'Silver lining.'

I had set up my first morning of online appointments, helped no end by the insurance companies waiving the co-pay for the duration of the downtime or whatever we were going to call it, and spurred on by the thought that if I did some on a Friday and it was a disaster, I'd have the weekend to work out what was wrong. If I waited until Monday, I'd have to plough through five long days of poor tech and ill-judged etiquette, making things worse for everyone.

So I jumped down from the Jeep as soon as Noleen opened the gate for us and bustled off towards the boat.

'How'd it go?' she shouted after me.

'Smooth as silk,' I shouted back. 'I don't know what we'll do if it rains but it was fine today.'

'I don't mean dropping off bundles of laundry on driveways,' she shouted next. 'How could that go wrong? I meant the . . . waddaya call it . . . not "wanking".'

'No!' I shouted louder than ever. 'Not wanking. Bunting! Stop shouting.'

'Well, stop shouting "wanking" anyway,' said Taylor, suddenly beside me. He gave me a smile. I didn't return it.

'I've got clients,' I said. 'I need to go.'

'I'll try to keep Molly away from you,' he said. 'She's pretty keen to get a follow-up interview.'

'What about?' I said, then waved away his answer since I really was late now and didn't have time.

In my office, I carefully started up the Zoom programme I had downloaded and installed. I considered reading the instructions that popped up in the 'let's get started!' dialogue box. But then another box popped up in front of that one telling me my client was waiting somewhere in the ether for me to click a button and get the show on the road.

'Hi!' I said, when her face appeared in a little window beside my own.

'Oh no!' she said, putting her hands up. 'I never even thought of this. Am I going to have to sit and look at it for an hour?'

I twisted round to see what she was talking about. There was nothing on the wall behind me that she hadn't been facing in every other session we'd had. 'Look at what?' I said.

'Can't you hide it?'

'Hide what?'

'This isn't going to work. This is torture for me. I can't bear to look at it.'

'It being . . .?' I said.

'Thank you for trying to be kind,' she said, 'but don't patronize me.'

'I'm not,' I said. 'Anyway, I'm glad you've got used to whatever it was and you're calm again.'

'I've draped a Kleenex over my screen,' she said. 'I can't see myself.'

I nodded sagely. Nodding sagely while inside you're going 'that's bonkers' is a skill therapists develop early. 'And that's better because there's an aspect of your appearance that you're unhappy with?' I said. We had had three counselling sessions already and this was the first I'd heard of body issues.

'Please,' she said. 'I mean it. It feels like you're laughing at me when you do that.'

'Carly,' I told her, 'I have no clue what specific thing about your appearance you think is out of line with the rest of it. Trust me.'

She frowned. 'Seriously?'

'Seriously. If you want to talk about it, you're going to have to tell me what it is we're talking about.'

'Seriously?' she said again.

'Seriously.'

'It's kind of hard to believe. I mean, you're looking right at it.'

'Listen,' I said. 'I went to a seminar on the psychology of plastic surgery once and the most interesting thing was the tiny number of plastic surgeons who can look at a new patient and guess what they're there for.'

'Scr—?' she began. 'Sorry.'

'Now, I didn't get many pre-plastic-surgery counselling sessions in Dundee,' I said. 'In fact, none. And since I moved here . . . none again. But if I ever do, I'm planning to advise my client to go in for a free assessment and if the surgeon can't tell what they're there for when they walk through the door, they turn round and walk right out again.'

'So you think I need plastic surgery?' she said.

'No! What did I just say?'

'If I was *going* to have plastic surgery,' she tried next, 'what would you think I'd be having done?'

'Well, I'm not going to answer that, am I?' I said. 'How could anyone answer that? You wouldn't answer that if I asked you, would you?'

'Cheeks,' she said.

Which is why I ended up draping a tissue hankie over my half of the screen too.

EIGHTEEN

M olly didn't catch me till lunchtime. I wouldn't have said she'd made enough visits to my boat that I'd recognize her tread, but as soon as I felt the dip to the porch end and heard the thump of feet climbing the steps, I braced myself.

'You here?' she shouted.

I came out into the passageway and looked at her along its length. 'Do you know what poor maritime etiquette it is to board a boat without asking?'

'Nah,' said Molly. 'Not the porch of a houseboat. This is your yard. I haven't entered your front door. And this isn't maritime. It's a slough.'

So she was in that mood.

'Are you here to take up the case of a wife-beater? Again?' I said. 'Because Meera co-owns that property and we had her permission.'

'Huh?' said Molly, which was good news. Scumspouse clearly hadn't gone whining to his buddies in blue this time. 'I'm here to interview you as part of the investigation into the murder.'

'Alone?' I said. But she was already thumbing her phone and, before another moment had passed, Officer Huang was with us. Molly pointed me back into my consultation room, set the phone up on a little easel and sat herself down, taking a notebook out of her back pocket in a practised move.

'So, the last time we spoke you told us you had offered several sessions of unsolicited and unwanted advice to Mrs Temple about her marriage and her parenting.'

'No, I didn't,' I said. '*You* told me I did that and I told you I didn't. Because I didn't.'

'Really nitty-gritty stuff like nutritional choices and the balance of care-giving between mother and father.'

'Nope,' I said.

'So you're changing your statement?'

'Look, for God's sake Molly, what is this about? We talked about a downstairs room, snotty doctors' wives, dinner choices, FaceTime, me-time – well, her-time – and that's about it.'

'Quite a conversation for two people who'd just met two minutes before.'

'It would be,' I said carefully, 'but it wasn't a conversation. And I'm pretty sure I told you that. It was four. One when she turned up, one at dinner, one when I filmed her kids and one when I caught her eating a PayDay bar instead of practising.' I cast my mind back and counted off on my fingers. 'Yep. Four. Plus she was around in the general area when the first two signs were found.'

'So roughly . . .?' said Molly.

'Not roughly,' I said. 'Exactly. Four.'

'I mean, roughly when are you claiming these conversations took place?'

'Claiming, eh?' I said. 'OK. Saturday, when she turned up. Saturday night at dinner, Sunday morning and Monday morning with the signs, and then twice more on Monday – the PayDay conversation and the one about filming her kids.'

'So,' said Molly, looking up after making a long note, 'three conversations on Monday.'

'Two and an interaction,' I said.

'On Monday.'

'Yes,' I said. 'Why?'

'And this "interaction",' she went on, ignoring my question. Power does nothing for your manners. 'How many people would you say witnessed it?'

'Finding the second sign on Monday morning?' I said. 'Witnessed that, you mean?'

'Witnessed Blaine Temple's part in it.'

'I couldn't say,' I said. 'I mean, she was there in her doorway, and so was everyone else, so, I suppose, everyone.'

'And yet you're not willing to say?'

'Well, to be honest,' I told her, although even while the words were leaving my mouth I remembered that they're supposed to be a sign someone's lying, 'I can't be absolutely sure she was there at all. I think she was, but the thing is that Sunday morning and Monday morning have blended together. The sign, the screaming, Arif and Meera scared, everyone standing around. I think Blaine was there both mornings. Why?'

'But it was definitely Monday that she ate a PayDay bar in her practice room?' Molly said, yet again declining to answer me.

'I wouldn't swear to it,' I said. 'I think it was but, since you're pressing me so hard, I'm not willing to swear.'

'And definitely Monday when you filmed her kids?'

'But,' I said. '*But* definitely Monday. Not "and", since I just told you I wasn't sure.'

'Ahem.' It was Officer Huang speaking from Molly's propped-up phone. 'If you have the film, it'll be time-stamped,' she said.

'Well, I don't,' I said. 'It was Todd's phone and he's obsessive about clearing stuff out of his camera. It comes from taking so many selfies every day while dressing. But if all we want to do is make sure what day it was, the message I sent to Phil might still be in the sent folder.'

'Oopsie,' said Molly. 'You tripped yourself up there.'

'I have no idea what you're talking about,' I said, 'but I can't have tripped myself up because I'm telling you the absolute unvarnished God's honest truth. No matter what flying carpet *you've* decided to go for a trip on.'

'If you have the message you used to send the film, then you have the film,' said Molly.

'Oh yeah!' I said. 'Good point. Thank you. It might not still have its time-stamp on it if it's in an attachment though.' Neither of them said anything. 'Would you . . . like me to go and get Todd's phone and see?'

'Er no,' said Molly. 'I don't believe I would like you to go and have a private conversation with Dr Kroger, and then be alone with his phone while you bring it back here, where you would no doubt discover that the folder has been emptied into the trash and the trash has been deleted.'

I didn't realize Officer Huang had left our meeting until he came back. 'He's coming,' he said.

'Who's . . .?' I said, then felt the dip and patter of Todd landing on the bottom step and trotting up to the porch level.

'Lexy, are you OK?' he called. 'Someone from the cops just phoned me and told me to come and . . . Where are you?'

'Office,' I called back.

Todd blew in on a wave of menthol and coconut. 'Meera just gave me the most restorative facial I've ever . . . Oh.' He'd seen Molly. 'What's going on?'

'Dr Todd Kroger has entered the interview room,' said Molly.

'Todd, have you still got the message I sent to Phil on your phone?' I said. ''Member, when I filmed Navy and Salem swimming on the tarmac?'

'No,' said Todd.

'Well, no, because you weren't there. You were . . . trying to make over Arif and you told me to take the phone in case it was something I can't remember, but it was Roger. That was Monday, right?'

'Oh my Gordon Ramsay Kitchen Nightmare!' said Todd. '*Now* I remember. I said take the phone in case it was the *Voyager*, because I pitched a listicle. Have you written it? It's due today.'

'Good luck,' I said. 'Let me know if you need me to proof-read it. But for now, gimme your phone.'

Todd handed it over and my heart soared. That was another one in the eye for Molly's cynicism. He didn't care why I wanted it; he had nothing to hide from me or from the cops. Well, actually as I scrolled through his camera I saw that he had plenty to hide, at least when he'd been away from his beloved for five long days. I tried not to look too closely until I'd scrolled way past last Monday and could confirm that the video of the kids was gone. I went to his email next and found the sent folder.

'Aha!' I said. 'Here it is.'

I opened the file, hit play, and angled it so Molly and Huang could both watch. I couldn't see it but then I didn't need to. I was there. Whatever ferret they had got down their jodhpurs this should sort it.

I watched Molly's face as she watched the video, waiting for the moment she realized that she was up a gum tree if she thought Todd or I had anything to hide. When the sound of the children's squeals ended and she raised her eyes to mine, the look she gave me was one of mixed puzzlement and pity.

'What?' I said.

'Yeah, what?' said Todd.

Molly shook her head and said nothing.

'What?' I said again. 'Do you want me to find the time-stamp? Let me just check and see.'

'There's absolutely no need whatsoever, Lexy,' she said.

'Why not?'

'Yeah, why not?' said Todd.

'The interview is terminated at 12.46 p.m.,' Molly said. She lifted her phone off its little easel and hit some buttons. 'Thank you for your time, Ms Campbell,' she said. 'You can go.'

'This is my house,' I said.

'If I can use this room to interview Dr Kroger now, things might go a lot smoother.'

'You've already interviewed me,' said Todd. 'I can help you with issues of personal organization, if you like. It's a question of careful record-keeping and I've just learned this amazing technique developed in . . . Oh, you mean, a *second* interview?'

'And if Ms Campbell is withholding access to this room, then you might need to go to the police station. Officer Huang can interview, with me dialling in.'

'Why can't you interview Todd in your room like you did me?' I said.

'Oh, now you're just being silly,' said Todd. 'I was multi-tasking. I wasn't even going to charge you.'

I didn't need to hear the details. Clearly, during his interview, he had opened her wardrobe and divided her outfits into a huge bale of nos and a few yeses; he might have gone into her bathroom and ripped into her cosmetics and skincare; he might even have opened drawers. Whatever had happened, he wasn't getting into her room again.

'Can't you go to Todd's?' I said.

'Oh yes!' He clapped his hands together. 'And I can give you a deep facial while you ask questions. I know we can all do it ourselves but there's nothing like a bit of pampering. Meera has just turned me into a teenager again with her magic thumbs.'

'You are not laying thumbs on me,' said Molly.

'A hydrating mask then,' said Todd.

'You can stay here,' I said. 'As long as I get it back by two.'
I didn't know how Todd could even consider a mask. I would
never use one again after seeing Blaine with those silicon armour
plates stuck to her poor dead face in that bathroom. I knew my
cheeks had paled as I thought of it and I hurried off to find a
distraction.

Della was sitting in a plastic chair in the bit of the forecourt
that was turning into the coffee shop, or gossip station, as the
days passed by. I had tried to get the notion off the ground that
we would call it the 'wash house' just for a blast of home, but
that sent Todd off into apocryphal stories – that he swore were
memories – of bath houses in San Francisco, and *they* made Kathi
want to bleach everything. Noleen had taken charge anyway, I
saw as I sat down. 'NO BICKERING IN THE LOUNGE' said
a folded cardboard sign on the plastic table.

'Lounge, eh?' I said, sitting down and putting my feet up
on one of the other seats. Was I getting old? I never used to
put my feet up every time I sat down, or slip my shoes off
like I was doing now. I used to laugh at my mum for it. Maybe
if I was starting to ease my shoes off and put my feet up,
Taylor wasn't too old for me. 'Who's been bickering?'

'Diego and Bob,' she said. 'Todd and Kathi. Noleen and
everyone. Only Arif and Meera haven't been. And José
and Maria.' She took a breath. 'And Devin and me. We haven't
had any difficult conversations.'

'Mkay,' I said. 'Still haven't told him, eh?'

'Nope.'

'Well,' I began, then I ran out of useful input. But I truly
believe that sitting side by side looking at the same view, in
silence, is restorative, even when that view is a chain-link fence
and a ghost town beyond. I was just about syncing breaths with
her, when three doors opened and the bathing beauties appeared:
Barb in her bikini, Amaranth in her bathing dress and mad hat,
Maria in another outfit pilfered from her husband – this one
looked like a football strip, and as she turned her back to clamber
down the pool steps on the far side, I saw that it did indeed
have someone's name on the back.

'Maria looks identical to José from behind when she's wearing his clothes,' I said, hoping to raise a laugh.

Della nodded solemnly. 'They're like twins,' she said. Then she gasped in dread, like she had the last time. 'Oh God, Lexy. Twins!'

'It won't be twins,' I said. 'They're pretty much always IVF. And this baby wasn't even planned. Was it?'

'Devin is twenty-one,' said Della. 'All the planning in the world . . .' She rubbed her face like they were telling us not to, and then smacked her hands together. 'Just need to get on with it, I guess. Find an apartment to rent. Or a little house. *This* can't go on for ever.'

'The being banged-up?' I said. 'Operation Cocker?'

'Living in two motel rooms,' Della said.

I didn't gasp but I felt the dread, like I felt it any time one of them suggested that things would ever change. I'd had enough changes in my life – marriage, emigrating, divorce, murders, and then the really big one: trying to shake houseboat permits out of the City of Cuento. Now all I wanted was for the seven of us, plus Diego and the twins, to grow old together at the Last Ditch.

I shook myself. No doubt Arif felt he had had enough upheaval in his life too, but he wasn't mourning and whining. He was getting on with being separated from the love of his life. And Meera too. She was taking single life in her stride. But then they had each other, if our suspicions were correct.

I shook myself again. I had Taylor, didn't I? And what Della had just said about young men outwitting all contraception was another reason to be glad he was approaching senility.

I dug out my phone and texted him. 'I forgive you.'

'Your benevolence is a blessing,' he texted back. I didn't know if it was an actual quote or just general smart-arsery but it made me smile. I loved that he was winding me up again already, and not mooching around like a kicked pup making me feel guilty.

'What are you smirking about?' said Todd, appearing round the corner of the office. 'Della, you look tired. You don't have a fever, do you? Are you ill?'

'No,' said Della. 'I'm . . . what is it in Scottish, Lexy?'

'Up the duff,' I said.

'Ew,' Della said. 'That's nasty.'

'Speaking of nasty,' Todd said, ignoring what I'd said, 'Molly just put me through the pasta machine on the vermicelli setting. Again. What the hell is *with* her?'

'What was she on about now?' I said.

'What was she not!' said Todd. 'Did I see Blaine arrive? What did she say about the big angry sign on Sunday morning. What did she say about the big angry sign on Monday morning. Where did she sit at dinner on Saturday night, and Sunday night, and Monday night. And, of course, where were we and what was the weather like and who was president when we had the big talk about tattoos that we *did not have.*' He had exhausted himself, and now he lay back in his seat. 'What the hell is Maria wearing, by the way? Is that a Hugo Sánchez replica jersey?'

'And shorts to match,' I said. 'What did you tell her?'

'That no I didn't, and she couldn't say anything because she had her masklets on, and I couldn't remember who sat where except that I sat with my back to the big light because it's very draining. And I reminded her that the only conversation we had at all was a tiny little heads-up about the importance of not letting the children leave candy all over the place because of ants. And that was Sunday afternoon.'

'What did she make of that?'

'Mincemeat,' said Todd, giving me a warm glow. I wasn't sure if that was an example of our shared language, or if he'd picked it up from me and it had stuck, but it didn't half make me feel at home.

'Did she say anything else about the video of the kids?' I asked him.

'Huh?' said Della. 'What video of what kids? What?'

'Show her,' I said. 'See if you can work out why this bugged Molly so much, Della. She looked at me like she felt sorry for how dumb I was when I couldn't see the trouble with it.'

Todd played the video on his phone and we all watched it together. Three times. Once looking at the kids, once looking at Meera and Blaine in the foreground, and one final time looking only at the street in the background.

'And this is a clue to Blaine's murder?' Della said.

'Molly thinks so,' I said. 'Where is she anyway, Todd? I haven't seen her come back round, and if she wants to poke about my boat I'm going to insist on a warrant.'

'Hm?' said Todd, then he bolted upright. 'Shit! She's waiting for Kathi and Noleen to go and be re-interviewed. I was supposed to tell them.'

'In my office?' I said. 'Tell Kathi she wasn't being paranoid about commandeering private homes for government business. What a bloody nerve the woman's got.'

'Oh, Lexy, let her get on with it,' Todd said. 'The sooner it's over the sooner we can all get together and compare notes. Work out what Molly's at.'

'Like we did last time with the first round of interrogations?' I said. 'Yeah, we really cracked that nut.' He said nothing. 'Oh, all right. I'll go and tell Kathi.'

'I'll go!' Todd said, leaping to his feet, for some reason.

'Oh my God!' said Della. '*I'll* go. Anything but sit here and watch that.'

I looked round to see what she was pointing at and caught the first swirl of Barb's bikini top, Amaranth's bathing dress and, this time, the football jersey of Mexico's national sporting hero.

'Synchronized aquatic stripping,' I said. 'It'll never catch on.'

NINETEEN

Miss Manners herself couldn't have worked out how to make Molly feel welcome at her first family dinner on the forecourt, while also huddling to work out what that sneaky Molly was up to. Just as well she got a delivery of pizza from Odie's Ovens to eat in her room. Once Kathi had sprayed the box and wiped it down, naturally.

Even at that, we could hardly sit under her window and plot her downfall, which is why dinner that night was served onboard my little boat, with everyone in attendance, and me leaning over the side to check the plimsoll line, in case seventeen people sank her. I told myself Navy, Salem, Bob, Joan and Diego didn't count as five, and Amaranth probably weighed less than most of them. But the food Maria brought – not to mention the two-litre bottles of pop – probably weighed slightly more, and I couldn't kick the idea that, as we consumed it, it got even heavier. I know I felt as if the ball of stodge in my stomach was twice the mass of what I had put on my plate. But that might have been because the conversation didn't aid digestion.

While Maria and José kept the little ones fed and entertained inside my living room, and Della and Devin went through to my office for An Important Talk, with Devin wondering aloud why Della wasn't having a beer and just about to find out, the rest of us sat on the porch and tried to make sense of it all.

Arif took the floor first. 'She didn't ask any more questions about the things we discussed,' he said. 'Although that was because she'd kind of rolled on and assumed that her accusations were right and my denials were untrue. But even that wasn't the play.'

'What was the play?' said Meera.

'Timing,' Arif said. 'It wasn't how often I saw Blaine anymore or what I said to her, it was *when* I saw her, *when* I spoke to her. No explanation of why it mattered. Just on and on and on.'

'Me too, when you put it that way,' I said.

'And me,' said Todd.

'Yeah, same,' said Kathi. 'At least, there was a lot of . . . where did she sit on which night and what did she eat? And was she definitely there on Monday morning when we found the second sign.'

'That's right,' said Noleen. 'I couldn't have summed up what the hell she was banging on about, but "timing" just about covers it. That's weird, isn't it?'

'Is it?' said Amaranth. 'Isn't it normal after a murder to try to pin down the time of death by finding out when all the suspects last saw the victim?'

'Mom!' said Taylor.

'Don't shoosh your mother,' I said. 'Yes, Amaranth, of course it is. It's just that we all saw Blaine at dinner on Monday night and we all found out that she had died at the same time on Tuesday morning. When I realized it was blood on the sign and Navy and Salem woke up and started crying. So Molly's questions seem a bit odd. That's all.'

A ringtone stopped any more discussion. I didn't recognize it, so I knew it was Todd's. He does love a personalized ringtone. This one was Olivia Newton John singing 'Hopelessly Devoted to You'. If it wasn't Roger on the other end, I'd have something to say.

But it was. 'Hey, babe,' Todd said. 'How are you? Home? How was your shift? What are you eating for dinner? Uh-huh. Uh-huh. Uh-huh. Ooooooh. OK. I'm going to put you on speaker. Everyone's here.'

'Hi, Dr Pretty,' said Barb as soon as Todd turned the phone to face us.

'Hi, Barb,' said Roger, sounding dog-tired, although whether from work or from his mother-in-law was hard to say.

'Hi, what?' said Barb. 'Hi, who's that now?'

'Hi, *Mom*,' said Roger. 'OK. News from Phil. He would tell you himself but he's asleep. I think it just hit him.'

'Poor guy,' I said. 'We think.'

'You wouldn't doubt it if you could see him,' Roger said. 'He's a wreck. I tried again to say he should go off on leave and get the kids home, but . . . I think work's holding him together.'

And not just him, I thought. But I said nothing.

'So what's the news?' said Todd.

'Right.' Roger audibly gathered himself. 'Well, you know Phil was having the blood tested to measure against Blaine's DNA?'

'From before we found her body,' Noleen said. 'Kinda moot now, ain't it?'

'Mootest thing I ever saw,' said Roger. 'But he had set it in motion and couldn't stop it. That's not the point. The point is, why did you include a hair?'

'I didn't,' I said. 'Wait. I might have. I looked away while I scraped the blood up because it was gross. If there was a hair there, I suppose I scraped it too.'

'There was a hair there,' Roger said. 'And not Blaine's hair. But before you say it could be anyone's who stayed in the room at any time—'

'Hey!' said Kathi. 'It could not be from "anyone's hair from any time"! What kind of joint do you think I'm running here?'

'Sorry,' Roger said. 'Right. But the thing is they think it's from *after* the blood, the lab said. The hair was stuck in the blood on one side, but still clean on the other side. You see? It wasn't like the hair was in the room and the blood had gotten splattered on to it. It's like the blood was in the room and the hair landed in it. Do you see?'

'I think so,' I said. 'I wish I didn't. Less detail would be fine by me.'

'So,' Roger said, 'unless one of the cops got sloppy or someone else crossed the crime-scene tape . . . it's the murderer's hair.'

'That is fantastic news!' said Todd.

'That's what I've been telling Phil,' Roger said. 'But he's so overwhelmed with it all, he can't take it in. And here's some even better news. It's a long, straight, dyed hair from a Caucasian woman.'

'It *is* a woman!' Kathi shouted. 'We were right!'

'Um,' said Arif.

'Oh, yeah, sorry,' Kathi said. 'It's a chromosomally XX hair, I should say.'

'Oh please!' said Arif. 'It's not that. It's this. How is it fantastic news that you found a hair when we can't tell the cops how we got the blood sample and can't hand it over for analysis?'

'Huh,' said Todd. 'Yeah. That's true.'

'And actually, how is it fantastic news to narrow the list of suspects to white women in California who dye their long hair?' said Kathi. 'What is that, like a million? Five million?'

'I haven't told you the best part,' Roger said. 'She's a natural blonde with hair dyed brown. That's got to cut it down.'

'It sure does,' said Todd. 'So we're looking for a white woman with blonde hair that she's dyed brown so she could do a murder and no one would be looking for a blonde?'

'Or she just wanted brown hair,' Kathi said.

But Meera pushed out her lips and shook her head. 'Nah. No blonde just wants brown hair. Goth black, sure. Disney rainbow, absolutely, even granny grey or Ariel magenta. But brown? That's a disguise.'

'Sorry,' I said, 'but can we stop talking about hair?' The vision was back in front of my eyes: Blaine's hair darkened and dulled with blood inside the plastic sheeting.

'And Phil can't take it in?' Arif said. 'That had to be freaky to get back a DNA analysis from his wife's killer.' I gave him a grateful smile.

'Phil's . . .' said Roger. 'Phil's . . . He's . . . well, it's hard to say. The other night—'

Todd lunged forward suddenly and took the phone off speaker, pressing it to his ear and walking off round the deck.

'You don't think,' said Noleen in the silence he left behind him, 'that Phil's sought comfort "the other night" and Roger . . .'

'Obliged?' I said. 'I hope not. I mean, surely not. Roger? And Phil? No way.'

'Sumpm's up,' Noleen said. Then she pressed her lips together firmly and smiled. It was a strange look and one she was directing with a lot of focus to something behind me. I turned to see Salem standing in the doorway.

'Fuw,' he said. 'Dada.'

'Oh, Jeez,' said Arif. 'Yes, honey. C'mere!' He beckoned and Salem came toddling over and clambered into Arif's lap. 'Phil is your daddy. We were talking about him.'

'Bain,' said Salem. 'Mama.'

'It's good to hear him speaking a bit more again,' I said. 'Right? No matter what he's saying.'

'Language explosion,' said Meera. 'It's a real thing. I reckon all the one-on-one from Maria and hanging out with Bob, Joan, and Diego has given him a boost.'

'Or he regressed because of stress,' Della said. 'And he's getting it back again.'

'Not stress,' I said. 'Because it wasn't since Blaine died. It was ever since he got here.'

'Bain,' said Salem again. He looked around the room at all of us. 'Mama?'

'That's right, sweetie-pie,' said Arif. He was speaking firmly but his eyes had filled and he pressed Salem to his chest and planted a kiss on top of the curly little head. 'Blaine was your mommy.'

None of the rest of us managed to say anything for a minute.

'All gone,' said Salem, in a singsong, holding out his hands as if to show that he'd eaten the last of the sweeties.

'Daddy's not gone!' said Noleen.

'Dada?' said Salem, looking up at Arif and then twisting to check the rest of the seats.

'Aw shit,' Noleen said.

'But who's this?' said Arif, slightly wildly, pointing at Noleen. 'Gramma Nolly!'

'Dama Nono!' said Salem.

'And who's *this*?' Noleen said, pointing. 'Gramma Kathi!'

'Dama Dadi!'

'And Auntie Lexy!' Kathi said.

'Addy Yeti!'

I got in quick before that could take hold. 'And who's this?' I said. 'Auntie Meera!'

Salem turned and gazed at Meera for a long, quiet moment. When he spoke again his voice was tiny. 'Mama?'

Arif managed to hand him over to her before he let go of the sob he was holding in, and he managed to make it sound like some kind of sneeze-boak hybrid and not scare Salem too much.

'Mama,' Salem said again, when he was in Meera's lap. He took hold of a piece of her silky hair and, grasping it firmly in his fist, he plugged his thumb in his mouth and closed his eyes. 'Mum-mum,' he said one last time and went to sleep.

'He's OK,' said Kathi. But right at that moment he was the only one.

Maria had come to stand in the doorway at some point, and she looked us over with a wise eye. 'Babies bounce,' she said. 'Recuperar. Not "boing".'

'It would help if they had some FaceTime with Phil,' I said. 'It's the strangest thing that he doesn't want them with him. It was weird enough when we suspected him, but it's really freaky now.'

'It's not even close to the strangest thing,' Meera said, speaking softly over the top of Salem's head. 'The strangest thing is how unhappy these two babies were when they were taken away from their home and their daddy, and how quickly they recovered when they lost their mommy too. That's the strangest thing I've ever seen.'

'Hm,' said Kathi. 'Is it, though? Maybe, if they usually go to day-care, it's easier for them to be with strangers than with their mommy in a strange place. Maybe it's just tough for you to think about.'

'In case Bob and Joan would be fine without *me*?' said Meera, laughing. 'You could be right.'

But right at that moment, Bob happened to pop his head out of the living room and, when he saw Salem all cuddled up in the lap of *his* mommy, he came charging over like a tiny ineffectual Godzilla to tear the fabric of the houseboat into kindling sticks if it would right the wrong.

Meera outwitted him by standing up and turning aside. 'Don't be mad, Bob,' she said. 'Salem needs a snuggle and his own mommy isn't here. Aw, poor Salem, huh? Poor baby?'

'Poor baby,' Bob agreed, technically, although his face stayed thunderous.

''At's another thing about Blaine,' Noleen said. 'That one – and even little Navy – couldna cared less who *she* snuggled with. Diego, Bob, Joan . . . they didn't blink. Right, Maria? Remember?'

Maria nodded and she didn't look much sunnier than Bob, as she cast her mind back over the memory.

'She was an enigma, right enough,' I said. 'From the moment she arr— Hey, what's going to happen to her car? They've taken the tent off it now. Does anyone know if they're going to drive it away or if someone needs to deliver it to Phil at home?'

'You could ask Molly,' Noleen said. 'And pretty soon would be good. Right now would do. We need to get the kids' booster seats out of it asap in case we need to bring them to the doctor's office or anything.'

'Why me?' I said, even as I was standing up.

'Cos you're dumb enough to go when someone tells you,' said Noleen.

It gave the rest of them a laugh at least and so I didn't fight it.

Molly had finished the pizza, apart from the crusts, and was now on two phone calls and some kind of meeting app on her laptop. 'I'm going on mute to take care of something,' she said, loud enough to have all three sets of people hear, then she dinked three buttons and turned to face me.

'Come to confess?' she said. 'Cop humour.'

'Hilarious,' I said.

'So what can I do for you? You remember something?'

'The long hair tangled in the bushes on the way round to the boat,' I said. It had occurred to me en route that I regretted ever mentioning it. If we could have got it and compared it to the other one . . . 'Did you find it when you did your sweep?' I asked.

'I'm sorry,' said Molly. 'Is this a press conference? Do you have your pass?'

'Because there definitely was one,' I said. 'I got it in my mouth and had to spit it out on Tuesday morning. If it could be matched to anything else from the crime scene, that would be good.'

'Our evidence collection is not up for discussion.'

'Except I want to say this though.' I didn't think I was being outrageous. 'Have you finished with Blaine's car? What happens to it now?'

I really hadn't thought I had crossed any lines, so it was a surprise when Molly's face drained of all expression and she stared blankly at me.

'What?' I said.

'It's been sitting in the sun.'

I thought that over and said, 'So?'

'I mean, technically, it's up to Blaine's heir, Dr Temple, to take the car away as soon as the property owner asks him to move it. It's not my job.'

'Okay.' What was wrong with her?

'But . . .' Her face wasn't just blank now, it was pale too.

'But what?' I said, 'He's not allowed to come here and no one's allowed to go there and we can't get a driver to do it either, you mean?'

'No,' Molly said. She looked physically sick, even. 'Not that so much as . . .'

'So much as the fact that Noleen and Kathi won't mind, because they don't need the parking and you hate loose ends?' I said.

She shook her head again.

'Well what then?'

Molly swallowed hard then sighed. 'I never thought I would miss the rest of those guys at the station,' she said. 'And we're on the phone all day long anyway, so how *can* I miss them? And yet . . .'

'And yet here you are dying to get something off your chest, even if it's to me?'

'The killer didn't move Mrs Temple's body straight from Room 102 to Room 201,' Molly said. I waited for her to say more. When she didn't, I tried to make sense of what she *had* said. Blaine's body hadn't gone straight from where she was killed to where I found it, huddled so pathetically in the little bathtub. And there was a problem with the fact that her car had been sitting out in the sun for a few days.

'Oh God,' I said.

Molly nodded. For once she didn't seem to be taking pleasure in making me feel wretched. 'What I don't understand,' she said, after a while, 'is why she brought it back.'

'Why who brought what back?' I said. 'Wait, you're confirming that the killer was a female?'

'Dammit!' Molly said. 'But if I don't talk to someone I'll lose my mind. She put the body in the trunk, presumably to drive it way and dump it somewhere, then she brought it back.'

'Drive it away through a locked gate?' I said.

'She put it in the bathtub in a locked room,' Molly said. 'She had a master key.'

'Yeah, but someone would have heard her if she'd started up that minivan in the night. Amaranth would have heard her. She's old' – I paused as I remembered exactly what Amaranth's advanced age meant for me – 'but she's got ears like a bat. And Noleen and Kathi would definitely have heard her. Have you asked them?'

'What a great idea, Lexy,' Molly said. 'Where would I be without you? Yes of course I asked them. They didn't hear anything. But I'm telling you, the killer put the body in the trunk of the SUV and then took it out again and put it in Room 201.'

'That's insane.'

'Go figure.'

'Maybe she meant to take it away and then – Hey, this'll work! – she didn't realize the gate was padlocked until the body was already in the boot.'

'Sloppy,' Molly said. 'She should have opened the gate first. In case someone saw her move it. Cleaner getaway.'

We shared another silence.

'Can I ask you one last question?' I said, eventually. 'Now that you're talking to me like this. Are we suspects?'

'Who's we?'

'Me, Todd, Kathi, Noleen, Meera, Arif.'

'Not if you come clean,' Molly said. 'You wouldn't have been in my sights at all except for . . . you know.'

'I really don't,' I said.

'Just be straight with me and I'll be straight with you,' Molly said.

'I have been.' I stared at her. 'We've all been straight with you. Someone else is messing you about, Molly. It's not us.'

'That makes no sense,' Molly said. 'Why would she do that?' I sat very still as if maybe she'd forget I was there and just keep talking. I used to try the same trick when I was wee, sitting like a statue as bedtime approached, hoping my mum and dad would overlook me and I'd get to see *Baywatch*. It never worked

then and it didn't work now. After a long silence, I was forced
to prompt her.

'Why would who do what?'

'If,' Molly said, 'I take you into my confidence, Lexy . . .'
I sat as still as I ever had while the Hoff came scampering out
of the surf in slow-mo. '. . . in an advisory capacity, on the
strength of your professional status. And you promise to keep
the confidence I place in you . . .' I tried to look trustworthy
and useful. It's a look a counsellor uses a lot, but it's much
harder when you can't look down and make notes in your pad.
'The thing is,' Molly said, 'she kept a journal.'

'Blaine did?' I said.

'Not exactly.'

'Right.'

'A journal is daily, yeah?' Molly said. 'This was more of an
outpouring. A splurge. A vomit, if you will.'

'I won't. But OK. Even if you don't practise daily, it's a
healthy habit . . .' I took a deep breath and steeled myself to
say 'journaling'. I failed. '. . . keeping a diary.'

'Make your mind up,' said Molly. 'Either it was a healthy
habit or her journal was full of lies. Can't have it both ways.'

I blinked. 'So . . . all that guff about tattoos and clothes . . .
was from Blaine's journal?'

'Every last curse and every last insult,' Molly said. 'Kroger
losing his mind over her butterfly tattoo. Muntz the neat freak
threatening her if she didn't pick up her room. Jafari green with
envy about her happy marriage. Same with Flynn. And the other
Muntz could start a war in heaven.'

'And Campbell?'

'You were never a serious suspect,' Molly said. 'You must
piss off everyone you meet every day.'

'Boy, that was bittersweet,' I said. 'I mean, it's always nice
not to be a murder suspect but what's with the sting in the tail?'

'What?' said Molly. 'I didn't mean anything by it, just that
your job is telling people things they don't want to hear and
picking at their sores.'

'As opposed to handing out cuddles and lollipops like a cop
does?' I said. Then, 'Never mind,' as she started to bristle.
'Listen, I'm absolutely sure these conversations Blaine recorded

weren't "drawn from life", let's say. Maybe she was giving rein
to her imagination, worst-case-scenario type thing. Maybe she
was doing some kind of behavioural reprogramming therapy,
trying to still unhelpful voices by playing out what she feared.
Or something.'

'And you charge for this?' was all Molly said in reply.

'For you, no,' I said. 'And I'm serious. None of it ever
happened. And even if it did . . .'

'Yeah,' Molly said. 'Pretty thin motive for a planned murder.
Maybe a shove and hit your head after a few drinks but not
what happened here.'

'So we're off the hook?' I said. 'Do you have other leads?'

'Don't you worry yourself about me and my leads,' said
Molly. 'And like I said: you're off the hook if you come clean.'

'About *what*?' I couldn't help my voice rising. Hadn't we
just done this?

'Like I said, you be straight with me and I'll be straight with
you.' We had definitely just done this.

'What am I not being straight about now?' I said. 'Because
I'll *tell* you what: nothing. You've got the wrong end of another
stick, Molly.'

'Not this time,' she said, and said it so definitely that she
almost convinced me.

'Is it something to do with why you keep asking us about
the last time we saw her?'

'What a lucky guess,' she said, still in that smug, sarcastic
tone. And the look she wore was the same one she'd worn when
. . . what was it? I knew I'd seen that expression once already.
'Hang on,' I said. 'Is all of this stuff about when we saw her
tied into the film of the kids?'

Molly's face shut like a trap. 'You're too old to pull off cute,'
she said. 'And I don't like people making a fool of me.'

I had no idea what any of that meant, and clearly Molly
wasn't going to expand. Without another word, she stood up to
show me out.

Which suited me just fine, as it happened, because I needed
peace to think things through. I walked down the stairs, and started
doing circuits of the forecourt, eyes trained on ground while my
mind whirred.

It was pretty lucky for the killer that Blaine filled a diary full of lies about the rest of us in the Last Ditch. Because, with all those suspects to interview, the cops had let the trail go cold on the real murderer. In fact, they might have played into the real murderer's hands.

After all, the killer came back. She kicked in the connecting door from Amaranth's room to get back into Blaine's room for something. What if she'd got it, whatever it was?

What if, while Molly was bugging us all about tattoos and business tips, based on a pile of garbage in a fantasist's diary, the killer had removed a piece of solid evidence that would lead to her undoing?

Nah.

She couldn't have found anything in Blaine's room because Todd and Kathi had given it such a comprehensive going-over. But that was surely beside the point. She couldn't have *meant* to come back all along. That was a terrible plan. So, maybe, just maybe, the door-kicking visit was connected to the way the overall plan went wrong, to the fact of having to stash Blaine's body at the motel instead of where she meant to stash it when she put it in the car. Oh God, the car that was six feet away from me right now! I stepped up my pacing until I was past it, but the thing about SUVs is they're enormous. I couldn't stop seeing it out of the corner of my eye. In blind panic, I knocked on the nearest door, badly needing someone to help me.

TWENTY

'Close your eyes!' Taylor's voice rang out in the dark. 'I can hear you blinking.'

'I was asleep,' I said. 'You woke me up.'

'You weren't asleep,' he said. 'I could hear your eyelids going click click click.'

'Go through and sleep in the other bed,' I said. 'Like you were supposed to.'

'You invited me back,' he said.

I did.

It had started post-dinner, post-Molly, mid-pacing, mid-panic, when I realized it was Amaranth's door I was battering.

'Hi,' I said, when she answered. 'It's Lexy.'

'I know who it is,' said Amaranth. She had been sitting with her feet in an electric spa and she splashed back across the floor and plunked them back in again. 'There's no need to patronize me,' she added. 'Telling me your name or wincing because I'm walking with wet feet. I'm blind not stupid. And my balance is perfect. I do yoga. Do you do yoga?'

'No.'

'I do. And I'm not going to take your side, you know. For one, he's my son and, for another, age is just a number.'

'OK,' I said. 'It was Molly I wanted to talk to you about, though. Sergeant Rankinson.'

'Oh,' said Amaranth. 'Good. Because that's been puzzling me. She was at me for what I might have heard in the night. She bought right into that tired old cliché about the other senses taking over.'

'Well, to be fair, Amaranth,' I said, 'you've got hearing like the NSA dialled up to eleven.'

'Did I hear a car start? Did I hear doors slam? Did I hear a scuffle? Did I hear the gate? Did I hear them drive off? Did I hear them come back?'

'And did you?'

'I told her I wasn't even here!' said Amaranth. 'I didn't get here till Tuesday when the poor girl was dead already.' I struck myself in the forehead with the flat of my hand. I couldn't blame Molly for that, because I'd forgotten too. 'So I told her it didn't matter how good my hearing was, there was no way I noticed a car coming and going on Saturday when I was still at home in my own bed with Alan Rickman on Audible and didn't even get here till Tuesday.'

'Monday,' I said.

'Tuesday,' said Amaranth.

'No, I mean Monday not Saturday. Not Monday not Tuesday.'

'Well, then you need to tell Molly that,' she insisted. 'Because it was Saturday night she was harping on at me about. Then she moved on to Sunday. *Finally* Monday.'

'Saturday?' I said. '*Saturday?*'

'Nothing wrong with *your* ears either, huh?' Amaranth said.

'Right,' I agreed. 'Amaranth, I'll need to shoot off and have a word with Noleen about something. When Taylor gets in, if you get the chance, like if he comes here first, can you tell him I'm looking forward to seeing him?'

'I can do that,' she said as I was leaving. 'Why the change of heart? He said you were mad at him.'

'I was,' I said. 'I'm over it.' Truth was, I didn't care for being told I was too old to be cute. All of a sudden, the notion of being snatched out of a cradle by Taylor didn't seem so terrible after all. I would have to brace myself when he said his actual age out loud for the first time, but Amaranth was right: it was just a number.

And then he was so great when we were all together having a nightcap on the forecourt too.

While I was with Amaranth, Noleen had decided the rest of them needed to leave the boat and spend some time at the trestle table or Molly would know they were hiding from her.

'Don't want to let her smell fear,' was how she put it when I met her switching the fairy lights on. Kathi lit the chiminea,

Meera made coffee and hot chocolate, and we all did a fair impersonation of normal. Normal for now.

Taylor arrived with an easy smile for me and said 'let's leave it' when I tried to apologize for overreacting. And he marched right up to the chain-link and fired off an impressive tirade of foul language and emasculating snark to Meera's husband, who came for an unexpected and unwelcome visit just as Maria was cutting the flan she'd made for an extra post-dinner pudding.

'If even a gun and a badge and a nightstick aren't enough to make up for what you're lacking,' Taylor said, 'what made you think bullying your wife would do it?' He wasn't shouting. I could only hear him because I'd hustled over with Todd, Kathi, Noleen and Della to stand like a kick-line and block off his view of Meera.

'I've got a right to see my kids,' he said, going up on tiptoes as if to look over our heads.

'Sure you do,' Taylor said. 'If the court says it's safe and there's a neutral venue available, you can see your kids in the presence of a qualified social worker any time at all.'

'I've never laid a finger on either one of them!' said Supercop, jabbing one of these unlaid fingers right through the chain-link at Taylor's chest.

'Can't make it a hat trick though, huh?' Taylor said. 'Can't make the same claim about your wife?'

'She gave as good as she got.' He looked like saying more but he glanced to one side and caught sight of Molly, who had come down to join us.

'Careful, Charlton,' she said. 'Don't incriminate yourself.'

'Charlton?' I said. 'Wow. And here's me thinking I had no pity for you.'

But for once what Molly called my 'mouth' wasn't needed. The fact of a fellow cop hearing his low-grade bluster and calling it out was enough to send Charlton Flynn back to his enormous compensatory truck to drive away with a failed attempt at a sneer.

'And you really didn't know what he was like?' Noleen said to Molly. 'You really found out when Lexy came to tell you just this week?'

'It's complicated,' she said. 'The job's a lot to take home.'

'Is this a confession?' said Todd. Molly stared at him. 'Do you take it home to Cheyenne? Yeah, I didn't think so.'

We went back to the table and kept an uneasy silence until the first chance to go our separate ways. It was a waste of a good flan, frankly.

Now, though, in the night, my thoughts turned to leftovers, and also to the fact that the sooner I started acting untraumatized, the sooner the memory of Blaine in the bath might leave me.

Or maybe it was just the leftovers.

I slid out of bed and tiptoed along the corridor to my living room with my shoes in my hand. Then I made my way out on to the porch, down the steps, round the side of the motel and all the way to the office door, where I paused with the key in my hand, looking out over the row of parked cars, where once again Blaine's seemed to loom extra-large and extra-dark. To distract myself from what was inside it, I tried some reasoning.

Surely, I told myself, no one could sleep through doors slamming, maybe even an engine starting up, all the kerfuffle that would go along with fruitlessly stashing a body in a boot.

Noleen had been less than helpful when I'd asked her, over cocoa under the fairy lights. 'I sleep like the dead,' she said. 'And Kathi sleeps with earbuds in, some dude whispering crap in her ears all night long. So I'll tell you what I told Molly: dunno.'

'But can I just check, did she ask you about Monday night?' I felt foolish; half-sure that my antiquated boyfriend's geriatric mother must be confused.

'Eventually,' Noleen said. 'After I'd told her I didn't know about Saturday and Sunday. Weird, huh?'

'Beyond weird,' I agreed.

Now, in the moonlight, I decided to test at least part of the theory. I opened Todd's Jeep – he never locked it and rarely took the keys out – climbed in and started the engine. Would anyone hear it and come to see who was on the move? As I rolled back, ready to turn, I watched Noleen and Kathi's room, and Todd's, since it was his Jeep, and Molly's, since she was supposedly a trained noticer, and I totally missed Della's door opening and all of them – every single last one of them except the oldsters and the youngsters – coming out to see what was happening.

I stamped on the brake and stared. At Della, Devin, Meera, Arif, Todd, Noleen and Kathi, all with glasses in their hands, all watching me. I turned the engine off and left the Jeep where it was in the middle of the forecourt.

'Seriously?' I said. 'You're having a party and I wasn't invited?'

'A summit meeting cum stock-take,' said Todd. 'And we texted you.'

'Oh,' I said. 'When?'

'After you and Taylor went quiet,' Todd said.

'Jesus!' I stared at him and my mouth dropped open. Every time I think I'm inoculated against Todd (because of saturating doses of Todd), he goes one step further. 'You listened?'

'Figure of speech,' Todd said. 'Actually it was more about the boat rocking.'

'Oh God,' I said.

'I did catch you saying that just once.'

'Todd!' I said. I could feel my face flaring in the dark.

'But you managed not to shout that out,' he said. 'Well done.'

'Knock it off, Todd,' said Noleen. 'We've got things to do. Are you coming, Lexy?'

Todd snorted. Because he was twelve. I packed myself into Della's room along with the rest of them, dying to change the subject.

'Where's Diego?' was the first thing that sprang to mind.

'Sleepover with the abuela,' said Della. 'Poor José. All four big ones are hopped up on sherbet and Navy is teething.'

'Eh, he loves it,' Meera said. 'And he's knows it's for a good cause.'

'Where are his pussycats?' I asked next, the sight of the aquarium reminding me about the rest of the menagerie. 'And the rabbit?'

'He took 'em,' said Noleen. 'Bob and Joan insisted. And stop saying "pussy".'

'Yeah, right, "kitty-cat",' I said.

'Or,' said Della. '*Cat.* Baby-talk is so . . .' but the word "baby" knocked the wind out of her and she subsided.

'So,' I said, hurriedly, 'stock-take. Who's going to catch me up?'

'We're doing it like a drinking game,' Todd said. 'Playing to our strengths. We all need to state an . . . something that's weird or suspicious or remarkable about the case . . .'

'He can't say "anomaly" because he's hammered,' Della said.

'And the first one who can't come up with an . . . example,' said Kathi, 'chugs a drink of our choice.'

'Anomaly,' said Della slowly.

'Except Della won't play,' said Devin. 'For some reason.'

I flicked a glance at her. She gave me back a look so inscrutable it was like the Sphynx had Botox. Whatever she'd said during The Important Talk earlier, she hadn't told him yet.

'For some reason,' said Todd. 'Della won't play *a drinking game*.' He might not know what 'up the duff' meant but he'd certainly twigged.

'OK then,' I said. I knew I had cards up my sleeve. 'Is someone keeping a note of what anomalies you come up with?'

'Duh,' said Devin. 'Let's start from the top for Lexy so she doesn't repeat moves. I'll go. Why did the killer put the body in the trunk of the car and then take it out again?'

'Oh,' I said to Noleen. 'You told them that?' That was one of my moves lost then.

'Why did Molly ask about the car on Saturday and Sunday,' said Noleen, 'when Blaine was killed overnight Monday to Tuesday?'

'Why,' said Todd, 'did the killer put face masklets on Blaine's body? Or stick them back on if they fell off during . . . the crime?'

'Why would any blonde dye her hair brown?' said Meera.

'Disputed,' Arif put in. 'If it was a disguise, it's not an anomaly. That's not my turn: my turn is why didn't the killer just wear a wig? It would mean so much less DNA all over the place for one thing.'

'Speaking of which,' said Kathi. 'Why did the killer come back, sprinkling even more DNA, and try to get into the room where Blaine was killed?'

'Why did Blaine lie so much about food?' said Della.

'I thought you weren't playing?' I said.

'I'm contributing anomalies,' said Della. 'I'm just not drinking. Apart from anything else, someone should be sober in case of a medical emergency.'

'Apart from *what* else?' said Noleen with an innocent look on her face. Kathi smirked. They'd cottoned on, too.

'What about Maria and José and Barb and Amaranth?' said Devin. 'They're sober.'

'Barb?' said Todd. 'Barb Truman, my mother? You think she went to bed sober?'

'Well, Maria and José then. And Amaranth.'

'Amaranth can't drive a baby to urgent care,' said Della. 'And Maria doesn't drive and José likes a beer after supper. Can we leave this?'

'We can leave it,' said Meera, winking at Arif. 'It's no one's business but yours.' So the penny had dropped there too.

'It's up to you, Lexy,' Arif said. 'Can you think of an anomaly?'

'Yes, I can,' I said. 'Why were the kids more traumatized by being in a strange place with their mum than after she'd gone? Salem losing his voice. Practically.'

'And why didn't Blaine want to FaceTime Phil?' said Devin. 'This is a new round now.'

'How could a mom be so bad at momming?' said Meera. 'No judgement, but you know she was.'

A few of us nodded.

'Why did she ask for a practice room and then sit and eat candy?' said Noleen.

'Why would the killer telegraph the crime with those first two signs?' said Todd.

'Why would any young mom spend time putting all that thick make-up on her face at a time like this?' said Meera.

'Because not everyone is naturally beautiful,' Arif said. 'That's not my turn. My turn is: how did the killer get a hold of the master key to Room 201?'

'How did the killer know that room was empty?' said Kathi.

'What was it that bothered Molly so much about the video of the kids at the pool?' said Della.

It was my turn again and I was about to drop a bombshell.

'Why,' I said, 'did Blaine write in her journal that Todd was on the warpath over a butterfly tattoo?'

'What?' said Todd. He had just taken a drink and he spluttered a bit.

'Yep,' I said. 'Molly told me. She got that tale about you and Blaine falling out from a journal.'

'Whoa,' said Devin. 'Hey, is it back to me? OK: why did Blaine write lies about Arif in her journal?'

'Hey!' I said. 'You don't know that. You're just guessing.'

'I'm right though,' Devin said. 'My guess is a fact.'

'*My* fact!' I said.

'And if it's not yours, it's mine,' Arif said. 'That's not my turn: this is my turn. Why did Blaine write lies about Kathi in her journal?'

'Hey!' Kathi said. Then very fast she followed it up with, 'Why did Blaine write lies about Meera in her journal?'

'Why did she write them about Lexy!' Meera shouted.

'Why Noleen?' Della said.

'Hey!' Noleen said.

'So use something else,' said Devin. 'If you've got something else. Or do you give in?'

'No way, I just need a minute,' Noleen said.

'Sixty seconds starting now,' said Devin.

Noleen chewed her lip and stared at the floor for a while.

'Give in?' Devin said.

'That was nothing like sixty seconds,' Kathi said. 'But it was more than thirty. Give in, Noll?'

'Jesus,' said Noleen. 'Stop bugging me. OK. Hair, face, dancing, food, clothes, kids, car, dates, diary, doctors, video . . . video . . . video . . .'

'Della did the video already,' Arif said.

'Oh yeah,' Noleen said. 'That's right. But will you let me have "Why does Molly have such a bug up her ass about a video that Blaine's not even really in?"'

'No way,' said Devin. 'That's the same.'

'I mean technically she is,' Noleen went on, half to herself. 'But it could . . .' She stopped talking.

'Give in?' said Devin.

Noleen was staring at the floor and chewing her lip again.

'You give in?' said Todd.

Then – and we all saw it happen – light broke over Noleen's face. She sat back in her chair as if someone had cut her strings.

'This is my turn,' she said. 'Why did it take us so long to understand what Molly thinks is hinky about that video?'

'That still doesn't seem different enough from Della's,' said Devin, always such a stickler. 'Drink, Noleen!'

'Sshh,' I said. 'She's on to something. Why's the video hinky, Nolly?'

'Give us a clue,' said Della.

'Watch it again for yourselves and ask what's weird about Blaine,' Noleen said. Todd had his phone out before she had finished speaking, and yet again we all watched the kids on the tarmac. Meera looking up and asking me what I was doing, Meera shouting to Blaine that I was filming her kids. And Blaine coming out of her room and . . .

'That's odd,' I said. 'Meera pointed at me and Blaine didn't turn round and look up to see what was being pointed at.'

'Some people are shy about having photos and films done,' said Arif, dipping his head as if he was one of them.

'True,' said Todd. 'But those people don't tend to wear the full Kardashian paint job on random days, or sleep in expensive hydrating masklets.'

'So why didn't that woman want her face on film?' said Noleen, asking a question to which she knew the answer and enjoying it.

'Same reason,' said Della, 'that she didn't want to FaceTime Daddy.'

'Same reason,' said Kathi, 'that she dyed her hair a brown colour that clashed with her make-up so bad.'

'Blaine did?' said Todd. 'Blaine dyed her h— Oh my gondola ride round Venice at dusk! I get it.'

'Ohhhhh,' said Arif. 'Me too! Same reason she didn't know whether she was a foodie or not.'

'A dancer or not,' said Meera. 'I get it now.'

'And *that's* why Molly thinks Blaine was killed on Saturday,' I said.

'I don't get it,' Devin said. '*Why does* Molly think that?'

'Who wants to tell him?' said Della. 'OK, we all want to tell him. But who gets to tell him?'

'Noleen,' I said. 'Because she thought of it.'

'Oh, OK,' Noleen said, as if she was forcing herself. 'Molly thinks Blaine died on Saturday because Blaine died on Saturday.'

'But . . .' Devin said.

'Oh come on,' said Della. 'Even you haven't smoked this much weed!'

'Come on, Devin,' I said. 'This explains why the body was in the SUV when the plan was to stash it in a room.'

'Think, Devin,' said Todd. 'This explains why the kids were so unsettled when they arrived and so much more settled after the murder.'

'Because,' said Devin, 'Maria is better with kids than Blaine was?'

'He's never going to get it,' Della said. 'Honey, we have no idea what kind of mommy Blaine Temple was. Because we never met her. Lexy is the only one of us who ever saw her.' Devin frowned.

'And she was dead by then,' I said.

Devin's eyes grew and grew until they were just shy of horror-film wide. 'She was in the trunk of the SUV from Saturday,' he said.

'Yes,' I said. 'When her killer came to stay.'

TWENTY-ONE

Saturday 21 March

'So you see,' I said to Molly, 'we weren't hiding anything. We really did spend three days with her, even though Blaine died on Saturday, because she wasn't who we thought she was.'

'Yeah,' Molly said. 'We reckoned so.'

'*You knew we weren't?*' It come out as a squeak. 'So why were you leaning on us all like a dead horse then?'

'Well, she wasn't killed in the room,' Molly said, addressing the first question. She would never address the second, because the answer was: *Cos I can*. 'That crime scene was faked. And she wasn't killed anywhere else around here as far as we can tell, and you've all been here since before the killer arrived . . .'

'Do you know where she was killed?'

'Not yet,' Molly said. 'But as soon as we find out, we'll be sure and not make any effort to tell random members of the public.'

I thought about saying a lot of things but in the end I went with, 'Can I go?'

'Sure,' Molly said. 'After you just run through all of that one more time, with another officer on video-link, and me recording.'

That was when I finally had my meltdown. I had lived through it and held things together. I had told her once and held things together. For some reason, running through it again, did for me. It was the masklets that started me off: the thought of that woman putting them on her face every morning when she couldn't hide behind make-up and then putting them on poor dead Blaine to trick everyone. To trick *me*. And then it was the thought of those poor kids not knowing where they were or where their mummy was or who this woman was who didn't even care if they fell off a balcony. Next it was the thought of all Blaine's blood splattered around the motel room, the thought of her murderer saving enough of it to daub an enormous sign and leave that carnage in an empty room, the thought of how so much blood was collected, where it was stored . . . in the end it was everything – Blaine huddled in the bath, Salem saying her name in his little lisping voice, the thought of someone having to tell Phil. It was even Molly looking at me with an awkward smile and handing me tissues. I'd never been on the other end of it before. I'd only ever been the one doing the smiling and offering, trying to be professional but not absolutely dead inside. I didn't care for it from this end one bit.

When I finally stopped crying, gave my nose a torrential blow and cleared my throat, Molly said: 'OK. Let's leave it for now, because you're not feeling great. I can circle back to you later today, or even tomorrow. I'll re-interview everyone else first.'

'Re-interview?' I said. 'Everyone? Why?' She didn't dignify it with an answer, but I caught on anyway. Of course! Even if we were no longer suspects, we were still witnesses, and the news that we'd spent three days with the killer meant we were much more valuable witnesses now.

'And we need to link you up with a sketch artist too,' she went on. 'To get an image of our suspect.'

'So she's not in the system then?' I said. 'If her prints haven't thrown up a match?'

'Don't you worry about any of that,' said Molly. 'Leave the investigation to the people in charge of the investigation.' She paused. 'But there is one thing you could do for me. At least, depending on how your licence is? Your state accreditation?'

'Acht, I'm still racking up hours,' I said. 'Why?'

'Because once we get permission from Dr Temple, we're going to have to get an early childhood interrogation specialist to talk to the little boy and we need an adult to sit in.'

'But if I get permission from Phil, surely I don't need to be licensed too,' I said. 'I'll ask him.'

'You ask no one,' said Molly. 'You ask nothing.'

'Is he still a suspect?' I said. Molly said nothing. 'Yeah, I can see that. If a woman killed Blaine, then one good motive

is that she wanted her out of the way so she can be Mrs Temple
Number Two. And so he might know about it. Is that right?'

'I'll be in touch about questions,' Molly said. 'Me asking
questions and you answering them.'

'OK. But can I just say this? You do know she dyed her hair
brown to look like Blaine but she was blonde underneath, don't
you?'

'Now how,' said Molly, 'do you know that?'

I considered my answer. If the information was useful, surely
Molly would overlook the small matter of how I got hold of
an accidental murderer hair in with the blood sample I nicked
from the crime scene. Surely. I looked at her face for reassur-
ance and decided on Plan B.

'Meera told me,' I said. 'She's a hairdresser and beautician.
She saw through the dye job. She knew Blaine – the woman
we thought was Blaine – was fair-haired really. The question
is' – I sailed blithely on; sailing blithely on is usually the best
way to get round an awkward corner in subterfuge, if kind of
risky in actual driving – 'would she have washed the dye out
as soon as the deed was done or will she stay brunette until the
hairdressers reopen?'

'You think that's the real question?'

'One of them. Was she already blonde again when she came
back to the motel and kicked Amaranth's door in looking for
whatever she was looking for? There's no way to know. Do
you happen to know what she was looking for though? Have
you worked that out?'

'Just concentrate on getting over the shock of finding the
body and all the associated upset,' Molly said. 'Leave the rest
to me.'

I left casually enough but, as soon as I was clear of her
windows, I put a massive spurt on, galloped down the stairs
three at a time and hammered on Meera's door. I had to tell
her about her hairdresser brainwave before Molly got to her.
There was no answer there and no answer at Arif's. (I was
pretty sure that was the next most likely place; they were being
discreet but the air between them crackled like a summer storm.)
She wasn't helping Maria and José do early morning aerobics
with the babies either. And she wasn't in the office, where

Noleen was tussling with more of Molly's city-approved-lodging paperwork and wearing a sweatshirt that said: 'Let's start with no'.

'Try the Skweek,' she said. 'Our kerbside service has took off big time styley. She might be helping Todd get on top of it.'

'Kathi's not tempted back?' I said. 'With a good mask and rubber gauntlets.'

Noleen shook her head. 'Kathi's cleaning,' she said, a cloud passing over her face.

'Don't be downhearted,' I said, 'I think she's doing pretty well, considering. She's expanded her family to seventeen people. She's taken *that* in her stride.'

'She's put another padlock on the front gate,' said Noleen. 'Since Meera got out without anyone noticing.'

'Baby steps,' I said.

'She made Taylor swear on the good book that he was only going to hang out with geese and ducks before she unlocked it for him.'

'Interesting point,' I said. 'Would Taylor lie on a Bible? You know he lied to me about his age, don't you?'

'I heard. Amaranth told me. But it wasn't a Bible. It was *Peterson's Field Guide to Birds*.'

'Ah,' I said. 'Probably OK then.'

Meera was indeed in the Skweek. So were Della and Todd. Unfortunately, so was Molly.

'We meet again,' I said, trying for breezy and failing.

'I was just telling Molly why I think it was a permanent dye and not a six-rinse vegetable-based tint,' Meera said. 'Mainly because of the tonal differentiation. If she was older she could have gotten that effect from putting a box-dye on salt-and-pepper natural hair. But at her age, a home kit would have given her one flat colour, and this was anything but, if you remember.'

Todd nodded. 'Beautiful,' he said. 'Chestnut highlights and mahogany low-lights with those honey slices along the part.'

'OK,' I said, thinking that all I had seen was brown hair and how the hell did you slice honey.

'And now we've thrashed that to death,' Molly said, making me think she knew fine well she was being conned, 'who's going first?'

'I'll get it over with,' said Della. 'Then I need to take the kids for a singing lesson. If I can bring myself to open my mouth wide and project.' She swallowed hard and gave a little shiver.

'Stomach flu?' said Molly. 'We can leave it.'

'Knocked up,' said Della. 'I'd forgotten this part.'

'Oh so it's out?' I said. 'You told Devin?'

'I did not,' said Della. 'I'm hoping it leaks but I gotta say, you guys don't deserve the name "gossips". Even you, Todd.'

Molly ushered her out and I stood looking after them. 'Why's she so nervous to tell Devin?' I said. 'He loves Diego and he's besotted with Della. I bet he'll be cool with being a young dad.'

'Her first husband left her when she was pregnant,' Todd said. 'What a prince, huh?'

'We need to tell him and stop her worrying,' I said. 'It's not good for the baby.' Then I turned to Meera. 'So . . . was any of that true? Or was it just excellent covering for me dropping you in it? Sorry about that, by the way.'

'Yeah, why . . .?' said Meera.

'It was either that or admit that we scraped up a sample,' I said.

'Well, *I* didn't mean it about the highlights and lowlights,' Todd said. 'But then I'm not a professional. I'm just a simple laundrymaid, rub-a-dub-dubbing my way through my days.'

'So you've stopped critiquing people's wardrobes?' I said.

'Don't change the subject,' said Todd. 'Meera was going to tell us what she thinks.'

'I don't think that was a home-dye job,' Meera said. 'They give me hives. I would have noticed and gotten hives.'

'I suppose the lab would be sure it wasn't a wig?' I said.

Meera nodded. 'They'd be able to tell if a hair still had a follicle or had been cut and stitched. Why do you think it matters?'

'Well, it might not, obviously,' I told her. 'But if it was a professional colour, and it's quite unusual for a blonde to go brown, then – depending, this is, on what like kind of hair-dressers' underground there might be in Cuento, Sac, Madding and Muelleverde, the person who did it . . . See what I mean?'

'I do, I do, I do see what you mean,' said Meera. 'And I

would say there's a pretty decent network. There are Facebook groups and WhatsApps. We share news of sales at Sally's and put the word out about scissor thieves.'

'Scissor thieves?'

'There was a spate.'

'Why would someone steal scissors?' I said.

'How much do you think my scissors are worth?' said Meera. I shrugged. 'Three hundred dollars. I rent subs when they go to get sharpened. Like a courtesy car. So yeah: scissor thieves.'

'So could you get in touch with the people you know and ask them to get in touch with the people *they* know and find out if anyone turned a blonde brown recently?'

'On it,' Meera said, and whipped out her phone.

One of the dryers beeped that it was finished and Todd turned a huge tangled bale of warm washing out into a basket, which he plunked on to the folding table. He sighed. 'And you want me to give these pitiful rags back to some poor woman and say nothing, huh?'

'Kathi does too,' I reminded him.

Todd put down the T-shirt he was rolling into a Kondo-burrito and rubbed his arms as if he was cold suddenly. 'I wish someone would take that SUV away,' he said. 'I can't stand to look at it, knowing that she was in there. All that time. She was right there.'

'I wonder how come she didn't—' I said.

'Stop!' said Todd. 'Don't wonder it aloud in front of me.'

'Probably packed in dry ice,' I said.

'No!' said Todd and, throwing down the next T-shirt, he stalked towards the door. Meera kept texting.

'Sorry, sorry, sorry,' I said. 'Come back. Listen, Molly said it's up to Phil what happens to the car. So maybe Roger could ask him to call the tow company?'

Todd didn't need to hear it twice. He was already dialling. 'Hey babe, you at work yet? Oh good, I caught you. I got a question for you to ask Phil when you see him. Oh he is? Who's driving? Yeah, maybe don't ask him when he's driving. No, I won't tell you now. Call me at lunch.' He paused. I gestured to the door, asking him if he wanted Meera and me to give him some privacy, although Meera was still texting up a storm and didn't seem to be listening anyway. He shook his head and took a deep breath. 'So . . .' he said, in a very bright voice. 'How did you sleep? No more *bad dreams*. I'm not! I wouldn't. I resent that. And I really resent *that*. Yeah you too, sideways.' He hung up.

'Trouble?' I said.

'Oh now you want me to tell you?' He glared. 'Because last night you were clutching your pearls at the very thought.'

'Meera?' I said softly. She didn't look up. 'Give me a dollar,' I said to Todd. Once I had pocketed it, I said, 'Now I'm your counsellor. So. Trouble?'

'The worst kind,' said Todd, dramatically. Even for Todd. 'And he pulled the hero doctor card to get me off his back too. I hate when he does that.'

'And he's sleeping badly?' I said.

'I hope so,' Todd said, weirdly.

I waited to see if he was going to add something and, when he didn't, I summoned all my training in communication and said, 'Eh?'

Todd heaved a sigh that fluttered the nightie he was folding as he let it out again. 'Oh, just that if I could put it down to night terrors or even sleep-walking, I wouldn't be feeling so freaked out.'

'Riiight,' I said, in the sense of 'keep talking'. Meera carried on texting.

'You think you know someone,' Todd said. 'Twelve years we've been together. I didn't think there were any more surprises to come.'

'But that's good, isn't it?' I said. 'Keeping it fresh? Surprises are a good thing.'

'*Nice* surprises are a good thing,' Todd said. 'But finding out your spouse holds beliefs he's been keeping quiet all these years . . .'

'I actually agree with you there,' I said. 'It's not the crime, it's the cover-up.'

'Oh no, it's the crime,' said Todd. 'It's definitely the crime.'

'Come on, Todd,' I said. 'How bad can it be?'

'Worse than you can imagine,' Todd said. 'My husband, my rational, scientific, won't even read a horoscope husband has just told me that he believes in ghosts.'

'So?' said Meera, looking up and completely blowing the story that this was a therapy session. 'I don't think I would mind if Ar— if a new partner of mine said he believed in ghosts.'

'And saw one?' said Todd. 'If "Ar— a new partner of yours" swore blind he'd seen one?'

'Tell us what happened,' I said. 'It was two nights ago, wasn't it?'

Meera's phone pinged and she glanced down at it, but I was all ears and agog for the Roger ghost story.

'He said he woke up – I say he didn't; I say he was asleep and dreaming – because he heard the back door open and close. And he got up – I say he didn't – and looked out – I say—'

'Todd! I've got it!' I told him.

'Hey,' said Meera, 'while you've paused your story anyway, can I—?'

But Todd wasn't listening. 'And looked out,' he said, 'and saw Phil go across the yard to sit on the swing set. And then Roger – my science-mad, rational husband – claims he was just deciding to go out and see if he could offer some comfort when a *ghost* appeared out of the shadows.'

'Huh,' I said. 'A random ghost? Like Caspar or a grey lady or something?'

'Can I—?' Meera said.

'Grey-ish lady,' Todd said. 'Roger said it looked like the ghost of—' He stopped as if he'd been put under a spell. A painful flush rose up out of his collar, past his necklace, through his stubble and all the way to his hairline. 'Oh. My. Gosford Park Wardrobe Mistress,' he said. 'Roger told me it looked like the ghost of Blaine, because it was pure white from head to toe.'

'Huh,' I said. 'She went back to blonde then?'

'Or there's ghosts,' said Todd. He was already dialling. 'There's no such thing as ghosts. Which means Phil's in this up to his neck and Roger needs to get out of there. Hey, babe. Where are you?' He covered the phone. 'He's in the locker room, changing.' He put it back to his ear. 'Well, have a good safe quiet shift and don't go home with Phil. He's the killer. Accomplice anyway.' As might be expected, Roger spoke for quite a long time after that. When it was Todd's turn again he said: 'I don't like that idea at all. I hate that idea. But I see your point. I'll talk to Molly. Can you offer to do a double at least? For me? Yeah? Thank you, love you, later, bye.' He hung up. 'Goddam hero doctors,' he said. 'Roger just pointed out that if he doesn't go home with Phil, it'll tip him off and he'll get away. But he'll try to keep on at work until they arrest him. So it had better be today.' He rubbed his face like we weren't supposed to any more. 'Or maybe there's ghosts.'

'No,' said Meera. 'That's what I'm trying to tell you. We were wrong. It *was* a brown box-dye from the market. *And* she dyed it blonde again with another one. Which wrecked her hair like anyone could have told her it would.'

'OK,' I said.

'And this girl from The Best Little Hair House, up in Madding, that I know from a ride-share to an expo, just texted me to say that a random stranger offered her five hundred dollars to break curfew and fix it.'

'Five hundred dollars on a traceable credit card?' I said.

Meera shook her head. 'Cash.'

'No!' I said. 'We missed her? We worked it out but we did it too late and we've *missed* her?'

'No,' said Meera. 'It's today.'

And now we had a real problem.

'She agreed to break the law!' Meera said. 'The shelter-in-place order! That's a fine right there, and just when the salon's closed and she's still paying rent with no income! I can't sic the cops on her.'

'An illicit hairdo against a murder, though,' I said.

'My buddy didn't do a murder,' said Meera. 'She just said she'd fix the colour.'

'But—' I said.

'OK, let me ask her,' Meera said. And we both watched as she punched buttons on her phone. After a minute, she looked up and said, 'I deleted the conversation and you can pull my nails out before I'll tell you her name.'

'How many girls work at The Best Little Hair House in Madding?' I said.

'Oh,' said Meera. 'Oh yeah. I forgot I already said that. Damn.'

'But you didn't say it to Molly,' said Todd. 'We can run it past Molly – hypothetically, no names. And see what she says.'

Meera's phone pinged. She glanced down. 'Toni wants to know why I'm asking,' she said. 'I gotta tell her. I can't let her meet a murderer and not tell her!'

'Let's ask Molly first,' I said. 'Chances are she'll say the hairdresser deserves a medal for helping catch a killer. Not a fine.'

'Chances are?' said Meera.

'*I* think the chances are Fake Blaine won't show,' said Todd. 'No one's that vain. Surely. And this is me saying it so you know it's true.'

Meera was shaking her head. 'You have no idea,' she said. 'You do makeovers, right? So all *your* clients are folks who don't care. Folks who let themselves get to the stage where they need a makeover. You seriously have no clue.' Her phone pinged again and she looked down.

'Another pal saying someone's stopping by her nail salon to get dried blood buffed off her acrylics?' said Todd. I think he was offended at being told he didn't know vanity; certainly he was bitching for some reason or another.

'It's Toni again,' said Meera. 'She needs to know why I'm asking and soon.'

'Wait, when's the appointment?' I said.

'In twenty-five minutes,' said Meera.

We stared at one another. Twenty-five minutes to run the hypothetical past Molly, get a favourable answer, tell her the truth, get the sting signed off on, find another officer not on desk duty to take over, and drive the twenty-minute route to downtown Madding.

'We're going, aren't we?' Todd said. 'We don't have a choice.'

'I'll give you directions,' Meera said. 'But I can't come. I'm the single parent of two young kids.'

'Just us then,' I said to Todd. 'It's weird to be saying "how will we get past Kathi?" instead of "Where's Kathi, because it's time to roll?"'

Then all three of us turned at the sound of footsteps

pounding up the outside stairs. The launderette door banged open and bounced off the wall. Kathi stood there, panting.

'Look,' she said, 'I know we're sequestered or whatever we're calling it and I know you might think this is a terrible idea and I know I'm asking you to defy Operation Cocker and put everyone at risk, but it's an emergency. Maybe.'

'Maybe?'

'Because I had this crazy idea about what I would do if I had dyed my hair brown to commit a murder and I have a lot of contacts in the linens-dependent businesses of Beteo County, as you know.' I could feel my mouth drop open. Was she really going to say what I thought she was going to say? Todd certainly believed she was. He was clearing his folding table, double-time, checking his keys and wallet, handing his phone to Meera, presumably to get directions to the Hair House plugged into his satnav. 'So I called around,' Kathi said, 'and you're not going to believe what one of my clients just told me. But we need to do it on the down-low because she could get in trouble and we need to do it now because we have less than half an hour. Are you in? I'll explain on the way.'

'Where are you going?' Molly shouted as the three of us jumped into Todd's Jeep and Noleen hauled the gate open.

'Delivering,' Todd called up to her. 'Laundry.'

'Where is it?' Molly shouted.

'I put it in last night to leave a time-lapse after touching it,' Todd said. He was good.

'And why's it take three of you?' Molly said.

'Just go!' Kathi hissed.

'I'm the emotional support human,' I shouted. 'It's part kerb-side, part therapy.'

Molly opened her mouth to say more but we were off, taking the turn out of the gate on two wheels and making for the underpass.

'We're on our way to your place, Toni,' Kathi said into her phone. 'We're over halfway there. Here's what I want you to do. When that bitch gets there, you put as much weapons-grade bleach on her as her scalp can hold, and then you lock yourself in the bathroom and stay put. OK?'

I could hear the high-pitched arguments and I gestured to Kathi to hand me the phone.

'Toni?' I said. 'I'm a psychologist-counsellor. My name is Lexy. Here's what to do. Tell this woman – what did she say her name was?'

'Navy,' Toni said.

'Ew,' I said. 'OK, tell her you're going to put on some ambient music to let her have space and tranquillity. Then get out of there!'

'What's going on?' Toni said. 'Lock myself in the bathroom? Get out of there? What's her deal apart from being rich and wrecking her hair?'

'We're not sure,' I said. 'Maybe she did nothing. We need to see her and see if she's who we think she is. Maybe she's just some rando that dyed her own barnet and wished she hadn't.'

'But if she's not,' said Toni, 'who is she? What's going on? What's a barnet?'

'What's going on is you're about to be a hero,' I told her. 'Because you knew who she was and you agreed to trap her in your salon so the cops could pick her up, OK? Otherwise, no way would you ever have agreed to break the shelter order, right?'

'Uhhhh,' said Toni. 'So I knew who she was and I lured her to my salon? Why didn't I call the cops?'

'Beeee-caauuuuse,' I said. 'Hang on.' I hit mute. 'Why didn't she call the cops?'

'Because there wasn't time!' said Todd. 'Wait. Oh yeah, that's a problem, isn't it?'

'Shit!' said Toni from the phone. 'She's here. She's right outside. She's at the back door. Wow, her hair *is* wrecked.'

'Let her in,' I said, unmuting. 'And we'll tell you why you didn't call the cops when the cops are on their way. OK?'

'Hanging up!' said Toni. And she was gone. Which felt horrendous. I imagined her opening her door and letting in the woman who had coolly and calmly lived alongside us all for three days while Blaine's body, packed in dry-ice I had to believe, waited in the SUV. The woman desperate enough to come back to the motel and break into her room again. The woman unhinged enough to go and have her hair done when having your hair done was a crime.

'Can't you go any faster?' I said to Todd.

'Than eighty?'

'OK.'

'We'll be there in five minutes,' Kathi said. 'Or we could just call Molly now. Her name *is* Navy.'

'But what if it's not her?' I said. 'Toni gets slapped with a fine. We probably get slapped with something, and we won't be able to explain why Roger needs to leave Phil's, which means he goes back there. So let's just take one peek at her before we phone anyone, eh?'

We were in the outskirts of Madding now, in that infuriating bit of town with a stop sign every five hundred yards.

'Why didn't she call the cops?' I said.

Kathi's phone rang. It was Toni, whispering from what sounded like a broom cupboard 'I've put the stripper on,' she said. 'And the music. And I'm locked in the supply closet in the break room. But, oh my God, Kathi, she's got a gun! I saw it in her purse! She's got a gun!'

'Good!' I said. 'That's why you didn't call the cops! Toni, you were in your salon clearing up for the break – making sure there was no milk in the fridge, all that – and this crazy woman pounded on your door and she had a gun and you let her in and you locked yourself in the cupboard and you called the cops.'

'Should I hang up and call the cops?' whispered Toni.

'We're turning on to your block,' said Todd. 'Wait two more minutes.'

He cut the engine as we rolled to a stop just shy of The Best Little Hair House. 'Here goes,' he said. 'Do you think we'll be able to see in?'

'One way to find out,' I said stepping down, and feeling a lot less brave than I sounded. The only time I had ever experienced this sensation in my legs before was after getting off a fairground ride. And my stomach was much the same as the last time it had been full of cheap hot dog and fried ice-cream too.

Trying not to look conspicuous, which is not possible in a main street deserted from end to end without another car moving or another living soul in sight, we edged up to the plate-glass windows of the salon.

'I'll look,' Kathi said. She squidged round and peered in. 'Aw jeez,' she said. 'She's at the basin and I'm looking up her nostrils. That could be anyone.'

'Here, swap places,' said Todd. After a bit of shuffling, he pushed himself up off the wall and squinted in through the glass. 'Um,' he said, 'it's a woman in work-out clothes and no make-up with a tinting cap on. I have no idea.'

'Swap,' I said. 'Let me.'

We shuffled once again and, with my heart hammering, my knees wobbling, and the imaginary fried ice-cream sitting just under my collar bones, I rolled round and peered in the window. 'Shit!' I said. 'She's not leaning back now. She's sitting up straight. She's bending down. She's scrabbling around in her bag.'

'Duck!' said Kathi.

'No,' I said. 'I don't want to move. She's not looking this way. I don't think she's seen us.'

'What's she doing now?' said Todd.

'She's still searching through her bag,' I said.

'For her gun!' said Kathi. 'Lexy, duck!'

'I don't even know if it's her,' I said. 'And she's still not looking this way. She's doing something, inside her bag.'

'She's taking off the safety!' said Todd. 'Lexy, duck!'

'It's her,' I said, and my voice was as calm as it has ever been. 'It's definitely Fake Blaine. It's not a gun. It's a PayDay.'

As the woman in the hairdresser's chair closed her eyes and bit into the bar, and just before Kathi combusted, I ducked. We all ducked. And ran. And managed to get ourselves into the Jeep, and the Jeep on the road, and a call through to Toni and . . . long story short we heard the first sirens before we were out of the business district, and had Molly phoning to tell Todd to tell Roger to get away from Phil, before we were back in Cuento.

TWENTY-TWO

Tuesday 24 March 2020

'You finished all your laundry drop-off pretty quick that fateful Saturday morning,' Molly said, squinting at me through the candlelight, during family dinner.

'That fateful Saturday morning?' I said. 'You make it sound like the opening of a Dickens novel. It was three days ago.'

Molly blinked and shook her head like a wet dog. 'Right,' she said. I felt for her. Time had gone a bit Dalí-esque what with one thing and another. The beaches were closed. The parks were locked. Gav the Gov had said it might last till June. June!

'Tell you what,' I said. 'If you answer one question of mine, I'll answer one of yours.'

Molly shook her head and laughed. 'It doesn't work that way.'

'Come on, no one's listening.' This was true. Devin and Della were up the other end of the table, Devin googling every foodstuff Della put near her mouth to see if it was safe for the baby, and Della concentrating on not throwing the whole gravy boat full of tri-tip dipping sauce at him. It was going to be a long nine months. Barb, Amaranth and Taylor were deep in discussion about something of their own. Arif and Meera were in another world, which was lovely, or would have been if only *my* boyfriend wasn't five seats away from *me*, talking to his mum. Again. José and Maria were tuned in to the kids as usual. Noleen, Kathi and Todd were in continuing negotiations about the plan to put Roger on the boat and move me into what I wished they wouldn't call 'the murder room'. Kathi didn't believe Todd wouldn't sneak on board for visits. Todd couldn't believe Kathi would accuse him of such treachery. Noleen was trying to referee, but it was all getting a bit fractious.

'What did you want to ask me?' Molly said. 'Why Navy posed as Blaine?'

'No,' I said. 'That must have been to muck up the time of death and give Phil a cast-iron alibi, wasn't it?'

Molly scowled. 'Is it why she ever believed that could work?'

'No,' I said. 'That must have been because after a few days in ice and a few days in a warm motel room, establishing a time of death would have been a nightmare. We just found the body too soon.'

Molly's scowl deepened and darkened. 'Is it why—'

'Why don't I just ask?' I said. The scowl was now a black hole sucking in the light from all around, but I pressed on. 'Why did Fake Blaine come back and kick that connecting door down?' I said

'*Navy* came back,' Molly said, 'to retrieve something.'

I shuddered. 'How sick was that? Pretending his baby girl was called her name. And how confusing for Salem.' I looked up the table to where he and his little sister, *Nancy*, were playing patty-cake. We had worried they might be taken away, but it turns out that even though their father was banged up for conspiracy to murder, he still had the right to choose foster parents. And he had chosen twelve of them. Thirteen if Roger came home. One of Phil's better choices, I thought. As opposed to his choice of mistress or his choice of how to end a marriage.

They'd almost got away with it; *would* have got away with it if his side piece had only been a bit less nuts about her hair.

'How about this, Moll?' I said. 'If I can guess what Fake Bl— Navy came back to retrieve, you confirm it. If I can't, I tell you our laundry delivery route from Saturday. But just you, Molly. Not you, representing the City of Cuento PD. You as a member of this family that might be living together till Junc.'

'Great deal for me,' Molly said. 'You don't stand a chance.'

I laced my fingers and stretched my arms out in front of me to crack my knuckles. Up at the other end of the table, Taylor looked at me and smiled. I smiled back. He might be avoiding me and whispering sweet nothings to his mother, and Todd's, but still: my boyfriend found my annoying habits adorable. 'OK,'

I said. 'It wasn't physical evidence because her DNA was all over the place. And it wasn't anything that incriminated Phil because, if it was, Phil would have been incriminated already, which he wasn't. You had stopped even thinking of him as a suspect by the time she broke in, right?'

Molly nodded, still looking pretty smug.

'So,' I went on, 'I was thinking it must be something to do with the fact that Phil *wasn't* a suspect, like they thought he would be. Which was a nice surprise for the pair of them, wasn't it? Must have been. They must have been all set for you to look at him pretty hard, even though they worked to make it look like Blaine died all the way down here in Cuento, when Phil was working all the way up there in Sac. And the notes on the bedsheets were supposed to make us believe the murderer was hanging round here in the night, for days beforehand. Again, when Phil wasn't. Anyway, Fake Blaine thought she'd add a bit to the plan. And maybe she told Phil about this little extra bit of plan when she met him in the moonlight and maybe he freaked out because it was too much, you know? Over-egging the pudding? And because he'd freaked out she thought she'd try to fix it. Another dumb idea from a not very bright, as well as really horrible, woman. And why have you stopped smiling, Molly?'

'Just say it,' she told me. 'Don't milk it.'

'She came back to get the diary.'

'What a moron,' Molly said. Meaning Fake Blaine, not me; because I was right.

'She came back to get the diary,' I told Taylor later, when he arrived on board after settling Amaranth in her room.

'Navy did?' he said. 'Wow, she's thick, isn't she?'

'Thick?' I said. 'You're starting to talk like me.'

'Nah,' he said. 'That's a Kathi word.' Where did he think *she* got it?

But it was late and I didn't want to argue. 'What were you cooking up with your mum and Barb at dinner?'

'They were advising me how to live my life,' he said, 'and I was pretending not to listen. But actually I think they're on to something.'

'Oh?'

'Devin's gonna be a dad before he's twenty-three,' Taylor said. 'And Barb's not sixty yet. Can you believe that?'

So we were getting round to talking about age, were we? 'Barb,' I said, 'has done a lot of sunbathing. What are you building to?'

'Life's short,' Taylor said. 'Love's rare. I love you, Lexy.'

'High-stakes move when I've already said it to you.'

'So,' he went on, 'will you marry me?'

If he had given me a karate kick in the kidneys he couldn't have taken my breath away more thoroughly.

'We've still got a couple of things to straighten out,' I said.

'Yes, we have.' He cleared his throat. 'I don't know how old my mom was when she had me because I never met my biological mother. Amaranth adopted me when I was tiny.'

'Huh,' I said. 'OK, well, that's a better answer than I could have hoped for, to question one. Now for question two: how old are you?'

He cleared his throat, chest and abdominal cavity. 'I'm twenty-seven,' he said.

'You . . .' I said, before my breath ran out. Then, 'Wait, you told me you were forty-four the first time we ever met. Why would you do that?'

'I liked you,' he said. 'I wanted you to like me too. Take me seriously.'

'How the hell old did you think *I* was?' I said. I'd got my breath back again.

He shrugged. 'I dunno. Why, how old are you?'

'None of your bloody business,' I told him. 'It's just a number anyway.'

FACTS AND FICTIONS

The timeline of events outside the Last Ditch is "what happened when" in California in Spring 2020, but none of the events inside the chain-link fence are based on reality. Nor, Gav the Gov aside, do the characters depicted or referred to here have anything in common with real people.

Beteo County, and the cities of Cuento, Madding and Muelleverde are all fictional. But there are some Easter eggs, which residents of and visitors to Davis, CA might have fun spotting. A list of these can be found on my website, www. catrionamcpherson.com. (Double points if you work out why Muelleverde is so-called, by the way.)

ACKNOWLEDGEMENTS

I would like to thank: Lisa Moylett, Zöe Apostolides, Elena Langtry and Jamie Mclean at CMM Literary Agency; Natasha Bell, Kate Lyall Grant, Carl Smith, Penny Isaac, Jem Butcher and all at Severn House; the Wednesday Ladies of Literature, Kris Calvin, Lisa Nalbone, Eileen Rendahl, Tamsen Shultz and Spring Warren, who let me join in online (since there was no yoga, where I usually am on Wednesday evenings, but then also Stacey de Barrios, for the yoga videos); the NaNoWriMo community who stood in for all the missed visits and hugs in the winter of 2020; Gigi Pandian, who taught me the difference between closed circle and locked room mysteries; Jessica Laine, who helped with knotty questions of Latinx culture; my family and friends, down the phone, on the screen, in the chat box; my lockdown buddy, Neil McRoberts; and of course, first and last and most and best and now and forever the medical professionals, other first responders, essential workers, scientists and policy makers who kept us going and brought us through that most extraordinary time following the few days I've revisited here.